CW00496799

ZERO HOUR

STEWART CLYDE

For Ema & Henry

FOREWORD

While this novel was published after the passing of Her Majesty Queen Elizabeth II, it is set at a time when she was still the reigning monarch and so, throughout the story, the author has referred to 'Her Majesty's Government' and so on.

ONE

THE INVESTIGATOR WIPED THE SNOWFLAKES OFF HIS eyelashes with a mittened hand and cursed. He hated the cold wind coming off the North Sea. He hated the crowds. And most of all he hated being away from his family at this time of year. It didn't snow in the south of France.

He pushed his way through the people near The Hague's Christmas market. Soon it would be over, he told himself. No more sneaking. No more paranoia. He could dump his burner phones and get back to being a nobody. British intelligence could leave him alone. He would retire. He would be gone.

He rushed along and wheezed as he breathed long plumes of crystalline vapour. Why they'd chosen a busy street he'd never understand. Bloody English. Bloody Roast Beef. If they were in France he'd have met at a quiet cafe. One where the owner was practically deaf and was paid well to look the other way. Instead, he was out—*oof*—he bumped into a woman with her shopping. She yelled out at him, but he looked back and wheezed an apology in French and kept on going. He checked his watch and glanced behind again. There she was again. The blonde. He was already late. And pressed on sure he would lose her in the throng.

IT WAS TO BE A STRAIGHTFORWARD SWAP MEET. Everett McKenna, the intelligence director overseeing the operation knew, could be something or could be nothing.

He stood in front of a wall of screens patched into the encrypted radio communications from the team on the ground. McKenna shivered as he watched the screens. It was warm in the command centre—too warm for him even as he stood in his collared shirt open at the neck—light snow fell over the Royal Christmas Fair in The Hague, Netherlands. The European Union Agency for Law Enforcement Cooperation's (Europol) headquarters was in the city and their informant, a middle-ranking investigator codenamed GASTRIC, was based in the city. The Frenchman was overweight and was known to wear an abdominal support brace to help with his back pain and protect his dying kidneys. It was also a useful instrument in which to hide a wire. Theirs was a transactional relationship based on one thing: money. It made McKenna uneasy. There was no European patriotism and certainly no love lost with the French, but cross-channel intelligence relationships needed to be robust.

"Survey One, this is Mobile One. This guy is a walking heart attack. You can't miss him, over," McKenna heard through his earpiece. The voice sounded annoyed. McKenna would've been too, standing out in the cold waiting for Survey One to pick the contact up on the closed-circuit television monitors.

Mobile One—Harry Metcalfe—was a young intelligence operative nicknamed Wilson. McKenna had asked why and they'd said it was after the cast-away volleyball from the film, the one with the drawn-on smile because that's how he looked ... always smiling. It was like he couldn't quite believe he actually worked in the Secret Intelligence Service. He was young and fit and dedicated to the cause. Mobile Two, the other intelligence operative on the ground was Sam Johnson. She was a similar age to Harry. Former army officer type. Smart. Slender. Seductive good looks that she knew how to use.

IN THE VAN, SURVEY ONE WAS ROBERT GORDON— Gordo—and Katie Rice. They sat in a surveillance vehicle parked nearby the L-shaped Lange Voorhout. A boulevard near the centre of the city. They watched a closed-circuit television feed and relayed what they saw back directly to the intelligence officers on the ground. They were a good team, McKenna thought.

"Roger," Survey One said.

"Survey One, this is Mobile Two. I'm watching the band set up now, we need eyes on GASTRIC now," Johnson said. The urgency in her voice was palpable over the airwaves.

IN THE EUROPEAN TASK FORCE COMMAND CENTRE, THE operation's second-in-command stood next to Intelligence Director McKenna.

"Brief me," he said.

"Julian Le Marche," Rocca said. "French. Very French. A retired *Gendarmerie Nationale* Colonel. Been with Europol since and on our books almost as long. Works in

O3, sir, Cybercrime Centre. Says he has information from a source from within Albanian organised crime."

"Concerning?"

"He won't disclose, sir."

"Ever produce anything useful before?"

"Nothing we've recorded." McKenna gave her a sideways glance. "Some files last linked to Director Soames."

"Hmm." McKenna put his hand on his chin. "Aren't they just a low-level human trafficking gang?"

"The Albanians, yes sir," Rocca said. "Until recently. They've branched out. Several factions—one in particular—are pushing their way into more exotic trades."

"Reptiles?"

"Weapons, sir."

"How much does he want?"

"Two hundred thousand."

"He says it is a threat to the national security of the United Kingdom, sir."

"I see. What isn't? What do the Albanians have to do with cybercrime ... I guess we'll find out. Here comes our man now," McKenna said and nodded to the screen. "Carry on, Sabrina."

"Yes, sir," Rocca said.

"Mobile One, Survey One. We have him," Rice said. "He's coming towards you now. You should have eyes on in approximately ten seconds."

"Roger," Metcalfe said.

"Who chose this location?" McKenna asked Rocca.

"The contact, Le Marche, sir. It's Mobile Two's show on the ground. She went along with it."

McKenna shook his head. If it was Sam Johnson's plan he knew could count on it being simple enough. There was an open-air stage at one end of the shopping street.

They were to meet at the start of the concert. A Rolling Stones cover band. With the crowds drawn towards the entertainment, Mobile One would hold GASTRIC's gloves while he fumbled with his camera to take a picture. Inside the glove would be the intelligence on a flash drive. Mobile One would hand it over to Mobile Two. Johnson would head straight for Survey One and confirm the contents of the flash drive. And, if it was what the informant said it was, get him paid. Private bank account through a shell company in the Caymans. All electronic and untraceable.

What McKenna was looking at had the potential to complicate the operation. The open-air. The darkness. Although there was a local police presence, there were no barriers or perimeter security. Anyone with any weapon could wander in. No doubt the French informant had chosen it for its escape routes, relative lack of surveillance equipment, and the crowds. These were all things an experienced field operative despised. People created problems. They were unpredictable and uncontrollable. McKenna's years of experience told him this had the potential to be a spook's nightmare. He hoped everyone stayed awake.

"Mobile One. I see him," Metcalfe said. "Wheezing fat bastard."

"He looks panicked," McKenna said.

"I would too —" Rocca said as they watched the black and white closed-circuit footage. Gordo was operating a stealth drone from the surveillance van. It was zoomed in on the informant. McKenna saw something on the screen.

"There, what's that he's looking at?" McKeen said and pointed at the screen.

"Survey One, Control," Rocca said. "Why's he so jumpy? What's he looking at?"

"Wait out," Rice said and relayed the message to Metcalfe and Johnson.

"Ask them to zoom out and track back so we can see what was behind."

The drone's camera zoomed in and scanned back along the busy street. McKenna thought he caught a glimpse of a shock of blonde hair and then it was gone, swept away by the tide of humanity moving to the stage. The drone footage floated back to the overweight Frenchman and Mobile One.

"Survey One, Mobile Two," Johnson said. "Target in sight. Mobile One is making contact, wait out."

McKenna watched as Johnson shadowed Metcalfe.

"Mobile One. I'm going in, over," Metcalfe went forwards and stood next to Le Marche.

"Where's the disk?" Metcalfe asked him.

"It's close by. What is my money."

McKenna watched.

Metcalfe shook his head. "That wasn't the deal, you're supposed to have it on you and give it to me. We need to verify the intelligence."

As they spoke a shorter, more Dutch version of Mick Jagger yelled, "I can't get no!" into the mic and the band started playing Satisfaction.

GORDO'S EYES WERE LOCKED ONTO THE FEED FROM THE drone's camera. He watched Metcalfe speaking to the informant without looking at him. Then there was a sound on the van's rear doors. Three rapid thumps from the back of a fist. Rice and Gordo glanced at one another.

"See who it is and get rid of them," Rice said. She'd made her decision quickly. It was a critical moment in the operation.

"It might be Survey Two," Gordo said.

"They haven't made the hand-off. See who it is."

Gordo set the drone to hover mode and left the camera on track mode. He went to the rear doors and pulled them open. He was expecting to see local Dutch police telling them to move the van, instead, it was a tall woman with Marylyn-Monroe peroxide blonde hair.

"Can I help —" before Gordo could finish his sentence he felt a sharp pain like he was punched in the chest and touched his hand to his heart. He lifted his hand away. It was oily and black. It smelled metallic. The woman was holding a suppressed 9mm handgun outstretched to him. He turned and looked back at Rice before he collapsed. Rice opened her mouth to shout out but was silenced by a bullet into her left eye before she could sound the alarm.

Johnson watched as GASTRIC handed his set of gloves to Metcalfe to hold. Metcalfe stuck his fingers into one of the gloves and lifted his hand to his ear.

"Mobile One. I have the package."

"Take your hand away from your ear," Johnson said to him. "Mobile Two, moving in, over."

Johnson pushed past a couple holding hands and zeroed in on Metcalfe as Le Marche fumbled with a disposable camera and snapped a picture of the stage. Mick Jagger was in full flow and the dark sunglasses-wearing Keith Richards broke into a solo. Johnson grimaced. The crowd cheered and exhaled mists of breath as their clapping was dulled against gloved hands. Metcalfe put the flash drive into Johnson's open hand. She took it quickly and walked past him to where Survey One was parked. As she hurried she heard the word "Code —" from Rice in Survey One and then nothing.

Johnson lifted her hand to her ear and put pressure on the earpiece to hear more clearly and said, "Say again, over."

Nothing.

"Survey One, Mobile Two. I am inbound. Say again over," Johnson persisted. She stepped through the gap between two of the wooden mocked-up chalets selling Christmas goodies and into the darkness away from the bright white spotlights of the shopping street. She saw a woman coming toward her. She smiled and was about to say good evening when the woman lifted her arm and Johnson felt a sharp pain in the base of her neck. God, she's shot me she thought as she collapsed to the ground. The woman was bent over on top of her and felt through the pockets of her jacket for the flash drive. She tried to warn the others. As she spoke she only made a gurgling sound and blood bubbled out of the puncture in her neck. She looked past the woman's blonde hair now at the snow falling through the white-lit trees above her. She closed her eyes.

"SOMETHING'S WRONG," McKENNA SAID LOUDLY TO the command room. He stepped towards the monitors. Survey One has just transmitted a single word: code. Code what? Second-in-command Sabrina Rocca was saying, "Say again Survey One. I repeat, say again Survey One."

Both Mobile One and Mobile Two were on the network asking Survey One to repeat the message. McKenna watched the monitor. Le Marche was getting jumpy.

"Sir, I can't get Survey One back," Rocca said behind him.

"It's gone sideways," McKenna said to himself.

"Sir?"

McKenna saw a blonde woman on the monitor approaching GASTRIC and Mobile Two. He couldn't believe it. She was an assassin. Someone knew about the operation. They had a leak.

He lifted his hand to his ear and shouted into the mic, "Mobile Two, Control. Behind you. Threat at your six a clock. Blonde female. Black coat. Abort. Abort —"

McKenna watched as the unknown woman lifted her arm toward the two men. Metcalfe spun around. The Frenchman's eyes followed. He saw Metcalfe turn and then he saw the woman pointing a weapon at him. His face contorted into a cascade of fat rolls as he flinched. Metcalfe ducked and tried to push GASTRIC to the side. McKenna saw the enhanced flash from the end of the suppressor as the woman fired. At the same moment, the informant's head snapped back as the bullet smashed into his forehead. Metcalfe got behind the big Frenchman as he was falling. The assassin's aim followed him. She fired and McKenna saw the flashes from the end of the suppressor. The rounds thumped into the thick torso of the informant. There was a moment of stillness, a calm, where the bystanders' brain's reconfigured and made sense of what was happening. Then, like someone fast-forwarding a tape, the scene sprung to life. Parents grabbed their children. People near the shooter scattered. The assassin checked over her shoulder and did a quick calculation. It was time to go. McKenna watched her disappear with the running crowd.

"Mobile One, Control. Come in Mobile One."

"Mobile One, send, over."

"Control. This is a Stage Three abort. I repeat. Stage three abort. Get to the safe house immediately. The operation is blown."

"What about Mobile Two?" Metcalfe asked.

"The mission is aborted, Mobile One. Follow protocol. Get to the safe house."

Metcalfe didn't respond. He climbed up and ran towards Survey One. McKenna saw armed Dutch police arriving on the scene. He turned to Rocca, "Pack it up, Sabrina. I want a clean-up team there immediately. We shut it down. And get someone in control of that drone before it is shot down and we have to explain what we were doing conducting an unsanctioned operation on a busy street in the Netherlands."

"I have control of the drone," one of the analysts in the room said.

"Well, see where Mobile One is going then," McKenna said, eyes locked on the screen. The video feed panned and McKenna saw Metcalfe crouched by Johnson's side, his fingers on her neck.

"No pulse," Metcalfe said. "Johns— ... Mobile Two is dead."

"Check the van," McKenna said quietly.

Metcalfe got to his feet and ran. He skidded to a halt at the rear doors. He stood there silent for a moment.

"SITREP," McKenna said.

He saw Metcalfe shake his head and say, "Control, Mobile One. Survey One has been—-they're both dead, sir."

McKenna held his breath and then asked, "And the intelligence, Mobile One. Where is the disk?"

"Gone, sir."

TWO

LAST NIGHT HUNT DREAMED HE WAS DROWNING AGAIN. The memory of the dream flashed in his mind's eye. Maybe it was because of the complete darkness. Or the vapid swish and wash of black water that was now all around him.

Hunt was four-hundred and ninety feet below the surface of the North Sea. He was knee-deep in mud near the bottom of a rig and feeling his way forward for something. He wouldn't know where it was until he touched it.

Children were often afraid of the dark. What was it, some kind of ancient fear in the shared unconscious in the evolution of the human brain? The innate feeling in every human being, like fear of snakes. Whatever it was, Hunt understood phobias better now. He tried to control his breathing as the fear crept up his spine.

He'd had the same dream for twenty-three of the twenty-six days that he'd been on the job. Only two more to go before decompression. He was counting down the minutes. Twenty-eight days in total. The same he'd spent in the jungles of Brunei. The same claustrophobia. The same disorientation. The same monk-like meditative state it took to control his thoughts, suppress his fears, and stay frosty. All while living in a twenty-foot by fifteen-foot pressurised capsule with four other saturation divers for a month. It was some of the hardest work he'd ever done.

Hunt's helmet light was off temporarily. If it wasn't for the faint particles of phosphorus floating past him in the darkness, he wouldn't have been able to tell if his eyes were open or closed. The job today was welding. He found the pillar and climbed.

When he was in position, he said, "Give me heat." The microphone in his helmet picked up his voice and transmitted it to the support ship on the surface.

There was a loud snap and a burst of white light. He closed his eyes and saw the white-hot image burned onto his retinas. He was holding an oxygen electric torch and moved the burning rod against the steel at the base of the rig. The rod sank into the metal. Gas bubbles rose from where he was cutting. As the water conducted electricity from the high amperage welder through his body, he had the familiar, bitter taste in his mouth. He got a slight shock from the torch and swore. His hand twitched. The torch hadn't been insulated properly.

Hunt clenched his jaw and gritted his teeth. He'd nearly cut through this steel. It was the last burn job he'd be doing before they finished. He was so close to the finish line he could almost taste the sweetness of it over the acridity in his mouth. He only had a few inches to go. He prepared himself for the moment it would come away. As he cut through the last of it the steel broke. The dull crack in the water sounded like a chunk of ice breaking off a berg. The metal slid away and disappeared into the darkness below him.

"Make it cold," Hunt said to the topside technical controller.

"Roger, it's cold," he heard the tinny hiss of the technician's voice come back and the blackness of the depths surrounded him again. Hunt turned his helmet light on.

"Have you burned it all off?"

"Roger," Hunt said and sat down on the cold steel of a pipe behind him. He was relieved. Now he wanted to get out of the water. Above him, in the gloom, like the hazy lights of a car in the fog was the bell. It was a capsule, big enough for two men and their gear, that was lowered down from the support ship.

"I'm finished with the burning rig," Hunt said. He wanted the support ship to pull the welding platform to the surface. "Standing by for you to pull it up."

"Roger," came the hiss in the helmet. "Confirm it is clear and ready for pick up."

Hunt stood up. He bent down and felt for what he was looking for. He grabbed the burning rig and, as he did, the warm water flowing through his suit was cut off. He immediately felt the freezing temperature of the water. He stood and released the rig and shook his hand out to try and get the warm water flowing through his suit again.

"Affirmative. Start pick up," Hunt said.

"Roger. Tell us when it is clear," the tech said.

Hunt's eyes were still dazzled and he saw flashes in the sediment floating in front of him. He held onto the burning rig until he felt tension on it and let go of it.

"Okay, topside, burning rig is clear. Ask the bell to pick up my hose. Diver is returning to the bell, over," Hunt said.

He watched the bell intently. The hose was his lifeline. His only connection to the silent hovering capsule. It was his air intake and connection with the surface. The hose went taut and Hunt took a deep breath. He was like a high-diver stepping off a ten-metre board. He stepped forward into complete darkness. He reached up for the hose and started pulling himself up in a slow, controlled, hand over hand movement. As he did, he swung out into the black emptiness of space like a trapeze artist, only he had no net. Bobby, the diver in the bell, pulled him in at the same time. As he was reeled into the bell, the descent of his arc slowed, and he seemed to drift, weightless, like an astronaut. It was the one enjoyable sensation of the whole Norwegian gas rig diving experience.

He kept his eyes on the lights from the bell. It was his only point of reference in the swirling darkness. He could see the open hatch rising above him like a bright round moon as he fell and swung and then climbed the hose towards it. He was preparing to climb the last few feet to the bell. He inhaled and then all of a sudden airflow stopped. There was no more oxygen. He stopped being able to suck in air mid-breath. He tried to inhale, but there was no pressure. His heart rate leapt. He stopped climbing and checked the regulator on his helmet with his free hand. He was drifting downwards again.

"Topside! Check diver's gas," Hunt said. As he did his feet unexpectedly hit the mud at the bottom. He looked up. The bell was twenty feet above him now. Without thinking, he grabbed the hose and started frantically pulling himself hand over hand towards it. He tried to draw on the regulator again as he climbed. Still no pressure. He was panicking. What if he lost consciousness down here? He'd heard the stories. It was one of the reasons the danger pay was so good. A fat bank account is no use to anyone lying at the bottom of the sea bed. Suddenly the pressure returned. He sucked in air. It stopped again. No pressure.

"Bugger it! Topside —" Hunt started to say. As he did the pressure returned and stayed with him this time. It was the type of thing fatalities were made of. Adrenaline coursed through his body. His heart rate was like a hundred-metre sprinter and he had to control his body to stop taking the big gulps of air it demanded.

Stay frosty. That's how you've got to stay, he told himself. Bobby was pulling the slack from the hose in as fast as Hunt climbed it. It was a rapid ascent. At last, his hand touched the ladder and he held onto it and took some long deep breaths and tried to calm himself down. He fed the last of the line into the bell. He put his foot on the base of the ladder and stuck his head up through the moon pool and into the atmosphere of the bell-shaped metal sphere. Bobby helped him and Hunt pulled the helmet off his head.

"Did the emergency gas go on a second ago?" Hunt asked, still hanging onto the ladder.

"Yeah, I dunno what the hell happened," Bobby said. He turned to the intercom and pressed the button. "Hey, topside," Hunt said, "What the hell happened? I just went on emergency gas."

"We have gas up here. Why're you on emergency gas?"

Hunt gritted his teeth and stared intensely at the intercom and said, "Because I lost gas pressure at the end of the goddamn hose, you snickering arseholes!"

There was silence.

"We just switched over to a new rack of gas," came the reply. "It would only have been for a few seconds though."

Hunt climbed swiftly into the bell. There was barely space for the two of them. Bobby hugged the wall while Hunt still had his hose secured. He grabbed the intercom and leaned into it. "I told you never to do that without warning, what part of that didn't you understand?"

"Listen, Hunt, we gotta change racks. You want to breathe empty? Fine. It was only a few seconds. Anyway, it doesn't matter now. That was your last dive. You're to start your decompression early and head back to the rig. Boss wants to speak to you. All of you."

THREE

DECOMPRESSION TOOK FOUR DAYS. ONE DAY PER
hundred feet of dive depth. Long hours of uncertainty,
locked in a narrow metal tube, kept at the same pressure as
the dive depth under the water below them. Hunt had
needed to make some big money. Big money, fast. There
wasn't a higher paying or more dangerous way to do it than
by being a saturation diver, except for being a mercenary.
Hunt didn't want that kind of work anymore. A deep-sea
diver on oil or gas rigs suited him just fine. It was still only
something a crazy person would do.

All the guys could discuss during the decompression
was the meeting. Why'd they pulled them off the job early?
No one on the radio was telling them anything. Either it
was bad, or so top secret that even they didn't know. The
rumour mill on an oil rig was as bad as amongst the rankers
in a regiment. Hunt thought maybe worse. Two hundred-
plus hardened men on a barren island platform in the
middle of the North Sea. Gossip was almost all they had to
hang on to for weeks on end.

Now, after four days, they were about to find out. Hunt

was let out of the saturation chamber with the others. They made their way from the dive support vessel that was docked onto the rig.

As Hunt stepped out onto the deck, he felt the whip of the freezing Norwegian North Sea wind. After nearly a month underwater, risking his life to lay and repair pipe, Hunt was ready for a rest.

They filed into the mess hall. Over a hundred men from the dive vessel who worked for a gas subcontractor called Technosub. Hunt went and sat in the back and crossed his arms. His hair was long from months at sea. He looked tired. He felt tired. Working at depths of over three hundred feet took a special kind of toll on the body. He was as fit and strong as he'd ever been, but it was a strange kind of work and environment, like being on the moon. The body takes a beating.

"All right, listen up!" someone yelled from the front. The men ignored him. "Hey!" the voice shouted again and banged his hand hard on one of the plastic tables. The murmur died down and the men started to pay attention. There were a few coughs and laughs as the conversations ended. Then silence.

"Right, thanks for coming. Billy O'Brien has a few words for you," the guy who banged his fist said. He handed over to a group of four executive looking gentlemen who'd walked into the room. They were clean-shaven, overweight, wearing dark suits and ties.

"Damn it," Hunt said under his breath.

"What?" the guy next to him leaned over and asked.

"It's never good news when the undertakers walk in," Hunt said and the guy grunted and sat upright again.

Mister Billy walked in behind them and stood to the side. He was the Technosub General Manager. He wore thin rectangular reading glasses. He would take them off and let them hang around his neck, before lifting them onto his nose again and looking at whoever he was speaking to. He was leathery, with deep creases in his skin. A voice that sounded like gravel turning in a cement mixer. He looked solemn and took his glasses off. He opened his hands.

"Ah, listen up guys. There's no easy way to say this," Mister Billy said. He scanned the room, squinted, and lifted his glasses onto his nose again. "Lot of good people in this room, lotta good people."

He paused. It seemed like his words caught at the top of his throat. He lifted his hand to his mouth and coughed once.

"I'm here to tell you that Technosub has been sold to a Russian company. A company called Novachem. They've taken over the dive contract, the vessel, the equipment. All as part of the sale. They're also bringing in their own crews. You're all being replaced."

"What the hell," someone said. An angry murmur ran through the room. In his peripheral vision, Hunt saw the guy next to him glance at him. Hunt stared dead ahead. Bloody Russians, Hunt thought.

"What about our contracts?" someone else in the crowd asked. Mister Billy raised his hands and tried to calm and quiet the room. He was well respected. Not seen as a company man, but rough and tough marine engineers and blue-collar guys only had so much patience.

"Listen, listen," Mister Billy said. "These gentlemen here," he gestured to the suits to his right, "Are going to oversee the transition and arrange your compensation agreements. You're to see them one at a time, sign your agreements, and make your way off the rig."

"When is this happening?" a voice asked.

"This is happening now, today," Mister Billy said. "Effective immediately. There'll be aircraft to take you back to the mainland, you will disembark, the new crews will board, from there you can make your own arrangements."

The men were unhappy. Hunt could understand it. He wasn't in the same category as them, but he could understand it. They were family men. Hard-working, hard-living, hard-drinking, family men. Sending their salaries home to their wives and kids. This might've been Hunt's last job, anyway. No sweat off his back. The way he lived, he could make the cash last. He didn't need the aggravation. But for the rest of them ...

"I know this is a shock," Mister Billy said. "Hell, it's tough to take. For me too, I am in your position. New manager coming in to replace me."

When the men realised Mister Billy's head was on the chopping block too the mood softened. Someone booed.

"Be professional now, gentlemen, please. You need to speak to these gentlemen, one at a time, sign your paperwork, and then grab your gear and prepare to disembark. Crew change by helo in," he checked his watch, "Three hours from now."

Mister Billy nodded to the double-chins in suits and turned and walked out of the mess hall.

"What're you gonna do?" the guy next to Hunt asked.

Hunt glanced at him and stuck out his bottom lip.

"I don't know," he said. "Find a beach somewhere and live frugally for a few months."

"Oh, yeah?"

Hunt shrugged. "Yeah, maybe I'll buy a boat and take dive tours for tourists in Guadalupe."

The guy next to him shook his head and laughed.

"What?" Hunt asked.

"Screw you, man."

"Huh. What do you mean?" Hunt said and furrowed his brow and smiled at the guy's attitude.

"Don't give me that, guy like you, no way you're doing tourists. You're an SAT diver, right?"

"I was, yeah. So?"

"So, that means you're crazy as hell. The only way you're going to be happy is going Mach-two with your hair on fire."

Hunt looked at his colleague out of the corner of his eye.

"Maybe," Hunt said.

FOUR

Hunt sat alone in the dive bar. It was right on the coast, overlooking a pale-sand, dull, and dark beach called Sola. Aside from the bar at the hotel, it was the nearest place to the Stavanger Air Station for him to have a drink and try to get his thoughts in line. Most of the guys in Thor's Tavern had been on the helicopter with him. The majority had been fired.

The crew change on the rig was a sterile and ordered process. Hunt felt glad he wouldn't have to fly out to the rig again. Rough seas had pounded the platform and strong crosswinds battered the side of the structure. Twenty-four souls per helicopter put a lot of trust in the pilots.

Like everywhere in Norway, the view was pristine. Opposite the sand was rolling green and yellow fields with that sense of nostalgia that he couldn't quite put his finger on when in Scandinavia. It was pristine and calm and clean.

It was also icy cold outside, but Thor's was natural light-coloured wood. There was a raging fireplace. A jukebox playing loud nineties rock. And a blonde waitress in a thin white tank top that was too tight for her. Hunt sat at the bar alone and nursed his coffee and enjoyed the view.

He needed to work out his next move. He knew he couldn't keep running forever. Sooner or later someone would recognise him. Someone would betray him. If they hadn't already.

He was looking down at his cup. He put his fingertips on the rim and lifted it under his nose, closed his eyes, and smelled. He'd taken to pouring cocoa powder in his coffees in the compression chamber. He found it improved his memory, attention, and processing speed. It also released serotonin, so while cooped up with four farting, fatigued, unfunny guys, he immediately felt better. Nothing like a good mood to relieve the stress he'd found.

He heard an unfamiliar voice at the bar. It was American. Not unusual. The oil and gas industry in Stavanger attracted all sorts, from all over. It was the tone and the tenor. The bar was full of rig workers and business people. Norway is a place of quiet moderation. The culture is serene, calm, relaxed. Hunt noticed a change in vibe. The American's voice lifted itself above the hubbub. The murmur died down low as the people paid attention to it and waited for the equilibrium to return. Hunt took a sip of his cafe mocha and tasted the grainy chocolate-espresso flavour. He listened.

"Hey, bartender. Yeah, you buddy. Come here."

Hunt couldn't place it exactly. It could have been from Texas. He opened his eyes and looked. Two guys were at the bar. A big guy stood with his hands in the pockets of his jacket and surveyed the room. The other one in a worn baseball cap was on his tiptoes and leaned forward on the bar like he was about to hop over it. The bartender was dressed in a white shirt and black waistcoat, he had a long blond biker beard and his hair was pulled back in a pony-tail. He went over to the Texan.

"I've just asked your lovely lady friend, right over there," the Texan said and pointed the way back to the wait-ress. "She said I should come and try here. We're looking for our friend, you see, and she said you might be able to help."

"Okay," the tall and serious Norwegian bartender said.

"Well, he's really tall, he's English, or British, or what-ever, but he has a bit of a strange accent. You'd notice it. Said he was working on a rig around here, maybe diving or something else. Don't quite know what else to tell you, you know anybody by that description?"

The bartender pursed his lips and shook his head once. "What's his name?" he asked.

"Goes by the name of John Beagles."

The bartender inadvertently looked in Hunt's direction and then back at the Texan.

"No, I don't think I know him," the bartender said.

Too late. Hunt put his coffee down and sat back in his chair. The big guy with his hands in his pocket turned and looked at Hunt. He tapped his friend on the back.

"Much obliged," the Texan said to the bartender. "You've been a big help."

Hunt sighed. He didn't know what these guys wanted, but he could guess. The guys came over. The din in the bar went back to a normal level. People had lost interest. Just two guys looking for their friend. Hunt didn't look up at them.

"Well, aren't you going to ask us to join you, John?" the Texan said.

Hunt knew these guys weren't going to leave him alone until they'd got what they wanted.

Hunt relented. "Sure," he said and motioned to the

barstools next to him. They pulled them out and sat down. The Texan took off his cap and dropped it on the bar and rubbed his hand through his short hair.

He looked around the bar. "Nice place," he said. "How long you been hiding out here?"

The big guy just sat there and stared at Hunt. Trying to psych me out or something, Hunt thought. "Is he supposed to intimidate me?" Hunt asked and matched the big guy's glare.

The Texan glanced over his shoulder at his colleague. "Oh, don't mind big Doug. He don't say much, but he's a lovely fella once you get to know him, ain't ya Doug?"

Doug didn't say anything.

"What do you want?" Hunt asked.

"What do we want! Well now, let's see. What do we want?" the Texan lifted his hand to his chin in mock consideration. "Well, John, we need you to come with us. You can leave your luggage, won't be needing it. Come with us and we can straighten out a few things."

"Who sent you?" Hunt asked and picked up his coffee cup. He drained it and set it down on the saucer without making a sound.

"That hardly matters, doesn't it?"

"Okay," Hunt said. "Meeting over then, I guess." He stood up.

"Where do you think you're going?" the Texan said.

Hunt scoffed. Wherever the hell I want.

"Listen, gents," Hunt said and looked at the big guy, "I'm not sure what you think is going to happen or how you thought this was going to go before you walked in, but I assure you it isn't going to go how you expect."

"Oh yeah," the Texan said and glanced around quickly.

"Is that how you felt about how it went in the catacombs too?"

Hunt stayed and stared at him for a moment. He suddenly sparked. How'd they known about Odessa? "Whichever you cut it, John, I mean, Stirling, the only way you leave this place is with us, you hear? So sit back down and talk to us."

Hunt pressed his lips together and then smiled. He nodded once with a dumb, blank grin on his face.

"Who sent you?"

The Texan scoffed and looked at him disbelievingly. "Really?" he said.

"Yes, really, who are you?"

"This is Doug and I'm Dougie," the Texan said. "He's very pleased to meet you. Now, why don't you sit down so we can get this straightened out."

"I don't think so," Hunt said. "I'm going to pay my tab and get on a flight and if I so much as sniff you behind me ... I'll put you in the ground."

Hunt went to step past the Texan. Doug quickly stood and blocked his path. He squared up to Hunt. The murmur died down again. A few people at the nearby tables pushed their chairs out and moved away.

"I ain't gonna ask you again," the Texan said. "Look here, you're causing a scene. Sit down and parley with us."

Hunt heard a click come from inside the pocket of Doug's jacket. He stared blankly at Hunt.

"Didn't think they allowed concealed carry in Norway," Hunt said.

"He'll put you down right here," the Texan said.

FIVE

Hunt stared right back at big Doug. Out of the corner of his eye, he saw a bald man move towards them. It was the bar's owner, he was wearing a maroon T-shirt with his name on a badge in black and gold.

"Please, gentlemen," he said and came to stand next to them. "You are disturbing the guests and I would ask you to refrain from this."

The people at the tables had stood and stepped back.

"We ain't doing nothing but talking here," the Texan said and stood. He went around the back of big Doug and put his hand on the owner's shoulder. "Don't mind us *compadre*, they're just old friends who haven't seen each other in a while, look, they're about ready to kiss." Doug was standing eye to eye with Hunt. "You can almost feel the tension," the Texan said, "It's electric."

Just then Doug moved. He pulled his hand out of his jacket. Hunt didn't wait to see what it was. He head-butted the big American on the bridge of his nose. A woman screamed and there was the sound of tables and chairs scraping on the wooden floor as people in the vicinity scrambled to get away from them.

The owner went reeling backwards and the Texan came at Hunt. Doug stumbled backwards and touched his hand to his nose. It was oozing blood. Hunt saw a black taser in Big Doug's hand. Big Doug glanced up at him and Hunt jumped forward and jabbed the big man in his right eye.

"Get him, Doug!" the Texan yelled as he got behind Hunt and tried to grab hold of him. He got on Hunt's left arm and Doug came at him with the taser. Hunt leaned back and into the Texan and put his weight on him. As Doug closed the gap, Hunt lifted his foot and front kicked Doug in the forearm and sent his hand and the taser skyward. The second kick caught big Doug under the chin. Hunt heard a crack as his boot connected with the jawbone.

Big Doug's teeth clattered and he dropped to his knees. The Texan got his arms around Hunt's neck. Hunt grabbed the wrist and used his grip to pry the Texan's thumb loose. Hunt clamped his powerful hand around the thumb. The Texan anticipated what was happening and loosened his grip, but Hunt had his wrist locked and twisted the Texan's thumb back violently.

Hunt snapped it above the joint and the Texan squealed out in pain and fear. Hunt pulled the arm loose and elbowed the Texan in the ribs. He grunted with the effort and the Texan doubled over.

Doug got to his feet and came at Hunt with the snapping voltage of the taser. Hunt let go of the Texan's arm and stepped inside big Doug and blocked the oncoming forearm. Hunt pirouetted and pulled Doug's forearm over his right shoulder as he turned. With his back to the big American, Hunt drove his elbow into Doug's sternum and then grabbed the big man's wrist in both hands. Hunt twisted the wrist so Doug's palm faced the ceiling. Hunt dropped low and brought all of his body weight down on the attacker's arm. Doug's elbow snapped under the pressure as his arm bent the wrong way. He howled and dropped the taser. It clattered to the floor. The Texan saw it and his eyes went wide, but before he could react, Hunt sank to his haunches and spun. He picked up the taser and held it out. Doug was on the floor writhing and holding his elbow. The Texan was frozen in a half-crouch. He'd been ready to dive for the weapon before Hunt reached it, and now he was stopped dead. Hunt looked at the Texan's thumb. It was bent backwards. His colleague was in as much pain as he'd ever been in. There was silence in the bar. The onlookers had backed away in a semicircle.

"Who sent you?" Hunt said.

"You know I can't tell you that, man," the Texan said.

The taser clicked and snapped ominously. Hunt jumped forward and jammed the taser into the guy's side. He screeched and tried to grab for it, but the voltage surged through him and seized his nervous system up and he went to ground shaking and juddering. Hunt jumped on top of him and pinned him with his knees.

"No, man, stop, please! Don't do this anymore," the Texan begged.

Rage surged through Hunt's veins. He was ready to kill. He'd left them alone. He'd kept his head down. Now he realised they wouldn't stop. So, neither would he.

"Who sent you?"

"Man, I can't …"

Hunt pressed the taser into the Texan's neck. He wailed and Hunt felt the body contort under his weight and he smelled burning flesh. Hunt pulled the taser off him.

"Who are you?"

"Ex-Delta, man. Okay? We're cleaning up other people's messes."

"Who sent you?"

"I can't ... they'll kill me —"

"Worry about what I will do to you," Hunt said and pressed his weight harder into the Texan's shoulders. He pressed the button and the electricity crackled.

"Okay, okay," the Texan gasped. "I'll tell you. I'll tell you ... The guy's name is Mansfield."

"Who?"

"Simon Mansfield ran an operation called Blacksand."

"Who is he?"

"He fixes problems that can't be fixed."

Hunt gritted his teeth. "Like me," Hunt said.

"Like you," the Texan was negotiating now. "Listen, we're tying up loose ends, it's business, not personal. Someone put a contract out on you. We've been after you since Ukraine. You got away in the catacombs and we've been tracking you —"

"Yeah? Well, it's personal to me. Who put out the contract?" Hunt already knew the answer.

"I don't know, man, I swear I don't know. Mansfield only told us it was sanctioned. Official."

Hunt had heard enough. He fired up the taser. He didn't know how long it would be until the Texan's heart gave out, but it would be useful to know for future reference. He lifted the weapon and the Texan struggled to get away. Just then Hunt heard clattering footsteps. The owner burst through the bystanders. Hunt snapped out of it and realised there was a group of fifteen or twenty eyewitnesses standing around watching.

"Please! The police are on their way," the guy said. He

was standing near the bar, leaning forward and looking at Hunt imploringly.

"You're lucky," Hunt said matter-of-factly and climbed off the Texan. The guy groaned and rolled onto his side and held his thumb. Hunt walked up to the bar's owner and handed him the taser and said, "You saw what happened, they attacked me."

The owner nodded.

"You all saw," Hunt said to the crowd. They were his people. He'd lived and worked with them. "It was self-defence." A few nodded. Hunt looked at the bartender. He nodded too. Hunt was calm. The white-topped waitress smiled at him. He walked out of the bar.

SIX

Hunt went back to his room. He needed to leave. His mind raced. They'd found him. How? He needed some answers. He needed to check if she was okay. He slammed the motel door shut and knelt by the side of the bed. He stuck his hand under it and reached forward until his fingertips touched it. He ripped the duct tape away and pulled out a cheap mobile phone. Had to wait for it to turn on and he punched in the number.

"Hello?"

"Hey, it's me," Hunt said.

"Is this—"

"Yeah, it's a burner. This is the first number I've dialled on it. Untraceable."

"Nothing is untraceable, Stirling. You know that," Robin said.

Hunt smiled wryly. Same old Robin.

"You can never be too careful," Hunt said.

There was a pause between them. A moment of calm. They seemed close together. They were so far apart.

"I was actually just thinking about you," Robin said. Hunt imagined her biting her lip.

"I had to make sure you were safe," Hunt said.

"Why, what's happened?"

"I was wondering if my name had lit up on any of your scans?"

He heard some keyboard keys tapping. "Umm. Not that I can see ..."

"A couple of guys tried to kill me just now," Hunt said.

Robin was quiet.

"God, Stirling, I'm so sorry. I really thought this was behind us."

"You're safe," Hunt said. "I'm not trying to worry you. Just wanted to check you were okay."

"I'm fine. I miss you though ..."

Hunt pulled the corner of the curtain aside to glimpse out.

"I miss you too," he said. Hurried. Impatient.

"Okay, Mister Tough-guy. Keep your crap together. Don't get all soft on me now," she said.

Hunt gave a single laugh.

"What do I do?"

"I can try and find out who sent them?" Robin said.

"They said they were in Odessa, in the catacombs."

"Secret intelligence?"

"I think so," Hunt said and sat on the bed.

He rubbed his forehead.

"What're you going to do?"

"What can I do?"

"You can put an end to it ..." Robin said.

"This won't end—"

"Not while that bastard is still alive."

"We don't know if it was actually him," Hunt said.

"Come on, Stirling—look I get that he was your mentor and all that—but the guy sold you up the river. You must see that."

"Down the river. Maybe," Hunt said and pinched the bridge of his nose.

"*Maybe?*" Robin scoffed. "I'm sorry to be blunt, but you've really only got two options. You can sit and wait for them to come and get you, or you can go and find them first —"

"I can leave—"

"You mean run? You've been running. Isn't that what you're doing now? That's the same as letting them come to find you. I mean, this can't go on—"

Hunt heard a loud bang.

"Is everything okay?" He asked suddenly, sitting upright, alert.

"There's someone—" she said. Then there was a loud crash. "Stirling! Help!"

Hunt stood up. He was concentrating on the background noises.

"Where is he—" Hunt heard a man's voice say. Robin screamed.

"Stirling, help me!" She shouted.

"Describe them to me, what do they look like?"

"*Uh-umm.* Black combat gear, helmets, night vision. Automatic weapons. No! Ah! Help! Help!"

Hunt heard Robin's voice further from the mic now. There was a scuffle and a bang. Hunt heard a man's breathing. Close to the mic. He was wearing her headset. Each man listened to the dead air on the line.

"If you want to see her again—"

"I'm coming for you," Hunt said. He spoke slowly and

calmly, but his heart was thumping hard in his chest. "Don't close your eyes. If you go to sleep I'll be standing over you."

"You want to watch me sleep, *ey*?"

Australian accent. All nasally and high-pitched at the end.

"I want to watch you bleed out."

"Good luck with that," the voice said.

"You're a dead—"

The line cut.

SEVEN

Down in the European Task Force command centre, McKenna and Rocca watched the screen. She looked up at him.

"Why'd he use a passport he knew we could trace?" she asked, thinking out loud. "He must know that we're looking for him. That he's burned."

"Either he doesn't know and, so, is oblivious, or, he knows and doesn't care. Which means he wants *us* to know that he has come back ..." McKenna looked across at Rocca and met her eyes. Her face was somewhere between confusion and shock.

"Why would he—"

"Want us to know? Because he's looking for us too. Whoever shows up to get him will lead straight to the people he wants."

"And who is that?"

"Right now it's us."

Rocca swallowed hard and McKenna stifled a grin. Old school espionage. A game of deceit and shadows. He missed it.

"So what do we—"

"I'd recommend staying in the office until he's appre-hended." McKenna leaned past Rocca and spoke to one of the analysts. "When was this captured?"

The analyst tapped on some keys.

"Approximately twenty minutes ago, sir. We're tracking him up the motorway on the road traffic cameras."

"Destination?"

"Unknown, sir. Right now he is following the signs north to London."

"How's his driving?" McKenna asked.

"He's taking his time. Driving in the slow lane. Doesn't appear to be in any rush."

"*Hmm*," McKenna put his forefinger to his chin.

Rocca was still watching him. "What does that mean?"

"That means he is one angry man."

"He's trying not to draw attention to himself."

"No," McKenna said. "He knows we're watching him. He doesn't care. He's planning his next move. Takes a lot of control, don't you think ..."

"Sir?"

"... To be seething with rage and drive under the speed limit?"

They both looked at the screen.

"What do you think it means?"

EIGHT

WILLIAM T. HUBERMAN III WAS CHIEF EXECUTIVE
Officer and lead investor at the venture capital fund he
founded more than thirty years before. He'd seen technology replace technology over and over during that time.
An early forecaster of the power of the Internet, he never
thought he would see an opportunity like it again.

Until today.

Bill Huberman's Hivemind Capital was on the top floor
of a chrome skyscraper in southeast Manhattan. His
personal assistant leaned around the door to the conference
room and said, "He's on his way up."

"Thanks, Gloria," Bill said.

While his first—and only—meeting of the day walked
down the long hallway towards the meeting room, Bill
looked at his associates and said, "Here we go fellas. This is
the big one, let's see if we can hook this monster."

Gloria pushed the conference room door open and Bill
and his team stood. He wiped his hand on his trousers and
licked his top lip and set his face in a smile that was ready to
get bigger the moment the prospect walked in.

He walked into the room. Smart navy suit, crisp, white, open-collared shirt, smart shoes, glinting Rolex, and smile to match.

"Derek!" Bill said. "Come in. Please meet my team." As he was talking Derek van den Krijl locked onto his hand and his gaze and flashed his boyish grin. He had dimples and smooth skin that Bill—now in his early sixties—would pay extremely well for.

Bill introduced his team, "This is Allison Avery our legal counsel, and Steve McKenzie my managing director and co-founder. You already know Simon Dillon, our partnerships director."

"How-do-you-do," van den Krijl said and took their hands one by one. The woman with him silently handed him an anti-bacterial wipe after he'd shaken everyone's hands.

He didn't introduce her.

"Please, take a seat," Bill said and indicated a chair opposite. Van den Krijl glanced at the chair Bill was offering him. It was in the middle of the long table and faced Bill.

"I don't like to have my back exposed," van den Krijl said. "I'll sit at the head."

Bill was taken aback, but said, "Sure, you're our guest. Simon, you move over here and let Derek sit there."

Dillon went through the process of collecting up his folders and documents and shifting seats. Van den Krijl took his seat at the head of the table and his hooked-nosed female colleague sat primly to his left.

Bill took his seat. There was a moment of silence. They all looked at each other for a moment. The silence dragged out. Van den Krijl's iceberg blue eyes were locked onto Bill Huberman.

"Right, let's get started," Bill said. "As I think you know —Derek—we're usually the ones being pitched to but considering the interest in your offering, I think it is only fair that we pitch to you."

Bill gave a lighthearted chuckle and glanced around the conference table. His team smiled and nodded in agreement. It was cordial.

"Roderick," van den Krijl said.

"Excuse me?" Bill said, mid-smile.

"Roderick, if you don't mind. That's my name."

"Oh, why, yes, of course, Roderick. My apologies. I was briefed—" Bill glanced at his legal council and decided to stop talking there.

"Well, as I was saying, I believe it is us at Hivemind who should pitch you."

"That would be best, Mister Huberman," van den Krijl said.

"Please, call me Bill."

"We are not on first name terms yet, Mister Huberman," van den Krijl glanced at his watch.

Bill smiled. Right you are. Not a great start to their meeting. The man sitting at the head of his conference table wasn't the man he'd expected. What little they knew about him was a fascinating prospect. He'd catapulted out of obscurity to launch one of the most exciting and evocative cryptocurrency offerings in the game.

Bill knew Roderick van den Krijl wasn't a fan of the term *cryptocurrency*, but it was the nomenclature in fashion. What Bill had expected was—to put it bluntly—a hippy. Someone with dreads and wearing loose-fitting cotton threads. Not this immaculately dressed businessman. And, he meant business. Bill knew the 'name game' and seating ruse was just a power play. A negotiating tactic. Or, more accurately, a negating tactic. Bill wasn't going to play. They both knew what van den Krijl was offering was more valuable than what Bill had. Which, after all, was only money. What van den Krijl had was potential.

Simon Dillon stepped up, "We've reviewed the filings and the documentation, Mister van den Krijl, and to say we're impressed, I believe, would be an understatement."

Bill nodded his approval as Dillon glanced at him out of the corner of his eye.

Van den Krijl sighed and said, "Gentlemen, I certainly don't mean to be rude. I've been swooned and serenaded and had the sirens singing to me all day today, haven't I Petunia?" He glanced at the thin girl sitting on his left and she stayed motionless. "We saved, I hope, the best for last—is the expression?"

Bill slammed his hand on the table good naturedly and said, "I read you loud and clear, Mister van den Krijl. Let's get down to it. Brass tacks."

Van den Krijl was French-Canadian, albeit with a Dutch name and, because he spoke with a kind of confused accent, Bill felt the need to explain English expressions and idioms. "Let's get down to business. What've we got."

It was a rhetorical question, but van den Krijl took it as an opening. "Simply put we have the next oil rush on our hands, Mister Huberman. Data. Not just any data. The comprehensive data set on greenhouse-gas emissions, production, utilisation, and distribution that now—and will ever—exist. It is an entirely new economy. A new petrodollar. An entire system of capture, analysis, automated reporting, and the sell- and buy-side for carbon offset all revolving around an impenetrable digital asset. My impenetrable digital asset. Gaia. The mother of the earth."

"And the mother lode," Bill said and grinned widely.

"Yes, sir," van den Krijl said. "That too."

Bill was impressed. This guy'd come from nowhere to create the code for a cryptocurrency that undercut not only the technology companies but the banks too. He undercut the top cutting-edge technology companies by starting his own. Something revolutionary. Something with such scale and mass appeal. Something with a real shot at making people take climate change seriously. He *was* a hippy. One who spoke the language of capitalism.

"You must understand, Mister Huberman," van den Krijl said and then looked at each of the people sitting around the table one by one, "Gaia started as a community. A way for people to gather under the flag of mother earth. People installed our air quality monitors in their homes. These devices used their electricity and internet connection to send us data—on the ground—from every city, all over the world. They were paid in GaiaCoin. The value of this data is valuable to us, it is valuable to governments, it is valuable to the carbon and emissions trading market. The next idea is our biggest yet—"

Bill glanced at his colleagues. They were enthralled. This guy was the real deal.

"—Imagine, if you will, peer-to-peer carbon offset and carbon credit trading. A giant marketplace. The travel booking sector—one small example—is a seventy billion dollar per year venture. What if Gaia managed an instantaneous carbon offset program for travellers? Trade your carbon footprint with your neighbours to remain net zero. There is money to be made buying and selling the green revolution, ladies and gentlemen. And there is a spread in this market too."

Bill's smile was growing with each word. He licked his lips.

"I must say, Mister van den Krijl, it sounds like you're pitching us now."

"Force of habit," van den Krijl said and flashed his straight-white smile. Everyone laughed.

"You've got quite an empire," Bill said. "Communes—followers—in some idyllic locations. Land. Water. Natural resources. Governments on board. Industry. Is there anything you don't have?"

"We're in the process of being completely carbon neutral," van den Krijl said. "Not only that, we've acquired some disused mines above the arctic circle. The location is a secret, but they are deep below ground, so they require no air conditioning for our servers. The entire system is cooled by the freezing temperature of the ground. It remains constant, no matter the season. With your help, Bill, we can build the largest carbon capture machine ever built. It will suck carbon straight from the atmosphere and deposit it deep underground in our mines. We will actually be carbon *minus* as a movement—and we're very much a movement—not a company."

van den Krijl finished speaking. He and Bill were looking into one another's eyes. Neither man blinked. Finally, Bill gave a little wry smile.

"Well, son, tell me ... how much do you need?"

They all laughed as the tension was broken. Bill reached in his back pocket and pulled out his cheque book with a flourish. He grabbed a pen and flipped open the book. "Aw, hell," he said, "Who am I kiddin', here," he tore off a cheque. "It's blank, why don't you fill it in yourself."

van den Krijl stood and Bill did too. The blank cheque was symbolic. One of Bill Huberman's negotiating tactics for when there was a bidding war from other venture capitalist funds. Bill was lighthearted on the outside and ruthless on the inside. He saw the potential in this cryptocurrency movement and the dollar signs. This was to be his legacy. One last swing at the fences. A chance he never thought Hivemind Capital would see again. Van den Krijl accepted the cheque from him and then they shook hands firmly. The kid had a strong grip, Bill thought. As they shook and smiled at one another, Bill wondered how much it would cost him. Ten billion, he thought. Maybe fifteen. Whatever, it was a drop in the ocean in terms of what it would return him.

NINE

Hᴜɴᴛ ɴᴇᴠᴇʀ sʟᴇᴘᴛ ᴡᴇʟʟ ɪɴ ʜᴏᴛᴇʟs. Eꜱᴘᴇᴄɪᴀʟʟʏ ᴛʜᴇ seedy ones. The rooms were always too warm without the air conditioning on and the fact that the mattresses had had ten-thousand sweaty bodies asleep on, or that someone might have died on them, disturbed him.

Hunt had woken early and done some exercise and meditation. One of the guys in the dive team had got him into green tea and tai chi. Now he was dressed and sitting on the bed. Hunt was waiting for a call from reception telling him his taxi had arrived. There was a knock on the door. He checked his watch. Strange. He went to the peep-hole and looked through it. He saw the concierge from downstairs and two other men.

Oɴᴇ ᴏꜰ ᴛʜᴇ ᴍᴇɴ, ɪɴ ᴛʜᴇ ʙᴀᴄᴋ, ᴡᴀs ᴛʜᴇ ᴍᴜsᴄʟᴇ. Smart suit and tie. The earpiece and shaved head meant he was one of the Mastiffs. MI6's internal security. A guard dog. There was another one. He looked more English-public schoolboy. He was definitely a Secret Intelligence

Service officer. Hunt undid the latch and opened the door. The concierge looked relieved.

"You can go," Hunt said to him.

He nodded. "Thank you, sir," and scurried off.

"Hector Reyes?" the clean-shaven, brown-haired ex-public schoolboy asked.

"Depends on who's asking."

The public schoolboy reached into his suit jacket and pulled out his identification. Hunt took it and looked at the bank card-sized ID. Hunt handed it back to him.

"Okay," Hunt said and stood in the doorway.

"We'd like you to come with us please."

"Where to?"

"We're not at liberty to say."

Hunt pursed his lips. "I can't, I'm leaving in a minute."

"You'll be back in a few hours."

"A few hours?" Hunt repeated.

"Unless something dramatic happens," agent schoolboy said. Hunt grinned and the intelligence officer looked worried and tried to smile.

"Okay," he said and stepped out of the room. The intelligence officer looked relieved.

"This way," he said. "We have a car waiting."

HUNT SAT IN A WINDOWLESS ROOM IN THE BASEMENT of the Secret Intelligence Service building in Vauxhall. It was part dungeon, part interview room. There was one wide-angle security camera in the top left-hand corner of the room silently blinking red at him. He closed his eyes and breathed. Part of his mind was imagining being locked away in a room like this for the rest of his life.

They could do it.

What did they do with spies that just wouldn't retire?

He'd been snuck in via the underground car park at the rear of the building and concealed from view. Almost like they were ashamed to have him around the place. Easier to get rid of the evidence if he'd never arrived in the first place. They wouldn't do it here though. It would be some accident. Getting rammed off a mountain road or pushed into oncoming traffic. An accident. That's how they operated. Hunt opened his eyes.

He thought he heard a sound coming from outside the concrete walls. The red light on the closed-circuit camera blinked off and didn't come back on.

The heavy door opened.

A smartly suited, middle-aged man came in. He stuck out his hand and Hunt pushed his chair back and stood. He had a narrow, long smile like he was trying to conceal his teeth. His eyes were bright. He looked relaxed and well-rested. Hunt shook the man's hand. They looked at one another for a moment and then the man said, "You must be the infamous Stirling Hunt. How do you do. Everett McKenna."

Hunt released his hand and McKenna gestured to Hunt's chair. Hunt sat. McKenna stayed standing. He spread his hands towards the corners of the room.

"Apologies for the secretive nature of our little rendezvous, Hunt, it's just a bit better this way," McKenna said.

Hunt decided to be polite. "That's okay, sir."

McKenna sat. He positioned himself forwards, arms and hands together in front of him, paying attention. He had a pleasant look on his face, but steel behind his eyes.

"I heard you were in town and thought it best we meet. Any idea why you're here?"

That was a euphemism for the fact that they'd been watching him. Since when, Hunt didn't know. Likely since he entered the country. Hunt said nothing. He just kept his blank expression and dull stare on McKenna's chin. He didn't want to be rude, but he didn't want to let on that he was anxious to find out what this was all about. He felt like he was waiting outside the headmaster's office and wondering what his punishment would be.

"Bit of a coincidence, isn't it?"

"What's that?" Hunt asked and felt like he'd taken the bait.

"You, turning up out of the blue just as my team of agents are killed."

Hunt sighed and put his hand on the table. "That *is* just a coincidence," he said. "I don't know anything about your agents."

McKenna frowned and said in mock confusion, "Aren't you going to ask me how they died?" Hunt was quiet and contemplated the question. "Or, am I to assume that you already know?"

Hunt crossed his arms and sat back.

"I received this," McKenna said and leaned back and looked over his shoulder and held his hand out. The door opened and a young-looking low-level analyst in a white shirt came in holding a large envelope. Post office works fast, Hunt thought. The analyst put the padded parcel in McKenna's hand.

"My agents pulled it from a letterbox near your hotel last night. Curiously, it's addressed to the chief. Do you know what it is?"

Hunt shook his head. "No idea."

McKenna placed the parcel down on the table. He sat up straight again and rested his fingers on the envelope and looked at Hunt from under his eyebrows.

"You're wanted in connection with the ongoing murder investigation into Tom Holland's death.

Hunt furrowed his brow.

"You didn't know?" McKenna seemed amused. He looked at Hunt for a moment before he glanced at the ceiling and opened his palms and said, "As you may or may not know, Thomas was found badly beaten on the kitchen floor of your old apartment in Notting Hill."

Hunt shook his head. "When was this?" he asked.

"A fingerprint of yours was recovered at the scene," McKenna said.

"When did it happen?" Hunt asked again.

"The police report places the time of death somewhere in a four-hour window on the twenty-ninth of December," McKenna said.

"I wasn't in the country on that date," Hunt said. "I was in —"

"You were in Odessa, making contact with another burned operative, one Miss Robin Adler," McKenna said.

He reached into the inside pocket of his jacket and pulled out a small black notebook. He opened it and raised his left eyebrow as he read. Hunt decided to play the game.

"Let's say that's right," Hunt said. "So what?"

"Well, if that is the case, then you'd no longer be a suspect," McKenna said and placed the notebook down. He sat back in his chair and put his hands on his lap. "I'd like to think that the murder investigation into Tom Holland's death would be put on ice."

"For how long?"

"Indefinitely, potentially. Once we're confident the murderer has been ... dealt with."

"You think it's me?"

McKenna shook his head. "No, of course not, but even the real killer will never be caught," McKenna gestured towards the envelope, "We have our suspicions," he said.

"But it's a matter of national security. Got it," Hunt said.

McKenna pursed his lips and stared blankly at Hunt. Then he took a deep breath and said, "The Clubhouse and all Clubhouse operations have been shut down effective immediately. The programme has been mothballed. I was in front of the Foreign Secretary all day yesterday. He agrees with me. Almost all Clubhouse operatives have been debriefed and reassigned. We've concluded almost all of them. All—that is—except you."

Hunt said nothing.

"I'm aware of your intention to quit the service," McKenna said. "But, I thought it prudent for us to have a discussion before you made up your mind."

"You're giving me a choice?"

"While the Clubhouse is no more—I am—with the Foreign Secretary's approval, of course, reinstating an old Section 7 programme."

Hunt's eyes narrowed. Section 7 was an umbrella term, coined because of the section of the intelligence legislation that it fell under. It gave operatives of the Secret Intelligence Service—who operate under the direct supervision of the Foreign Secretary of the United Kingdom—immunity from all prosecution. It was also the reason the training programme Hunt had graduated from was nicknamed the 'Kill School'. Section 7 of the law, among other things, gave British overseas operatives legal sanction for murder. The Clubhouse had been one such division within multiple Section 7 programmes. Now it was being shut down.

"I have authorisation from the Foreign Secretary for a new programme, Hunt. And—"

"You want me to be your first recruit. Thanks for the offer, sir —" Hunt said.

"I haven't made it yet," McKenna interjected.

"— But I'm not interested."

"Just cool down a bit and hear me out," McKenna said and gave him a slightly irritated smile.

Hunt relented.

"You'd be working alone with the full backing of the Prime Minister. The threats to the country have changed, Field Agent Hunt. We need people like you, with experience, who can operate confidently in places that others could only dream of like you did in Ukraine."

"I was being hunted."

"Yes. By us, and you escaped and completed your mission. We owe our ongoing relationship with the Americans to your ingenuity."

Hunt was quiet. He was thinking. He took shallow breaths through his nose. He felt his pulse rising in his neck. Flattery made him nervous.

"The programme is code-named Oberon," McKenna said. "It'll be a new specialist programme. Only the best of the best from Section 7 are to be recruited in. You already know how tough the training is. It'll combine the best in modern cyber warfare and technology with the real-world tradecraft of operatives like yourself. You could be the foundation that the programme is built on," McKenna said.

"It'll be nothing like the sideshow that Soames was running. The Clubhouse was a relic. It turned trusted men into monsters. There will be oversight here, Hunt. You'll operate entirely alone, but you'll also be supported."

"I'll think about it," Hunt said.

"Come on," McKenna said and smiled warmly. "Join us. Your entire career could be built on this."

"*Your* entire career you mean," Hunt said.

"Our career then," McKenna said and nodded.

"I'm not interested in careers. If I was, I would have become a lawyer."

McKenna maintained his warm smile.

"No, I'm getting that sense. You're only interested in justice, isn't that right, Hunt? You don't care where your next meal is coming from, only that the person who serves it is getting a fair wage."

"I never expected to live too much longer than this," Hunt said.

"So every day to you seems like a bonus," McKenna said. "I understand."

"Have you ever been in the field, sir?"

McKenna just smiled and studied his tie. Hunt nodded.

"I don't want to spend my days climbing an invisible ladder and bowing and scraping to senior people in an organisation who are in turn only looking at ways to climb the same invisible ladder and don't mind stepping on people to get to the top."

McKenna sighed. "That's why we need you, Hunt. That's why we need Oberon, and Oberon needs you. The country needs you. Unfortunately, this culture doesn't seem capable of producing the people we need at the rate we need them. You might not believe it, but I am not in this to climb ladders, real or invisible. I want what you want."

"What's that?"

"To see justice done."

"For your agents?"

For the first time, Hunt looked at McKenna and thought maybe, just maybe, this guy was the real deal. Someone he could work with. No games. No hidden agenda. Just assessing intelligence and acting on it. Maybe he was just telling Hunt what he knew he wanted to hear.

"You'd have complete legislative freedom for our operations," McKenna said. "The Foreign Secretary would be directly involved, no one else."

"You talked about support?" Hunt said.

"Yes, absolutely. Anything you need. The best available," McKenna said. Hunt saw that McKenna had sensed a change. An opportunity.

"I'll have to think about it," Hunt said again. Noncommittal. McKenna sat back in his chair for the first time. His face hardened.

"I think we're both clear on the carrot here, wouldn't you say?" McKenna said.

Hunt closed his mouth and studied the new intelligence director. Now he waited for the stick.

"The Metropolitan Police aren't going to get too far with their investigation into Holland's untimely demise," McKenna said. "But that's not to say a new piece of evidence that helps with the case doesn't turn up the moment you go off the reservation."

Hunt clenched his jaw.

"It's just business, Hunt. You've been known to act erratically on occasion. It's my insurance policy. Stay close to me and the case against you disappears. Stray too far and perhaps some previously classified material finds its way to one of the detective's inboxes."

"So you'll hang me out to dry whenever you want," Hunt said.

"If you join Oberon you'll have immunity. Unfortunately, as a matter of national security, the only people who know your whereabouts on the night in question are MI6. We're the only ones who *can* ever know. We're in balance here, you and I. You need us to maintain your freedom, and we need you to maintain the freedom of the country."

Hunt was seeing that he might not have a choice after all.

"You think I care about what happens to me?"

"No—I don't actually—that's why we're offering one Miss Robin Adler as part of the deal."

"You know where she is?"

McKenna looked at Hunt blankly.

"You're the ones who took her," Hunt said.

"We can un-burn her. Bring her in from the cold," McKenna said.

Hunt looked dubious. "You'd do that?"

"Well, I understand you make quite the team. Keep your friends close, and all that ..."

"And if I refuse?"

"You'd be signing her death warrant. And yours."

"How do I know you took her?"

The Intelligence Director lifted a scrap of paper from his notebook.

"She doesn't live at this address?" McKenna asked and glanced at the paper, before sliding it across to Hunt. In blue, capital letters McKenna had written Robin's address out. "This is where she lives, isn't it?" he asked and tapped his finger near the scrap of paper.

Hunt didn't respond.

"So," McKenna asked. "Where does this leave us then?"

Hunt was quiet.

"Still uncertain?" McKenna asked. Hunt sensed another arrow in his quiver. McKenna looked at him.

"She is in our custody now, while you decide what we do with her." Hunt furrowed his brow. "She's in our custody, Hunt," McKenna said, reading the doubt on Hunt's face.

"What're you going to do with her?"

"That's up to you ... the Crown Prosecution Office feel they have a strong case against her under the Official Secrets Act. She was a very naughty girl ..."

Hunt's face hardened and he looked directly at Everett McKenna.

"Fine," Hunt said. "Robin Adler then. I want her freed. I want her off the burn list. I want her living in the West again, without fear of prosecution, or murder. And I want it in writing, a Royal Pardon and guarantees signed by the Foreign Secretary."

"I'm not sure if I can —"

"Yes, you are. You said you wanted the best," Hunt said. "You said I would get support. Well, without Robin, we wouldn't be sitting here. The Russians would have won. She deserves a second chance."

McKenna lifted his hand to his mouth. He was thinking about it.

"I don't work and play well with others, isn't that right?" Hunt said. "Isn't that what your file says? Well, I can work with Robin. It's my life for hers."

McKenna was quiet. His lips were pushed firmly together and his brow was squashed in firm straight lines on his forehead. He was concentrating hard. While he was, Hunt stood up. His chair scraped as he pushed it backwards. McKenna didn't move. He stared at the empty chair where Hunt had been. It seemed they'd reached an impasse.

"Get in touch if you can make it happen," Hunt said. "Until then, if you send anyone after me, the next guy in your chair will also have an envelope. It'll include a gunshot on tape."

TEN

Hunt hailed a cab outside the front of the river house and climbed in the backseat.

"The Victory Club, please," Hunt said to the cabbie.

The internal security Mastiff and the young schoolboy-haircut intelligence officer had tried to insist on escorting him back to his hotel. His blood was still up. In the large marble foyer, the schoolboy had tried to put his hand on Hunt's arm. "Get your hands off me," Hunt had said. "Unless you want to touch your next prostitute with broken wrists."

McKenna had given them the nod. Hunt had walked out on his own terms. And, for now, he still had a choice to make. The cab driver kept glancing at him in the rearview mirror. Hunt was sure he didn't mean anything by it, but it made the hair on his neck stand on end while he was trying to calm himself down. He looked out the window as they drove past Hyde Park.

The cabbie managed to get his attention and asked, "You servin' in the forces?"

Hunt forced a smile. What gave it away, he thought. "Used to," Hunt said.

It reminded him of the same conversation he'd had with the cabbie who'd dropped him at 85 Albert Embankment all those years ago. Before his first mission. Before the Kill School. After he'd met Gerald D. Soames at Headley Court. The Special Boat Service hadn't wanted anything more to do with him. They'd used him up and spat him out. Gerry Soames though—some sort of spook—had offered Hunt another chance. A chance to do things even the UK Special Forces didn't do. He didn't remember ever being a nervous guy. Now his cuticles were bitten back and the inside of his cheek was raw. Soames had offered him a chance. He'd wanted to find out what happened to his parents. He wanted to look the opaline-green-eyed murderer in the face and show him just how big a mistake he'd made by leaving that young boy alive. To know that Hunt was coming for him.

Soames had dangled the lure of working for the intelligence services on a top-secret mission to eliminate a Chechen *myfioso*. His first covert kill. Hunt had struck hard at the bait. Now he was wondering exactly what he might have signed up for. Sold his soul about summed it up.

The cabbie didn't ask any more questions. Hunt's mind wandered back to his first meeting with Soames. His first meeting with Robin Adler. Near enough half a decade ago now. As they drove through London, Hunt remembered back to the day he was recruited.

HE FLICKED THROUGH THE MAGAZINES ON THE GLASS coffee table in the large marble foyer of the Secret Intelligence Service building. He stood up to pace. Better than sitting on his arse which was still sore from the gunshot wound in Afghanistan. He saw a type of shrine. A thick book on a lectern. He wandered over to a large black leather-covered book, thick with pages. Hunt flipped through the declassified missions of the past that Military Intelligence 6, MI6, were involved in.

"Stirling!"

Hunt heard Soames' voice boom out from somewhere behind him. He turned to see Soames and he looked just as he remembered him. He hadn't dreamed it, after all, Hunt thought. Soames was a tall man, with loose skin under his chin like an old, loyal dog wearing a double-breasted pinstripe suit. They shook hands briefly and lightly. Soames walked by him and tapped the pages of the book with his long fingernail.

"Rule number one: don't get caught. If you do things right, neither you nor anything you do will ever get recognition in something like this ..."

Hunt pursed his lips and nodded like he was talking it all in when he just wanted to know what the hell was going on and when he could get started.

"What's rule number two?" Hunt asked.

Soames ignored the question.

"So, are you ready? The best few hours will be busy," Soames said and led Hunt through the electronic glass barriers to a lift bank. They went up. Soames didn't speak as they elevated, he just watched the numbers blink above the door. Hunt said nothing.

The lift doors opened and Soames walked ahead of Hunt. Soames took him to a blue carpeted floor of the building. It had high ceilings and he led him to an undecorated open space. There were more black leather sofas. Soames led Hunt to a woman waiting with a clipboard.

"Stirling, this is Mavis. She'll look after you from here. I'll see you a bit later. You're in good hands."

Soames turned and left him standing there. She made a note on the clipboard and said, "Come with me, I'll take you right in."

Hunt followed. He watched her smart business suit skirt move. She had long blonde hair tied up at the back and the bun bounced as she walked. They came to a large wooden double door and before he could offer to help, she'd pushed the heavy doors open. There was a sucking sound as the pressure in the room let them go.

She ushered him in and Hunt said, "Thank you," as he walked past her and then looked up and saw a full auditorium. He just stood there. Mavis came and touched his arm and whispered, "Find an open space. The test is waiting for you."

"Test?"

She nodded, "*Mhmm.*"

"I'm not late am I?"

Mavis just smiled and then pursed her lips and gave him a light push into the room and shut the big double doors. The room fell silent and there must have been five-hundred eyes in rows looking at him. He went to the first open seat, right at the front of the room and directly in front of him. He sat down on the end. He looked straight ahead with his hands clasped in front of him on the desktop.

A nice-looking and even better-smelling young woman was sitting in the seat next to him and gave him a nudge on the arm and said, "Hi," under her breath. He glanced at her. She had bobbed deep ruby hair. She reminded him of a film star. She was wearing big silver hooped earrings and a black denim jacket. He felt overdressed in his suit. Better over than under though. She was really pretty. If the girls in the intelligence service were like her; where did he sign?

"Hi," he said and looked forward. He saw her smile in his periphery. He still felt self-conscious, like all the eyes were still on him. A woman was standing in front of the auditorium. Her ears stuck out like flaps and she had cropped peroxide blonde hair. Not all the women looked like the one next to him in the intelligence services.

The woman at the front of the auditorium held a clicker and there was a giant projection on the screen behind her. She looked directly at Hunt and said, "As I was saying ... this is your test day. For some of you, this is the closest you will ever get to the Secret Intelligence Service. For others, it is the start of a long fruitful career defending your country from threats both foreign and domestic."

She looked around the room like she was expecting a question, or hands to go up. No-one moved.

"Statistically only two of you will be selected. Don't be upset by that. The Secret Intelligence Service receives over fifty-thousand applications from young hopefuls every year and we select less than one percent of those that apply. Ninety-nine point nine percent are not selected. So, try not to take it personally. Even if you get through and are successful here today, your training is only just beginning."

She pressed the clicker and a large stopwatch opened on the screen. She glanced over her shoulder at it and pressed the button again. The clock started counting down from ninety minutes. Eighty-nine minutes, fifty-nine seconds, fifty-eight, fifty-seven.

"In front of you, you have a stack of psychometric tests. When I tell you, open the envelope and take out the tests.

Inside you will also find notepaper and a pencil. Don't break it. You won't get another. Good luck. Begin."

Hunt sighed. "Should have brought a sharpener," he said out of the corner of his mouth to the red-head next to him. She reached in her denim jacket top pocket and showed him a plastic red pencil sharpener she leaned a bit closer and said, "Always come prepared. If you're really good, I might even let you borrow it."

He grinned and tore open the envelope and emptied it on the desk. The bottle-blonde pixie-looking woman paced along the front row with the clicker held close to her chest. Hunt scanned the papers. There were hundreds of questions each with the same six options across five different booklets. He sighed and put up his hand. The pixie-looking lady walked over and leaned down. There was the sound of papers shuffling and pencils scraping and Hunt felt the people around him prick their ears to listen. He spoke softly, "Um, I think there's been some mistake. I'm not sure I was supposed to fill in these forms and do these tests, I was told to come for an interview ..."

The woman listened to him and nodded and then said, "Director Soames says to stop effing around and complete the test, your time is running out."

Hunt sat still for a moment with his mouth slightly open. It took a while for the words to make sense to him. The woman nodded and gave him a single nod, which said 'okay?' and lifted her chin up to the back of the room. Hunt turned slowly to look over his shoulder. At the back of the auditorium, looking down on the rows of people was a panel of mirrored glass running the length and height of the back wall. Hunt looked up and saw a camera hidden in a black bowl on the ceiling. Now he knew why he'd felt like he was being watched ...

"The only thing they don't know are your thoughts. They still can't steal those, but if you want an invite to the party, you have to play the game," the red-head next to him said under her breath as she marked off boxes on the test. Better get started in that case. Hunt turned over the first one and read the question.

AFTER TWO HOURS OF MULTIPLE-CHOICE FORM filling, they were allowed to leave. It was like they'd finished their final exams at school. People came out chatting and discussing the answers to different questions. Hunt left the room and went over to a trestle table covered with a navy blue cloth. There were white cups and saucers, milk in clear glass jugs and a tall coffee thermos. He took a cup and filled it with hot, weak, black coffee. He smelled her perfume before he saw her. She came bouncing up and stood close to his shoulder and said, "What did you get for question five?" He glanced at her and she smiled and showed him her straight-white smile.

"I think I put 'C' for that one."

"And, number ten?"

"I put 'C' for that one too," he said and took a sip of the bland hot coffee. "I put 'C' for all of them. Statistically the same chance of getting it right as all the rest of the choices."

"I don't think it was a right versus wrong kind of test ..."

"Oh, yeah."

They stood and looked at one another for a moment. He was a bit tongue-tied.

"What're you doing here?" he asked.

"Same as you, I imagine. Trying out to be a spy."

The blonde pixie-lady came out of the auditorium doors

and shouted over the din, "Right! That's it for this section, please disperse and go to your next assessments."

People said their goodbyes and meandered off in different directions.

"How do you know where to go next?" Hunt asked.

She held up a little yellow booklet that was colour coded with different times and room numbers on it. He didn't have one of those.

"See you," she said and turned and then looked back over her shoulder and gave him a little wave. He watched her go and shook his head. Damn.

"Mister Hunt," Mavis called out to him. She looked serious, still holding her clipboard. She adjusted her rectangular glasses. "Do you know where you're going next?"

He had a mouth full of hot coffee so shook his head and swallowed. He set the cup down and cleared his throat and said, "No. No idea."

"This way," she said, "Follow me."

He followed her along. There were dozens of frosted-glass encased meeting rooms on the floor. He could hear murmuring and see people moving around inside them, but he couldn't make anything out. She stood to the side of an open door and gestured with her hand.

"This is the lie detector suite, all of the assessments are run by experts. You don't need to know their names, so don't ask. After this, there is a psych profile, physical medical assessment, word association, some problem solving and a few others. Good luck ..." she drew out the last word like it was more of a note of sympathy rather than a genuine wish of excitement. It was like she assumed it would be difficult for him. The lump of meat with the square jaw who she didn't think could spell 'interrogation' if his life depended on it. Hunt shook his head and raised his eyebrows. Being underestimated and coming out on top was his speciality. He went in.

An obese man with a grey goatee sat behind a long row of white tables that formed a horseshoe shape in front of him. The guy's neck ballooned over his collar. It reminded Hunt of a blowfish. In front of the guy, Hunt saw a polygraph machine. It was a suitcase with an open lid and wires protruding from it.

There was one chair opposite the large guy in the middle of the room. Hunt sat down and the man wheezed and stood up and came over and plugged him in. He strapped a blood pressure monitor cuff on Hunt's upper arm, put a black coiled sensor around his chest, and placed a headset on his head that had a camera in a lens and measured his pupil dilation.

"You ready?" the man wheezed.

"Yes," Hunt said.

THE FAT MAN WAS SWEATING AND HE USED A WHITE handkerchief to wipe his brow.

"I thought I was supposed to be the nervous one," Hunt said. The polygraph tester just grunted and wheezed.

"We're going to start with some baseline 'yes' questions. These are just to get started with the assessment."

Hunt was silent.

"Are you Stirling Hunt," the man asked.

"Stirling James Hunt."

"Just yes, or no."

"Yes."

"Were you born on the twenty-third of February?"

"Yes."

The questioner ticked off answers on a sheet in front of him as they went.

"Are you ready to take this lie detector test?"

"No."

The fat man looked up at him and grunted and then continued. Hunt was looking directly at him with a blank stare. He felt his pulse was normal, breathing clear and slow and controlled, face relaxed, pupils undiluted. Signs of the truth.

"Have you ever worn women's clothing?" the fat man asked with a wheeze. Hunt felt his pulse in his neck throb. He paused for a minute to think if he had.

"Yes," he said.

The interrogator raised an eyebrow and ticked the paper. A night out in the Marines often involved fancy dress. Hunt once went as Marilyn Monroe, complete with his real stubble, smudged lipstick and hairy chest on a dare. He didn't mind making a fool out of himself for a good time.

"Have you ever been associated with the CIA?"

Hunt swallowed. This was a weird one. It depended on what he meant by *associated*. Hunt was going to assume 'worked for' and not 'interviewed by on suspicion of being a suicide bomber.'

"No."

The lie detector analyst ticked his sheet.

"Are you an agent of a foreign power?"

"No."

"Has anyone in your family ever been associated with any foreign intelligence agency?"

"No."

"Have you ever killed anyone?"

"Yes."

"Did they deserve it?"

"Yes."

"Ever been cruel to an animal?"

"Yes."

"Did they deserve it?"

"Kill or be killed," he said as he thought of the guard dog he had to injure to save his own life to survive in Afghanistan.

"Yes or no."

"Yes."

"Are you here to serve your country?"

"Yes."

He marked the paper. Hunt felt his breathing become shallow. He felt hot. His heart rate was up. He tried to calm it.

"Pizza or pasta?"

"Pizza."

"Are you willing to kill for your country?"

"Yes."

BY THE TIME THE POLYGRAPH WAS OVER, THE OBESE goatee was smiling and had cooled down, and Hunt was the one sweating and relieved to be out of there. He felt like he'd just been to a proctologist for his feelings. Someone unearthing a skeleton from a grave that had long been buried. The pixie-lady was standing outside the glass door as he left.

"Why're you following me around?" Hunt asked. He opened his top button and pulled off his tie as they walked.

"What do you mean?"

"You're following me. No one else is getting a chaperone. Have I done something wrong?"

"Do you feel like you've done something wrong?" she asked. He stopped and turned and scoffed and then kept going.

"What's next?" he asked.

"In here," she said.

A room with a view. An oriental man, possibly of Chinese or Taiwanese heritage was sitting behind a desk. Same solitary chair in the middle of the room. One of the walls was mirrored glass. Someone was watching. Hunt sat down.

"I'd like to start with some simple word association," the dark-suited, slender Chinese-looking man said in an upper-class English accent. "For instance, I might say 'day', and you might say ..."

"Dream," Hunt said.

The man's face creased in a sympathetic smile and he lifted his hand in submission and said, "All right." He lifted his chin and narrowed his eyes and said, "Rifle."

"Tool."

"Assassin."

"Ate."

"Agent."

"Nerve."

"Mother."

"Dead."

The Chinese man made a note. Hunt clenched his jaw. Did he want this, this much? To put up with all this?

"Grief."

Hunt shrugged, "Pain."

"Heart."

"Diamonds."

"Heads."

"Target."

"Sunshine."

"Home," Hunt said.

"Moonlight."

"Darkness," Hunt answered.

"Loyalty."

"Sacrifice."

"Country."

"England."

"Secret."

"One."

The man made a note. "Okay, thank you. We're done here. One of my colleagues will come in next. You can stay seated." He stood up and left. Hunt heard the door clip closed and he glanced at the mirrored wall. Who was behind it? He waited. After about fifteen minutes the door opened again and a professional-looking woman walked in. She had black-rimmed rectangular glasses and short, bobbed hair. She sat briskly and pulled her pen from a leather notepad.

"Good morning," she said.

Hunt didn't respond. She looked at her notepad and said, "When you get angry, Mister Hunt, do you have trouble staying in control?"

He took a deep breath and crossed his arms and looked out of the window behind her. The view was out onto the Thames. It was cold and grey outside and he could almost feel the coldness radiating off the glass.

"Yes, I suppose so."

"How do you manifest your anger?"

"I don't know what that means."

"How do you deal with it?"

"I look for an outlet."

"Are you angry now?"

"Yes."

"Why?"

He shook his head once.

"I don't know. Not angry. Frustrated."

She made a note.

"Do you worry about the future?"

"Yes."

"So you like to be in control?"

"Yes."

"So why do you allow yourself to get angry?"

"Allow myself?"

"Do you enjoy it?"

"Excuse me?"

"Well, you said you like to be in control, and you lose control when you get angry. So why do you prefer to be angry more than you prefer to be in control?"

"I never said I prefer it."

"Yes, but we all choose our emotional state. We all choose our reactions to certain situations. Certain triggers. If a person can't control their thoughts and their feelings, then is that person really in control of themselves?"

"Isn't that just the human condition?"

She looked down and made a note.

"Are you a happy person?

"No."

"Why not?"

"I am too focused to be happy. I have moments of happiness. Things make me happy, but I am not a constantly upbeat, optimistic person."

"Why not?"

"Because I am not crazy. I live in the real world. I have seen what the world can do to people, and I've experienced it."

"And you're here because ...?"

"I have nowhere else to go. Nowhere else to be," Hunt said. It was true. He'd spent years training himself to be able, to be deserving, of the chance to put al-Zawahiri in the ground, and he'd lost. Now he was looking for penance and retribution. A second chance. He knew that when he left the building and walked along the river, instead of getting a cab, and felt the icy-cold blast of winter wind on the tips of his ears that he was going back to a fifty quid a night single ex-services hotel room with shared facilities. One black deployment bag. That was all he had. If he didn't do this, where was he going to go... what was he going to do?

"Look," Hunt said to the woman behind the desk but addressed whoever was behind the mirror. "I came here today to join up. I thought I was starting my training. I'm not going to stay and be prodded and poked and turned inside out anymore. You know my background. You know what I am willing to do. And, you know where to find me. I'm leaving. Okay?"

He stood up. The woman didn't move, she just watched him. He walked to the large glass door and pulled on the cold steel handle. The door was heavy and he let it glide open. He stepped out and walked to the lift bank. He saw Mavis and her business suit in his peripheral vision walking briskly behind him. She called up, "Wait, Mister Hunt, no one can move around this building unaccompanied. Wait!"

He kept moving and went to the lifts. She came up behind him out of breath and swiped her identification card and it beeped and she pressed the button to call for the lift. He saw her look up at him, but he didn't look down. The lift pinged and the doors opened and he stepped inside. She followed him in and pressed the button for the ground floor. They didn't speak. Hunt watched the lights.

.   .   .

WHEN THEY GOT TO THE BOTTOM, HUNT STEPPED OUT first and walked ahead. He was stern and serious and sure of his choice. This was all bullshit. They were trying to impress him, test him, or mess with him. Maybe he'd just failed. If they wanted him, they knew where to find him. She hurried to catch up and put her identification on the automatic gates and it beeped and the glass slid open. Hunt saw Soames standing at the reception desk. He was waiting for him.

"So," Soames said as Hunt approached and put his arms out, "How was it ... did I miss anything exciting?"

Hunt laughed once. Was he for real? Hard to tell.

"Where are you going?" Soames asked.

"I'm leaving," Hunt said.

"He's not finished the assessments yet," Mavis said sternly.

Soames scrunched his face and said, "It's okay Mavis, I'll take it from here," and he waved her away. Hunt heard her heels clacking away on the marble floor. He put his hand on Hunt's back and guided him away from her. "So, where are you headed?"

"Don't know," Hunt said.

"Come on, let me buy you lunch," Soames said.

SOAMES TOOK HIM TO AN OLD GEORGIAN HOUSE THAT had been converted into a restaurant called Brunswick House. It was an antiquated decor. Hard, dark woods, Persian rugs, contrasted with modern bohemian touches and clean, white lines. They were seated at a long dining table in one of the rooms with old brick walls and exposed rusted pipes. It was quiet, before the lunch rush.

"Two Campari sodas, and a Gin-Gin Mule for me," Soames said to the waitress without asking what Hunt wanted. He put the white paper menu down and crossed his arms as he leaned on the dining table and looked at Hunt with his bottom jaw protruding forward.

"I played the game, Mister Soames -"

"Call me Gerry," Soames interrupted him.

"I played the game, Gerry. I sat through their tests, but you know what, I'm not sure I need you as much as you need me."

"Oh, is that right?" Soames said. Hunt shrugged. Maybe. "There are things you don't know, things you need the answers to," Soames said. "Am I wrong?"

"No, you're not wrong, but -"

"We're the only place you're going to find the answers," Soames said, speaking over him. The waitress came with the drink and set them down gently and decided against asking them what they wanted to order. She shoved off like she sensed she'd interrupted something. Hunt spun the tumbler and made the ice tinkle. Soames watched him. He took the white napkin and shook it out and placed it on his lap and said, "All right then, why don't you just ask me."

"Ask what," Hunt said.

"Just go ahead and ask me your questions."

Hunt looked up and looked at the upper-class Englishman sitting opposite him. "Did you know him?" Hunt asked.

"No. I knew of him. Our paths never crossed with your Daddy's."

"I met your grandfather once, in London."

"How was he involved with you?"

Soames shook his head. "Think, my boy. I can't confirm mission specifics with you. Even if I wanted to. I just can't."

"Did my grandfather get involved with six?" Hunt meant MI-6.

Soames shook his head. The waitress came back. Soames picked up the menu again and said, "Dry-aged Tamworth pork chop, St George's mushrooms, shorthorn onglet, rare, smoked bone marrow, burnt shallots."

"Anything else?" she asked as she finished scribbling down the order on her notepad. Soames shook his head. She collected the menus and walked away. Hunt leaned back and crossed his arms.

"What did he do?" Hunt asked.

"Your father? You have to get over it, Stirling. You really do. He died too young. They left you too young. If you keep looking back, you're going to miss your whole life. He left you. That doesn't mean he didn't love you. He wanted what was best for you. I have no doubt. And, so do I, want what's best for you. I am offering you the chance to do something to put the past behind you. To look forward to knowing the man who took him from you is not a problem anymore."

"You mean not a problem, for *you* ..."

"Hey, it's a win-win. You do for me, I do for you. Like that."

The cafe was filling up. More and more tables and people chatting. The space seemed smaller. Less inviting. More threatening. Hunt didn't like having his back to the room and at the moment his back was facing the bar.

"It's a mystery you cannot solve, Stirling. And, neither can I. Who was Harvey Hunt? Well, I can show you the man who could have answers for you, and we want you to neutralise him for us. And, for yourself."

Hunt saw Soames' eyes drawn to the front door and watched him follow some people as they came in.

"Don't look," Soames said. "I think we're being followed."

Hunt lifted his head and focussed on his peripheral vision without turning his head.

"Are you sure?" Hunt said.

"Yeah," Soames said. The waitress arrived with the food and asked whose was whose. She put the plates down. It smelled fantastic, but Hunt wasn't in the mood for food.

"Sometimes these guys just like to loiter around. Follow people out of the River House, see if they can gain intelligence on the building, who's working there."

Hunt moved his seat. He dropped his napkin and bent to pick it up and saw a tall guy in a leather jacket leaning on the bar. He didn't look right for the place. He was alone. He had slicked-back black hair. Sharp features. He looked Albanian or Romanian. Anything but like he was meant to be in this busy central-London chic cafeteria. Soames pulled out his mobile phone and said, "Don't worry, I'll get someone on it."

Soames was eating his pork chop. It looked very good. Now Hunt was hungry. He picked up the steak knife and sliced through the juicy thick chunk of perfectly cooked beef.

After they'd eaten and the waitress had taken their plates, Soames scrambled up his cotton napkin and put it on the table. He sat back and looked at Hunt and said, "Look Stirling, I know I said you would be good at this, after all, I'm the one recruiting you, for my team, but if your heart isn't in it, I understand. I'm going to have enough explaining to do after you walked out of there," Soames crossed his arms, "But, turn up tomorrow morning, same time as today, and there will be a bus leaving from there to take you to the south coast for the start of training. If you don't, I'll know you weren't interested and we'll never mention it again." Soames stuck out his right hand, to shake on the deal. Hunt took it.

WHERE DO YOU GO WHEN YOU NEED TO TALK TO someone, but have no one to speak to? After he left Soames, Hunt wandered around Leicester Square and people watched tourists and busy suits as they rushed by. Maybe it was to the theatre, or a dinner reservation, or after-work drinks. It was late and it was cold. There was a heavy blackness around him of the night pushed back the glowing neon lights. People's faces appeared and disappeared in the gloom. His hands were deep in his pockets and he moved more slowly than everyone else. His strides were slower, longer and more careful like he was walking along a white line.

He saw a casino and decided to go in. People tended to talk to each other more. There was a sense of community in a casino. It was the scum against the house. Gamblers all wore the same tired expressions of faded hope on their faces. Deep frown lines from lives spent looking at cards, spinning wheels, or forlornly down at their air conditioner wrinkled dry hands.

Hunt didn't gamble. He walked past the rows of flashing lights and green card tables. He went to get a drink. The staff were all young and attractive in casinos. They looked like they were mostly from central and eastern Europe. Their expressions said they worked hard, despised the customers, and saved plastic smiles for the regulars who tipped well. Even Hunt's broad smile and boyish good looks didn't persuade the dark-haired girl behind the bar to soften her expression towards him. She was busy taking glasses out of the little silver dishwasher behind the counter and barely had time to look at him and ask what he wanted. She didn't care. She glanced at him.

"Coffee please," Hunt said.

"What sort, we have a cappuccino, latte, americano, what you like?"

"Americano, with milk."

She looked over her shoulder and shouted, "Marco! Cappuccino with milk."

"Americano."

"Marco! Americano. No milk."

Hunt just left it. Black americano was fine. He saw the guy go lazily to the coffee machine. The coffee came and it spilt over the side of the cup and into the saucer. Hunt picked it up and swallowed it in one gulp. It wasn't even hot. He wasn't going to find anyone to talk to here. He wandered out of the Empire and turned left. The streets were still bustling with people. A drizzle of cold rain started. He saw a sign, Platinum Place, and went in. He shook off the rain. It was warm and welcoming and he saw a beautiful girl. Looked like a bar. He walked in and saw the pole and the stage. Turned out it was a gentleman's club. The vibe was great. The music was loud. The lighting was low. It had beautiful women walking. Only a few customers were sitting around. It was a high-end place by the look of it. Hunt went to the bar and sat down. He glanced over his shoulder.

"It's quiet. Still early though," a woman's voice said. Hunt turned back and a blonde bartender with a bouncy ponytail, sleeve-tattoo on her forearm and cutoff, buttoned-low stood in front of him. "What'll it be? We've got a special on Jägermeister at the moment."

"Sure, I'll take a Jägermeister."

"What brings you in here tonight," she asked as she poured his drink.

He shrugged. "Dunno, just wandering around."

She furrowed her brow and put a double shot of black liquor in front of him and poured one for herself.

"Something on your mind?" she asked and lifted her shot glass. He lifted his and they clinked the glasses and knocked them back. They both pulled scrunched-up faces.

"Another," she said.

Hunt laughed, "Sure."

"You wouldn't think it to look at them," the bartender said, "but, most of these girls are great listeners. Get yourself a lap dance. You can chat away to your heart's desire ... cost you much less than a psychiatrist and you get to look at some premium boobs at the same time. I can arrange it for you." She raised her eyebrows and poured the black stuff into the glasses again. She bent down to put the bottle back in the fridge and glanced up as one of the girls approached. The blonde bartender said, "Here's a good listener now. Speak of the devil, Rubes! I was just saying to this guy," she looked at Hunt and said to him, "What was your name, darling?"

"Stirling," he said.

"... This guy, Stirling, what a good listener you were."

Hunt smiled and turned to look at the ruby-red-headed woman standing at the bar. His eyes locked on hers and her face dropped. That haircut, that lip-piercing, that smell. He'd seen her before. Not dressed like this, she had long dangly silver earrings and a tightly intertwined rope choker. All she wore was black lingerie and stilettos. He knew her.

She turned away quite suddenly and tried to leave. Hunt stood up off the barstool.

"I've got to go," she said to the bartender.

"Hey! Wait," Hunt called after her. "I know her," he said and looked at the bartender. She didn't look impressed.

"We doing these shots, or what?"

They picked up the shot glasses and swallowed the neat Jäger. Hunt stuck his tongue out and gave a little cough. He wasn't looking forward to tomorrow morning.

"Where'd she go?" he asked.

"What's it to you? What'd you do to her?"

"Nothing, I've only met her once. Today."

"She's probably hiding in the back, I'll tell the doorman to go and get her."

A FEW MINUTES LATER, ROBIN WAS STANDING THERE again. She'd come out by herself this time, not because the doorman had asked. She stood square on, close to his shoulder, and looked at him. She had her black denim jacket on this time.

"Look, ah, please don't tell them you saw me here, okay? If they find out I am out of the programme," she said all doe-eyed.

"You got through then?"

She nodded. Hunt hadn't even looked over at her yet. He just stirred his gin martini with the olive. "Haven't seen a thing," he said and ran his index finger and thumb across his mouth like they were zipped shut.

"Look, if you want to talk, we can, but I am not allowed to talk to customers out here. If you buy a lap dance in the VIP suite we can chat all you want and no one can hear us and you can ask me anything you want."

Hunt looked at the blonde bartender. She cocked her head and raised her eyebrows. Hunt felt weird about it, but he did want to speak to someone. He glanced at her standing there. She was also really pretty.

"All right," he said. "One dance."

She smiled. She seemed happy. "Pay her," she said and tilted her head towards the bartender and then clapped her hands and spun around and hurried into the back. Another dancer came and took his hand and led him through a purple velvet curtain, down a corridor lined with full-length mirrors separated by blue-neon strips of light, and past some separate leather sofas and chairs. She led him through a door and into another room. It had navy-blue tufted leather benches that ran around three sides. It looked like the vintage leather furniture you find in a private member's club. Each wall was a floor-to-ceiling mirror and faint pink neon lights and draped satin material hanging from the ceiling. He sat down and she blew him a kiss and walked out. As she left, Robin glided past her and into the room. She was wearing a bobbed bright pink wig and had her lingerie on again. She also had a frilly garter on her left thigh. Hunt suddenly felt nervous and sat forward and rubbed his palms together to get rid of the moisture. He was starting to feel warm.

"So what are the rules here?" Hunt asked as Robin stood on the mirrored tabletop and swayed.

"We can talk, but I have to dance, otherwise they get upset ..."

"How will they know?"

"Security cameras, in the ceiling," she said. "But, don't worry, they don't record sound."

Hunt looked up at the black bulge on the ceiling. The unblinking eye in the sky.

"Just don't get undressed, okay?" he said.

She giggled, "Why, do my boobs make you nervous?"

"Yeah, they do. And, I wouldn't want anyone to get the wrong idea."

"Oh, what idea is that?"

"That, I, you know, paid you to ..." he gestured with his hand at her dancing there. "You know."

"Get naked for you?"

He nodded and looked away. She climbed down and went and sat next to him and put her hand on his arm. He felt how warm and soft her fingers were and he felt how sharp her nails were as she rested the tips of them on his skin.

"So, sailor, what seems to be the problem?" she asked and put her fingers into the back of his hair and massaged it. Hunt was quiet for a moment, thinking.

"I thought we weren't supposed to touch?" he said.

"I can touch you. You can't touch me. Do you want me to stop?"

He shook his head. "No." He sat back and moved slightly away from her. She looked slightly surprised.

"Are you going to do it? Sign up, I mean. Become a spook," he said, looking at her.

"Course, aren't you?" she seemed surprised. "At least it'll get me out of this dump."

"I don't know. Pink neon and lace lingerie really suit you ..."

"Oh," she said and gave him a dirty look as she rubbed her flat stomach, "Does it?"

"Definitely."

She looked incredible to him.

"Why're you having second thoughts?" she asked.

He wasn't sure. Something felt off. Maybe it wasn't

right. If there was doubt, there was no doubt. He never seemed to follow the adage he lived by. He was at a fork in the road. One path was forgetting the past and moving on. Being free to do what he wanted and leave all the pain behind. The other involved a lot of pain. Him inflicting it. Him finding the truth. Him getting payback for the things they took from him and made him suffer.

"I'm tired of being so angry," he said, honestly.

"Angry with whom?"

He shook his head. Did he know? Fate. Destiny. The path that he was setting out on. He missed his family. He missed his parents. He wanted to look the man in the eyes that took them from him. He wanted to look the man in the eye that took Kelly from him. People needed to know that they couldn't get away with it.

"People who took things from me in the past."

"What sort of things?"

"All the good things. Why do you want to join up?" he asked, moving the conversation along. She glanced involuntarily at the ceiling and then away.

"I thought you said they couldn't hear you?" he said. She stayed quiet. She looked vulnerable. He decided to leave it.

"Are people listening to us?" Hunt asked. He was suspicious. He watched her reaction closely. She looked up at him and her face loosened. She looked directly at him. Her pupils were dilated, but it might just have been the dim light.

"No, it's video only," she said. "I have no reason to lie to you. We're on the same team ..." He decided to believe her. After all, he had something on her he could use if it came down to it. "You do, believe me, don't you?" She asked.

Hunt nodded. "Yes, I do."

She was pleased. She smiled. The tension was broken. Now he felt they were just having a coffee and a chat. He'd almost forgotten she was a stripper in a gentleman's club.

"They've offered me a chance to get one of the bad guys," he said.

"One of the guys who took something from you?" she asked. He nodded.

"Yeah."

"I feel sorry for them ..." she said.

He furrowed his brow. "Who?"

"The guys that crossed you. You're not someone I would want to get on the wrong side of."

He shook and laughed at her assumption.

"Come on!" she said. "You can't leave me at the Kill School all alone! Come and see what it's like and if you have fun, you can stay."

"I don't think it is going to be very fun," he said.

"Sure it is. All those guys, and their secrets, and their acting lessons."

"Acting lessons?"

"Of course, it's behavioural psychology, isn't it? Human programming. Getting people to do what you want, monitoring them, learning them, and then using that information to get what you want. Isn't it?"

"Is that what is happening here?" Hunt asked.

She pursed her lips and shook her head and sighed. She stood up. "Oh! Look at that. Time's up, sailor." She grabbed her clutch to leave.

"Wait," he said. "Don't go. I want to talk to you."

"Sorry, I have another client waiting for me. If you want to talk, I'll be on the bus from the River House tomorrow. Seven o'clock sharp." She blew him a kiss. "Don't be late."

He watched her bum as she walked out of the suite.

. . .

THE NEXT MORNING, THE BIG BLACK GATES OPENED and Hunt saw the greyhound start to depart. He had his duffel over his shoulder and the same black trench coat pulled up against the wind. He heard the airbrake hiss and the front door to the bus opened. Mavis came down wrapped up in a scarf and shouted, "Well! What are you waiting for, effing Christmas? Hurry up and get on board."

Hunt stepped aboard and saw Robin sitting next to a South-East Asian guy. He was leaning over speaking into her ear. She lifted her half-mittened fingers and gave Hunt a small wave and an imperceptible smile. Hunt walked along and looked for a seat. Most people looked like they either wanted to be alone or already had someone next to them. He found an empty row and sat down and looked out of the cold glass at the miserable winter weather outside. He jolted as the bus pulled forward and out of the gates. They were headed southwest to Fort Monckton. It was a historical military fort on the eastern end of Stokes Bay, near Gosport, in Hampshire.

It had been built on the ruins of Haselworth Castle, which was originally built to protect Portsmouth harbour, at the start of the American War of Independence. It was secretive and remote, and no one knew what happened there. From the air it looked in the shape of a five-pointed star, flat on one end against the beach. It would be home for the foreseeable future.

"Oi, mate," the cab driver said. Hunt looked at him. He'd been lost in space. The cabbie pulled a face and gestured to the pavement. "We're 'ere."

Hunt shook his head at himself. "Thank you," Hunt said apologetically and leaned forward with a ten-pound note.

"Nah, you keep it. The ride's on me today," the cab driver said and looked at Hunt in the mirror. "Just make sure you do us proud, whatever you do."

Hunt put the note back in his pocket as the cabbie waved him away. He stepped out in front of the Victory Club and knew he had another decision to make.

ELEVEN

Alone in an empty aircraft hanger, Hunt stood inside the vast doors and looked out at the rain. It fell straight down and the sound of it hitting the concrete reminded him of the static from a dead television channel. It was soothing and cold and he zipped his bomber jacket up and crossed his arms. He heard the sound of jet engines.

A modern private jet taxied in front of the hangar doors. Hunt heard footsteps behind him. He smelled McKenna's musky aftershave before he saw him. The intelligence director came and stood next to him.

"You're early," McKenna said.

Hunt didn't reply. The new head of the Oberon programme held a plastic folder in his right hand. "It wasn't easy, but I have what you asked for."

Hunt looked at him for the first time and McKenna held out the document. Hunt took it from him. "So we have a deal?"

Hunt nodded. "Yep - we have a deal," Hunt said.

The aircraft stopped in the middle of the gaping hanger doors and the front passenger exit opened and Hunt saw an air hostess. The automatic stairs unfolded out of the bottom of the door. A moment later Hunt saw her. She was wearing large sunglasses, her hair was pulled back, and she had a cashmere roll-neck sweater. She still looked elegant. Despite the harsh treatment, no doubt. Hunt glanced at McKenna. He was watching the private jet. Hunt would honour their deal. That wasn't in doubt, but deep down he knew McKenna was lucky he'd agreed to the terms. He felt strongly about her. He wasn't sure what McKenna could've expected from him if she'd been mistreated. Robin was carrying a leather cat carrier and had a matching leather backpack on. The air hostess opened an umbrella for her and she took it in her free hand and thanked her. She stepped carefully down the wet stairs in ankle-high boots and onto the tarmac.

"See," McKenna said. "All very civil. Now you can relax."

"I'll relax when I know what the mission is."

Adler glanced left and right and then up and into the hanger. When she saw Hunt standing there her face beamed. She ran towards him through the rain and he stepped forward to meet her.

"Oh my god," she said when she was close, "It's so good to see you!"

She put the carrier down. Hunt heard her cat meow and Robin wrapped her arms around Hunt's neck.

"Are you okay?" Hunt asked.

"Now I am," she said. "How did you get here?"

"Just came to see that you're okay," Hunt said. "Here, I got something for you." Hunt handed her the plastic folder.

"What is this?" she said as she took the plastic enve-lope from him and opened it. She half-pulled out the papers and her eyes scanned over them. Her mouth opened and she looked up at Hunt's eyes and then back at the letter.

"You did this?" she asked.

"You're free," he said.

"Oh, Stirling," Robin said. She looked down and touched her hand to her mouth and composed herself. She hugged him again and then stepped back. "You cut a deal?"

Hunt nodded and saw Robin glance to her right and heard McKenna step forward.

"Right, as heartwarming as this little reunion is, we do have more pressing issues to discuss," McKenna said with a broad smile. "Welcome back into the fold, Miss Adler. I look forward to working with you. We have a state-of-the-art facility set up for you. Obviously, your direction and input to optimise the technology will be greatly welcomed."

"Who's this?" Robin said to Hunt under her breath.

McKenna stuck his arm straight out. "Your new employer," he said.

Hunt gave him a look.

"If you so choose," McKenna said. "Right now though, of course, you need some rest. It's been a frightfully torrid journey from what I understand. For that, I can only apologise on behalf of Her Majesty's Government and try to reassure you that we will do everything in our power to make it right, starting, of course, with those documents I've procured on your behalf. Hopefully, that goes some way to remedying the situation?"

Robin forced a smile.

"Is this your new boss?" she asked.

"We have a car waiting for you Miss Adler," McKenna said and stepped back and held out his arm in direction of the rear exit of the hanger.

She looked at Hunt, "You're not coming?"

Before he could answer, McKenna said, "I'm afraid Stirling has a more pressing engagement, a matter of national security that we need to discuss. In fact, I am about to debrief him on the mission now. I will brief you later on your support role. The Field Agent is going to need you to be at your best for this operation, Miss Adler. So, if you don't mind ..." McKenna said.

"I've got to go," Hunt said quietly to Robin. McKenna took a few paces back.

"You're leaving already?"

"Duty calls."

She looked up into Hunt's eyes. "Okay," she said and stepped forward on her tiptoes and kissed him on the cheek. "Thank you," she said. "Be safe."

She picked up the cat carrier and took her documents and walked between both men to the back of the hanger.

"We'll be in touch," McKenna called after her and waved. He went and stood next to Hunt. They both looked out at the aircraft being refuelled.

"So, I trust our transaction was concluded to your satisfaction, Stirling?"

"What's the mission?" Hunt asked.

"Straight to the point. Good lad. It's an Executive Action, I'm afraid," McKenna said.

Hunt looked at him out of the corner of his eye. McKenna looked straight ahead. The mission was an assassination of a high-ranking target.

"Who's the target?"

"A retired admiral of the Russian Pacific Fleet, Stepanovich Isakov."

"What's he done?"

"That's what we need you to find out. The who's who of the black market in international arms dealers and charitable fronts for known terror groups are amassing on the island of Sicily where we believe Admiral Isakov is planning to sell intelligence of great value to the terror groups of the world."

"What sort of intelligence?" Hunt asked.

"The sort that is of great danger to the citizens of Western democracies. One of our agents, embedded inside Enver Dushku's Albanian arms-dealing operation, said he had some vital information about the sale. He was found with bullet holes in both his eyes and with his ears cut off before he could relay it to us. A message. He'd been tortured and thrown off the top of a high-rise parking lot in broad daylight."

"So these are nice people," Hunt said.

"Oh, extremely. Very welcoming," McKenna said. He lifted his chin to the waiting jet. "This will take you directly to Catania airport. You'll hire a car and make your way to Taormina, posing as a luxury property developer. The area is very popular with the global elite. Sicily has a criminal underbelly that creates the conditions for this type of behaviour like a warm, damp room creating the condition for mould. It'll give you the freedom and cover to move around. You're to locate Isakov. Carry out the executive action, and recover the intelligence. Not necessarily in that order."

Think through to the finish. That was one of Hunt's rules. It's no good having half, or three-quarters of a plan. How was he getting out alive?

"And exfil?" Hunt asked.

"We have a shell company that has leased a superyacht. It'll be moored offshore. Once you're on the ground, let us know the best mode of exfiltration, and we'll arrange it from our end. I'll send the updated coordinates as we have them."

"That it?" Hunt asked.

"That's it," McKenna said. "The usual files and travel documents are on the plane. Any questions?"

Hunt thought for a moment. "Any preference for the hit?"

McKenna looked at him for a moment and shook his head slowly. "No, Agent Hunt. Use your judgement, you have complete tactical command, but if you can, make it public, make it violent, and make it known to the assembled guests that there is a new power in the world that is not afraid to exert lethal force. We will not stand idly by ..."

"Okay," Hunt said.

"We need to stop that intelligence from falling into the wrong hands. So, whatever you do, make sure you recover the information."

Hunt gave McKenna a single nod. His new boss stuck out a hand and said, "Good luck."

TWELVE

Hunt was driving north on the island's narrow and uneven roads from Calabria on Sicily's eastern coast to the sought-after and expensive town of Taormina.

The car dipped and leaned as he swooped over the undulating and pothole-scarred road. He was travelling as John Mason, a British luxury-property developer, in town to survey properties on behalf of his employer, a wealthy tech businessman who preferred his affairs to remain confidential. Money was no object and Mason's benefactor trusted him implicitly with making the decisions on his behalf.

Hunt thought, if that was the case in reality they could have stumped up for something more than the mid-market, American-made sedan that was trying its best to keep hold of the road surface. He'd have to have a word with McKenna's travel agent in future. The weather was pleasant and mild for winter. The car's dashboard read fourteen degrees celsius. The sun was low and glinting off the water down a cliff to his right-hand side. After being in the deep darkness of the North Sea, besides the fact that he'd have to kill a man, this was the kind of thing he could get used to. The

Mediterranean Sea was a deep azure blue that seemed to be skimmed with silver as sunlight reflected off it. Hunt was driving fast.

He came over a rise and saw an old, baby blue farmer's pickup truck trundling along in front of him. He checked his wing mirror and glided out into the left lane. All of a sudden, as if from nowhere a sleek, black Maserati Gran-Turismo with the top down and red upholstery, was right on his rear. He looked in the rearview mirror as he swept past the farmer's pickup and saw a black-haired girl with a scarf over her head, red lipstick, and dark sunglasses. She had both hands on the steering wheel and was sitting forward driving with concentration and intensity. Next to her was an older gentleman. Hunt changed down and put his foot on the floor. The family sedan lurched forward and Hunt kept his foot pressed down as the rev counter climbed. He moved into the right-hand lane. The Maserati stayed left and started to pass him. They went up another blind rise and there was a small city car in the oncoming traffic.

"Bloody hell!" Hunt said.

The Maserati braked and Hunt saw a puff of white from the tyres. The convertible ducked in behind him as the small Fiat flashed by with the driver leaning on their horn and the passenger shaking their fist at them. Hunt grinned and glanced in the mirror again. The girl behind the wheel was laughing and the man next to her was holding tight and giving her an ear full. Hunt heard the grunt of the big V8 Ferrari-manufactured engine and prepared to be overtaken. They were flying along the coastal road. Hunt saw them coming up to another car in their lane. He indicated and the Maserati surged forward. She wasn't going to let him stay ahead of them. Hunt had to time it right. He didn't want to slow down too much and let them get away. This was too much fun. Not only did Italians make fast cars. They didn't care about the rules of the road. The Maserati started to pass him. He lifted off the accelerator slightly. He was barrelling up towards the white car in front. As soon as the convertible was in front, he changed down rapidly and pulled into the next lane. They went past the slower car together. He saw the driver looking at him. She pulled into the right-hand lane. Hunt stayed left. The family sedan's engine was screaming in third gear and sitting almost at maximum revs. He couldn't compete with the muscle of the Italian sports car. They were neck and neck. Then Hunt saw an oncoming car in the left lane. His only option was to press the brake and get behind her. He diligently did and she looked over her shoulder and stuck her tongue out at him as he slotted in behind. His heart was racing and his pupils were dilated. His focus was like a laser. They were coming up to a corner. The road started winding down towards Taormina from their elevated position. Hunt saw the red lights on the back of the Maserati light up. He didn't brake. It looked like a long left-hander at a downward gradient.

Screw it, Hunt thought and as she braked, he pulled into the inside lane and swept under the GranTurismo. He saw her mouth open in offended shock and she punched the accelerator. The Maserati kept pace with him through the corner. It was a sharper bend than Hunt had anticipated and he leaned hard into the corner and held the juddering steering wheel tightly. He was right on the edge. Then, he saw the Maserati drop back and he pulled into the right-hand lane. He started laughing. He could see her in the rearview mirror with her face in a scrunched-up scowl. He saluted into the rearview mirror. They were pulling into the village and the signs had lower speeds on them. Hunt slowed and so did the Maserati. She didn't try to overtake him again. There was an unspoken understanding that the race was over.

Hunt followed the steep, windy road that snaked down the side of the valley towards the middle of the town. It seemed like, even if they hadn't come through on the car, McKenna's new programme, flush with cash, had done the right thing and booked him into the San Domenico Palace. A five-star Four Seasons hotel that jutted out overlooking the wide horseshoe bay and calm blue waters below. Hunt pulled up in front of the hotel and climbed out. He was greeted by a uniformed porter.

"Checking in, sir?" the porter asked.

"Yes," Hunt said.

"May I take your luggage from the car?"

Hunt handed him the keys and told him to carry on. He heard the growl of the Ferrari engine and saw the black Maserati pull up behind him. Damn it, here we go, Hunt thought. He was sure the old man wanted to have some strong words with him. After all, he had been driving a bit erratically. A bit full-blooded.

The gentleman climbed out of the car. He had a thick head of curled salt and pepper hair and a manicured beard to match. He was very smartly dressed. Blue blazer, open-collared shirt, moleskin shoes. He pulled off his sunglasses and smiled broadly.

"Are you English?" he asked, well enunciated with just a hint of an accent.

"Yes," Hunt said and turned to him, returning his smile.

"I must apologise about my daughter," he said. "She has a bit of a wild streak and likes to see if she makes me crap in my pants every now and again!"

He laughed and Hunt did the same.

"That's quite all right," Hunt said. "It made the drive more interesting."

"I'm sure, I'm sure, is this your car?" the gentleman asked and pointed at it.

"Oh! No," Hunt said. "Just a rental."

"You sure you didn't steal it?" he asked and grinned. "Because you drive it as if you stole it."

Hunt laughed again at the joke.

"Ernesto Enrique," he said and put out his hand to introduce himself. Spanish, Hunt thought, not Italian as he shook it. Enrique half-turned and indicated the woman in the car. "That is my daughter, Raquelle."

Hunt nodded hello. Raquelle pouted and lifted her sunglasses to inspect Hunt more closely. She had Mediterranean features. Smooth skin. And round dark eyes that glinted with a kind of hidden cheekiness.

"At first I thought maybe you were a racing driver in disguise, but now I see you, you're too big to race. What is it you do, Mister ...?"

"Mason," Hunt said. "John Mason. How'd you do. I'm a property developer."

"How interesting. Buying and selling? Asset management?"

"I'm a developer for a private buyer. A small private equity operation," Hunt said.

"Fascinating," Enrique said. "Around here? They must have exquisite taste. I, myself, am actually a lawyer. I am sure you noticed, but I am Spanish, so I know both markets and legal systems very well. Let me give you my card." He stuck his hand in his inside jacket pocket and felt his in his trousers. He turned to his daughter and said something rapidly in Spanish. She leaned across and opened the glove box with slow, elegant, bored movements. She opened the

Maserati's heavy door and swung her legs over the seat and stood up gracefully. Both men stood and watched her. It was like a piece of performance art. She walked up in high designer shoes and held the card out at almost full length. Her father smiled and took it.

"You were driving like that in high-heels," Hunt said.

"Raquelle, this is John Mason," Enrique said. She moved her extended arm out towards Hunt, slightly cocked at the elbow and limp-wristed. He took her hand lightly. Her nails were perfectly manicured. Her hands were soft and warm.

"A pleasure, I'm sure," she said.

"Mister Mason is in luxury property," Enrique said. Raquelle raised an eyebrow and gave Hunt the slightest of polite smiles. "And Raquelle has just finished a fine arts degree at the University of Oxford."

"Congratulations," Hunt said and she withdrew her hand.

"Did you go to university, Mister Mason?" she asked and turned away from him.

"For a little while," he said. "I left to pursue more thrilling ventures."

"So you can appreciate art?" she asked.

"You'll have to excuse my daughter, Mister Mason," she has her own style. "We all have to get used to it."

Unflustered and as if her father had said nothing, she continued, "If you'd care to, I am having a little exhibition of my work this weekend. Just a small get-together at the family estate if you'd be interested in attending?"

"I'd be delighted," Hunt said. She took a step closer to him and he smelled her perfume on the breeze. "There might be some dancing too."

Her father held out his business card. "Then it is

settled, here, take my card and we can go over the finer details."

Hunt took the card from Enrique and shook his hand. Raquelle glanced back at her father as he went to the car and took out a briefcase. She turned and stepped towards Hunt and put her manicured index finger on his right pectoral, looked up at him, leaned in and said, "So you like a bit of luxury, Mister Mason?"

"Sometimes, but mostly I like creating it."

"If you move like you drive, I might be inclined to create some luxury with you."

"Why don't you give me your number?" Hunt asked.

"Why don't you give me yours?" she said and handed him her smartphone.

Hunt took it and went to the phone's settings and noted her email address. He also toggled the option to automatically back up her contacts to the cloud.

"You okay, you know how to use a phone, right?"

"Yeah, just fat fingers," he said.

"My favourite," he said. He glanced up at her and grinned. He inputted his mobile phone number and called himself. "There," he said. He handed the device back to her. She put her hand on it, leaned forward, pecked him on the cheek and spun around and went back to the car. Hunt touched the place where she'd kissed him. Hunt dropped his hand from his face. She stepped into the car and started the engine. It sounded like a pride of angry lions. She pressed the accelerator, checked over her shoulder and drove off.

"Are you staying in the hotel?" Hunt said to Enrique as the car pulled away. He started to walk towards the reception and Hunt walked next to him.

"No, no. I am meeting a client. Very impressive man.

Staying in the Royal Suite, here. You know how much that costs per night?"

Hunt shook his head. "No idea, sir," Hunt said.

"If you had you would realise that this man was very, very valuable."

"You mean, wealthy?" Hunt asked.

"No, I mean valuable. With valuable people, you always make sure they are treated like a Faberge egg. You must look after them, keep them warm, and then, like a real egg, they hatch."

THIRTEEN

Hunt walked through the panelled glass door and stepped onto the classic terracotta-style clay tiles. They glistened under a chandelier. He was greeted warmly at the high-shine mahogany reception counter.

"Good morning, sir, welcome to the San Domenico Palace," the bright-smiling, bobbed-blonde receptionist said.

"Good morning, John Mason, checking in please."

She tapped on the keyboard.

"Yes, Mister Mason, you're staying in one of our sea-view deluxe rooms, I'll just need your passport and," she grabbed some papers from the printer, "Please sign, here," she indicated with a pen, "And here."

Hunt took the pen.

"Also," she said as she bent down, "We've had a delivery for you. It's quite heavy." Her voice strained as she lifted it onto the countertop.

"Fantastic, thanks," Hunt said. "Actually, I had a quick question."

She looked up at him expectantly with a white-toothed

plastic smile stuck on her face. She looked like a wax statue of an artist's impression of a person posing for a photograph.

"I was wondering if I could possibly upgrade," Hunt said.

"Of course, sir," she said and tapped on the keyboard again.

"I was wondering if any of your rooms had a private garden."

"Oh, no," she said. "The only room with a private garden is the Royal Suite and I'm afraid it is occupied at present."

Hunt nodded and showed his disappointment on his face.

"We do have executive suites with a plunge pool and include the sea view you currently have."

Just then, Hunt smelled the unmistakable sweet fragrance of spray-on deodorant. He glanced across. A man, with a one-millimetre buzz cut, his off-the-rack suit sticking impossibly tightly to his muscled body, and the top button of his shirt undone to accommodate his overly-thick neck came and stood next to Hunt. Closer than someone would normally. He was almost touching him. He didn't excuse himself or ask if he might interrupt.

He simply said in a thick Russian accent, "My boss need book boat for trip. Private."

Hunt should have known. Russia is the only country in the world where men spend more on deodorant and fragrances than women do. By the smell of it, this guy had subsidised a large portion of the overall spending.

The receptionist looked apologetically at Hunt for a second and then re-plastered her wide smile back on her face.

"Yes, Mister Igorevich, of course. When will you be needing it?"

"Tomorrow evening," he said. "Tell pilot to be ready from one hour before sunset."

"Captain," Hunt corrected him.

She scribbled a note on her pad. The henchman looked at Hunt for a moment with a deadpan, serious expression and then walked off. He walked like he was having difficulty pulling his bulk along and his shoulders rolled with each step and his head moved from side to side. Hunt watched him go and turned back to the receptionist.

"I'm so sorry," she said and seemed flustered. "His boss is staying in the Royal Suite you were asking about. They've been very demanding."

"What was that all about?" Hunt asked, taking advantage of her being slightly off balance.

"The hotel has a private jetty for guests. Many have their own speedboats, but we also have a water taxi service to take people on short hops around the island," she said.

"Interesting," Hunt said. "I'll bear that in mind."

"Why," the receptionist cocked her head and looked up at him from under her eyelashes, "Going somewhere nice?"

Hunt laughed once and smiled and said, "Possibly. Might just need to make a quick escape."

"Oh, are you one of those types of guys?"

It seemed as though they'd broken the ice. There was a momentary silence between them. Then she said, seeming to have forgotten herself, "Did you want to go ahead and upgrade your room, sir?"

"I arrived at the hotel with a lawyer, a man I'd just met. I wanted to thank him for the introduction and maybe buy him a drink, but he seems to have disappeared," Hunt said.

"Mister Enrique?" the receptionist asked.

Hunt nodded, "The very same."

"He visits our guest in the Royal Suite, there is a private elevator and entrance to the far side of the hotel," she said.

"I see," Hunt said and then smiled charmingly, "How the other half live, hey?"

She smiled.

"Let me take the room you've booked me and I'll have a look and call down if I'd like to change?" Hunt suggested.

"Yes, sir," she said and slid a leather keycard holder across the counter. He went to take it and she left her hand there for just a second longer and their hands touched. She blushed. "If there is anything else, sir," she said huskily, "My name is Alice, you can ask for me and I'll make sure you are well taken care of ..."

Hunt smiled politely and said, "Thanks, Alice. I'll remember that."

"Should I have the porter bring this up to your room?" she asked and gestured towards the package.

"No, that's okay. I'll take it up with me now."

WHEN HUNT GOT TO HIS DELUXE ROOM HIS LUGGAGE was already waiting for him. He put the parcel on the desk and went to the balcony. A plunge pool would have been a nice upgrade, but he doubted he'd be there long enough to enjoy it. His room was on the second floor and overlooked the gardens. They were pristinely manicured and full of maze hedges and fountains. Hunt leaned over the railing and looked to his left. As the property of the old fifteenth-century monastery curved around the cliff face, he could see a walled-off garden behind a hedge. The Royal Suite was like another private villa within the hotel's vast grounds. He went back inside and dialled reception. Alice answered.

"The room is great," Hunt said. "I'll keep it."

"Wonderful, enjoy your stay, Mister Mason."

He hung up and opened the package that had been delivered to reception for him. He tore open the tightly taped outer layer and cardboard box and grabbed the black handle of a carbon-fibre case. He got rid of the cardboard and laid the black and grey ribbed case on the bed. He put his thumbprint on the scanner and a light flashed green and the case unlocked. He pulled it open.

Inside were two carbon fibre handgun cases. He opened them. A Glock 19 with a suppressor. In the other was a more specialist weapon. A B&T VP9. A single-shot handgun with an integrated suppressor and chambered for 9x19 Parabellum rounds. It was developed from an almost identical assassination handgun from the Second World War called the Welrod Mk IIA. A specialist weapons course was one of Hunt's favourite sessions at the Kill School. The VP9 had two major benefits, not only was it a single shot but it also didn't expel the cartridge once fired because the bolt was silent. The firing pin was compressed by closing the bolt. The integrated suppressor had metal baffles, as well as solid rubber wipes which not only slowed the gas but the bullet too. The wipes once shot through, needed to be replaced. It was highly specialist. Hunt set it aside. There was a secure smartphone and tablet device. Biological-based trackers and receivers no bigger in size and shape than a contact lens which could be stuck onto any surface and disintegrated after twenty-four hours. The benefit is that they would never be discovered and there was no requirement for a clean-up team to remove any evidence of surveillance or intelligence gathering. There were also fewer intelligence weapons, but ones that required more skill to use properly. There were two knives, Hunt's favourite and go-to, a Fairbairn-Sykes fighting knife, created as an expert close combat weapon. There was also a fixed-hole dagger in a nylon sheath. It was a simple double-edged blade with a finger hole instead of a handle. It was easy to conceal and in the right hands, specifically Hunt's right hand, it was quick and deadly. Hunt also had Robin in his corner. If he was the blunt instrument, she was a precision laser-guided missile.

He turned on the mobile phone and waited. It prompted him to scan his iris and verbally enter his access code. Once matched, it unlocked. Uniquely, his phone had a global positioning transmitter and receiver. It was a small technicality, but Hunt knew that it was a misconception that a global positioning signal could be tracked. The Global Positioning System was receiving only. Whereas GPS in a mobile phone with a transmitting cellular signal could be tracked, GPS alone could not. His device had both. Even if he was not connected to a cellular tower, the operations room would know where he was, if he had the device on him.

Hunt opened an application and inputted the intelligence he'd collected and submitted the form. As soon as he had, a call came in from the operations room. He connected to the call and was prompted to input his personal identifier to pass security on the encryption-secured line.

"You took your time," Robin said.

Hunt smiled. "I had some business to take care of."

"Blonde or brunette?"

Hunt raised his eyebrows.

"Neither," Hunt said. "But I do have her email address,

phone number, car registration and her father's business card."

"I see that," she said. "Let's see what we're dealing with."

"The car is registered to a company based in Andorra. It looks like a tax write-off," she said as she accessed information. "Enrique, Ernesto. Fifty-three. Spanish and Italian dual national. Founding partner of Lazarus-Zollinger, a Dominican Republic registered international law firm. Details are sketchy. I'll have to do some digging here."

Hunt sat on the bed and leaned forward. He rested his elbows on his knees and massaged his temples and waited.

"Let's see," Robin said. "Raquelle Simone Enrique Guevara. It'll take my programme a few minutes to hack her cloud data storage."

"I uploaded her contacts to the cloud," he said.

"Good work. Now —" Hunt could tell Robin was busy working hard. Her distracted and professional tone was like that of an experienced insurance agent tapping information into online forms. "— Let's see. Twenty-four years old. Five-foot-eight, black hair, blue eyes, a hundred and forty pounds. You sure know how to pick 'em, Stirling ..."

Yeah, he thought. If it keeps you safe and gets me out of this corner, it'll be worth it.

"For Queen and country," Hunt said.

"More like princess and pantomime."

"I'm going to a little soirée tomorrow night at their villa."

"Lucky you."

"I think Enrique, the father, is connected with elements around or close to Isakov."

Hunt heard McKenna's voice. "Have you had eyes on him?" he asked.

"Not yet," Hunt said. "Can you get a satellite image of the Royal Suites private garden?"

"Working on it now," Robin said.

"Good work, Hunt," McKenna said.

"Roger," Hunt said. "Out." He hung up and laid back on the bed.

FOURTEEN

Hunt sat in the back of the taxi and leaned forward and pressed his nose against the window. He looked out on the high stone-walled compound as they wound their way up the sand and gravel driveway. It was lined with conical-shaped trees and exquisitely manicured grass.

The taxi stopped at the gatehouse and he stepped out. An athletic-looking man was waiting in a dark suit with a clipboard. There were rows and rows of high-end sports cars and chauffeur-driven Bentleys and Rolls-Royces. The man with the clipboard looked at Hunt expectantly and Hunt said, "Mason. John, Mason."

The security guard scanned the list. He turned the page over the back of the metal clip and then popped a highlighter lid off with his mouth and highlighted the name Hunt had given. He folded the paper down, stowed the highlighter, and bent down to open the roped-off entrance.

"John Mason coming up," the security said into his wired earpiece.

"Thanks," Hunt said and stepped through the open

wooden gate and under the high stone wall. He walked up a long maroon-red carpet that led to a brightly lit mansion-like villa. He passed another suited security guard as he entered and the man nodded once to him and stood there with his hands folded at his crotch.

People were standing throughout the large open-plan living space, chatting and taking drinks from the waiters as they moved through the palace. There were black-and-white photographs placed strategically around the rooms. Mostly artsy, close-up portraits. Some landscapes. Everyone was in evening wear. Hunt lifted a champagne flute from a passing waiter and walked out onto a terrace that over-looked the Ionian Sea. It was late evening and the sun was fading. He held the glass in one hand and put his hands on the yellow-painted concrete railing and looked out over the party below. There was an infinity pool surrounded by Greco-Roman statues and clay-potted shrubs and flowers. The light shimmered off the now dark grey sea. It almost seemed like criminal enterprise made it all worth it for a view like this.

"You're fashionably late," he heard Raquelle's voice behind him. He smiled and turned. She looked radiant. Her dark hair was pulled tightly back and parted in the middle. She had thick hooped earrings and a matching necklace and a long, floral, black dress. It was timeless and elegant.

"Couldn't find anything to wear," Hunt said and nodded towards her outfit, "Unlike you, I see. You look —" he paused to consider.

"Ravishing?" she said. "Beautiful, *magnifique?*"

"All of the above," Hunt said.

"You look rather remarkable yourself, Mister Mason," Raquelle said and moved closer to him. Hunt was wearing a classic navy-blue blazer and khaki trousers. She held out her glass and they clinked them together. She took a sip of her champagne and watched him closely over the top of her glass.

"You know my name is John, right?" he said.

She nodded. "I do."

"And, you know you can call me that?" he said.

"No, I can't," she said and smiled slightly.

"Why not?"

She leaned her head back and squinted at him and said, "I don't know, you don't seem like a John to me at all, or a Johnny ..."

"What do I look like?"

"Not a John," she said. "Maybe an Albert, or Albie."

She smiled cheekily at him.

"Albie!?" he said. "Well, pleased to meet you, I suppose."

She took another sip of her champagne and Hunt could tell she was enjoying the little back and forth. She didn't seem like the kind of person who gave much away. She seemed cold and distant, but it was probably more a defence mechanism to stop herself from being hurt than anything else, he decided.

"Quite a turnout," Hunt said. "Congratulations on your opening, by the way ..."

"Thank you," she said.

"And on your beautiful home," Hunt said.

"None of this is mine," she said and looked around. "It's all my father's. It was an old fort before he bought it and restored it. Now it is like being held captive behind high walls and security cameras. I don't like it."

"Do you know all of the people here?"

She stepped to the railing and stood next to him and

they looked out at the cliques and packs of assembled guests.

"Most of them," she said. "Some, actually the majority, are my father's business associates. In town for some big hoo-ha or other."

She looked up at Hunt, then looked out over the sea. He turned and rested his hips against the railing and looked at her.

"What?" he asked.

"Nothing," she shook her head.

"Come on, tell me," he said.

She shrugged. "It's just that, I'm getting the impression, maybe the main point of all of this was to get his clients together, not to exhibit my work."

Hunt pressed his lips together in empathetic pity and kept studying the outline of her face and features. He thought she was beautiful.

"In fact," she said and looked at him again, their faces close to one another, "I feel like you're the person I know best, and I don't even know you!" She laughed morosely and put her hand to her cheek and said, "God, how pathetic!"

"I'm sure that's not true," he said.

"It is."

He turned around and faced the pool and the sea again.

"Go on then," he said and gestured with his glass out of the crowd. "Tell me who you recognise and we'll see if it's really true or not."

"Okay," she said. "I like games." She looked out over the crowd. "So, besides you, Albert, I know... Oh, that short man with curly hair standing there is my father's head of security. His name is Richard Draper. Everyone calls him

Dickie." She leaned closer to Hunt's ear and whispered, "He's gay but pretends he isn't, but everyone knows."

Hunt dropped the corners of his mouth and nodded. "Good knowledge," he said.

"A lot of the others are business partners and colleagues of my father. See that girl over there," she said and lifted her chin towards a very tall blonde in a golden-yellow dress. She was surrounded by a group of suited younger men.

"Yes," Hunt said.

"That is a friend of mine, Sylvia, she is a *Baronessa* from the old Italian nobility. She's a Normanni, and all of those boys around her are only trying to get in her pants and get her pregnant so that they can marry into her Sicilian royal household. She's got her eye on the good-looking one with his back to us, but little does he know that she has been on the pill since she was twelve and has been with more guys than she can even remember. We now just pretend to be friends, she's gotten all snobby and *la-di-da* now that she's realised we're from new money. It's so dull ..." she said and sipped her champagne.

"Wow," Hunt said and laughed.

"Enjoying this game?" she asked and gave him a big smile.

"Very much," Hunt said. As they were talking a motor-boat approached in a wide arc from behind the swell out to sea. They both looked. They stood silently and watched as the sleek and shiny black speed boat turned into the path of the jetty and slowed. An old man was on board. He stood at the front with his hands on the cream-coloured trim in a flat cap and scarf, dark glasses, and a black overcoat with the collar up against the wind. There was a man in a suit and dark glasses sitting at the back of the boat too. As they got closer, Hunt recognised him as the bodyguard from the hotel. He'd booked a boat. Isakov was a guest at the party. There was another man in the boat that Hunt didn't recognise. He was also in dark glasses, slicked over dark hair, and an open-collared shirt showing off a collection of chain necklaces. Hunt noted that these guys weren't going to be on any list held by Dickie Draper's security detail.

"Who's that?" Hunt asked as they both watched. The bodyguard climbed out onto the jetty and put his hand out to help the Russian Admiral off the boat. The slick-haired, open-collared guy climbed off last and said something to the boat's captain. They walked up the jetty and started climbing the stairs toward the villa.

"I don't know," Raquelle said unconvincingly and finished her drink. "Another?" she asked him and waved her empty flute at him. Hunt downed his and said, "Yes, please."

She took his empty glass and went to find a waiter. He watched her swaying hips as she left, like a lioness flicking her tail, and she turned and smiled when she saw him watching her. Hunt smiled back, but his hand was already on his smartphone. He unlocked it as soon as she was out of view and used two fingers to zoom in on the old man climbing the stairs towards the old fortifications. He held his thumb down and took a burst of pictures. He felt someone behind him and quickly turned. It was Raquelle with the drinks. She must have seen him taking a picture of the old man, but she didn't say anything. She had the champagne glasses in each hand and said, "My father is here, I told him you came and he'd like to say hello," she said.

"By all means," Hunt said and stuck the phone back in his pocket.

FIFTEEN

Hunt followed Raquelle inside. She half-glanced over her shoulder and stopped just outside the double sliding doors. Hunt bumped gently into the back of her and he felt her firm body beneath her loose dress and her warm skin and smelled the fragrance from her neck.

"Sorry," she said and smiled. He knew it was no accident. Then she looked straight and stepped through the door. Hunt saw her father standing in the middle of the room with his hand in the pocket of his white trousers and swirling the other in the air as he talked to someone.

"Papa!" Raquelle called and Enrique excused himself and spread his arms. She went towards him and they kissed each cheek and he put his hands on her waist. Hunt stepped down into the open living room and Raquelle smiled broadly and turned away from her father to face him.

"Papa, you remember Alfie, don't you?"

"John, good to see you again, I trust you've been well? No more drag racing the coastal route I hope!" Enrique said and they shook hands.

"Nice to see you," Hunt said.

Enrique was about to respond and was still holding Hunt's hand when a suited security guard with an earpiece came up and touched him on the shoulder and whispered something in his ear. The security guard gestured to the other side of the room. They all turned to look. Hunt saw the old man. Former Russian Pacific Fleet Admiral Isakov. He was flanked by the bodyguard from the hotel and, behind him, the sharp-faced, open-buttoned shirt guy from the speedboat. At closer range, Hunt saw that he had gold incisors to go with his gold chains and a tattoo that curled out from under his collar up the left side of his neck and down his left arm.

"Excuse me," Enrique said and as he left then added, "Buy some art!"

As they watched him go, Raquelle handed Hunt his drink.

"Sorry about my father," she said.

Hunt was still looking at the new arrivals. Enrique went up to them and welcomed them to his home. He was short and slight but full of energy and bounce. None of them shook hands, but he guided them into the living room and they cut through the low angled rays of setting sun that were shining against the mantlepiece and the group filed silently through the room. No one paid them any attention. Hunt watched as they climbed a staircase to another level.

"How about a tour of the house?" Hunt suggested.

"What'd you have in mind?" Raquelle asked. He dropped the corners of his mouth.

"I don't know, we could get away from these people. You could show me your room."

Raquelle furrowed her brow slightly. She looked amused.

"And ... what then?"

"I'm sure we could find something to entertain ourselves ..." Hunt said. "Don't you have any puzzles or board games we could play?"

"I can think of another game we could play," she said.

"Does it involve getting out of these clothes?" he asked. She fluttered her eyelashes exaggeratingly and had a look of bemusement on her face.

"Mister Mason, I do declare," she said dramatically in a put-on southern accent.

"Lead the way, Miss O'Hara," Hunt said.

"You go up and wait for me," she said, "We need to be a bit more subtle. Lots of eyes and ears in this place, don't you know. I'll get us some drinks."

Hunt nodded and went to the railing of the stairs. Raquelle made her way through the clumps of people and glanced at him and then tried to hide her smile as she went to the bar. Hunt slowly climbed the stairs. At the top, they opened up onto a long corridor. It was lined with open archways of columns on his right looking down onto a courtyard. The other side of the wall was decorated with century-old portraits of nobility. There was also antique furniture with blue and white vases on them and other Ming ceramics. Whatever Enrique and his clientele were into, they were making a fortune. He heard footsteps and turned and saw Raquelle coming up the staircase carrying a fresh bottle of champagne in one hand, two glasses in the other, a designer clutch under her arm, and a naughty look on her face. She walked past him and said, "Come on this way. God, I hope no one saw me."

Hunt furrowed his brow. "Thanks very much," he said. "Real vote of confidence there."

As he followed her he saw another short staircase at the end of the corridor. The door was ajar and he heard Enrique's throaty laugh echo down the hall. Ahead of him, Raquelle leaned with her elbow on one of the handles and pushed the door open with her hip.

"In here," she said in a forced whisper. "Quickly, before someone sees you." Hunt slipped past her into the darkened room and she said, "I feel like I'm back at Catholic school sneaking boys into the convent behind the nun's backs."

"Is this your room?" Hunt asked.

She put the glasses down on a bureau and placed her clutch down next to them. She turned and flicked on the lights. It was a grand room with a four-poster bed, an en-suite, and a view onto fields at the back of the estate.

"No," she said. "It's for guests ... "

Hunt turned around from looking out the window at the fields and she had her arms outstretched above her head and pushed her body into his and said, "Now, where were we?"

She pressed her lips into his and he put his hands on her waist. Her body was warm against his chest. Her lips were soft and she tried to stick her tongue in his mouth. It took him by surprise. She wasn't a good kisser, too rushed and sloppy. Hunt was thinking fast. He needed to get out of this room and find out what was going on in the office down the hallway. He pulled back slowly and said in a low suggestive tone, "I think you were just telling me about how you liked to get undressed in front of strange men," he said. She leaned her head back and said, "Oh, was I?"

"You were ... so, take your dress off and get onto the bed."

"Yes, sir."

She pushed herself away from him and lifted her hand above her head and looked down and bit her lip sensually. All Hunt was thinking about was trying to get out of here. Plus, he was sure Robin had hacked into the mic on his smartphone and was probably listening in on the whole thing. Not that they were together or anything, he just knew Robin liked to play the jealousy card.

Raquelle crossed her arms and grabbed onto her dress and pulled it over her head. She was wearing black lingerie. Suddenly she got shy and hopped onto the bed and curled her legs up and pulled a large pillow in front of her body.

"Where are you going?" she asked. Hunt stopped at the champagne and pulled the gold foil off. He undid the wire cage and popped the cork. He filled the glasses and carried them over to the bed. He handed her a glass and she took a big sip.

"I can't believe we're doing this," she said and put the glass down on the bedside table. "Now get over here," she said and grabbed him by the lapel and pulled him towards her. She kissed him and started trying to pull his jacket off. Hunt set his glass down next to her and undid his tie and moved forward. She laid back and while they were kissing he put his hand around her wrist and pinned it to the pillow next to her. She stopped kissing him and opened her mouth and looked at where he had pinned her wrist. He expertly wrapped his loosened tie around her wrist and pulled tight, then flipped her on her back, and before she realised what he was doing, he'd tied her wrists together. She rolled over and before she could say anything he took his silk handkerchief out of his breast pocket and held it in front of her mouth. She looked at it and then opened wide and he put it in. He looked at her for a second and then said, "Stay right here, I just need to go to the bathroom."

Her eyes went wide and she tried to mumble something like, 'there's a bathroom right here', but Hunt couldn't make it out over the handkerchief in her mouth and was already out the door. He pulled it gently shut and straightened his jacket.

The door at the end of the corridor was still ajar and in the faint dusk light coming through the window, he couldn't make out any human figures. He walked towards it. There was a flight of four steps that led up to the darkened room in front of him. As he approached he saw a light shining from an adjacent room. He crept forward. The voices grew louder. They were still obscured. He reached the base of the stairs. There was another door directly to his left and he saw there was a light on inside, shining out from under the closed door. He climbed the stairs and heard the voices more clearly. There was a voice speaking in Russian. Then another spoke, in accented, broken English, seemingly translating what the Russian voice had said. Hunt reached into his jacket pocket and pulled out a small plastic box about the size of a cardholder. He clicked it open and took out one of the contact lens-sized adhesive voice receivers. He put his arm around the wall and stuck it into the inside of the wall and attached one. The nanotechnology was extremely sensitive to sound and started recording and transmitting the audio data automatically the moment it was removed from the case.

Behind and to his left, Hunt heard a toilet flush. Quickly he closed the case and put it away and hopped down the steps. He was standing on the bottom step when the door pulled open violently and he found himself looking directly at the bodyguard from the hotel reception. Isakov's bodyguard was looking down, but when he looked up and saw Hunt his face scrunched up in confusion and anger and he said, "You cannot be here, you must leave."

"Sorry," Hunt said and tried to pull the dumb lost-tourist card. He put on his best pompous Brit-abroad shtick and said, "I was just looking for the toilet, and there you go, I found it, but you were in it."

Hunt saw a movement out his peripheral and saw Enrique's head pop out of the room. Hunt lifted his hand and said, "Just looking for the loo."

Enrique pulled the door shut without saying anything. Damn it, Hunt thought. Busted. Badly busted.

"May I?" Hunt said to the security guard who was trying to leave the toilet. As the guy stepped in front of him, Hunt tripped down the final step and bumped into him. The bodyguard was made of granite and he twisted away as Hunt fell into him. Hunt recovered his footing and turned back to the bodyguard and smiled apologetically and said, "Sorry, my man, apologies. Too much of the old bubbly in me I'm afraid!"

The Russian glared at him. His face was red and his fists were clenched by his sides. He looked like a kettle that was about to boil over. He expected steam to bust from his ears and a high-pitched whistle to emanate from his mouth. Hunt felt like if it wasn't a party, the bodyguard might've shot him.

"I'll just go," Hunt said and walked away from the bodyguard and back down the corridor. Hunt glanced over his shoulder and saw the bodyguard climbing the stairs back to the outer room. He entered and closed the door at the top of the steps. When he'd gone, Hunt pulled out the bodyguard's wallet. He'd lifted it when he pretended to fall. He opened it and scanned through it. He saw what he was after, the keycard to the Royal Suite at the Sun Domenico

Palace. Hunt took the keycard out and put it into his inside jacket pocket. He glanced behind. The door to the meeting was shut. He went back to the bathroom and placed the bodyguard's wallet on the white sink. Hunt rinsed his hands and shook his hands of excess water and ran a hand through his hair. He looked quickly at the door again and then hurried back down the corridor.

SIXTEEN

ALEKSANDR ARKHIPOV CLOSED THE DOOR TO THE meeting room.

"What was that?" Admiral Isakov asked.

Arkhipov shook his head and put his hand flat against the buttons of his suit jacket. "Nothing," he said. "Just some drunk guest looking for the toilet."

"Speak in English, please gentleman," the voice said over the speakerphone.

"Of course, Mister van den Krijl," Enrique, the lawyer, said. "I believe we are all here now."

"Fine. Where are we?" van den Krijl said over the speaker.

The men in the room looked at one another.

"We are here," Isakov said. "At Enrique's house."

Enrique grinned.

"Where are you?" Isakov asked. "Are you not joining us?"

"I mean where are we with the operation, Admiral. I am well aware of where you are. I haven't been able to attend, unfortunately. It's nothing personal, it's business."

"I think what Mister van den Krijl means is, what is the status update?" Enrique said.

"Yes," the voice over the speaker said.

"I believe Dushku should go first," Isakov said.

The Albanian arms dealer lifted his fist to his mouth and cleared his throat and shrugged. "Once we know the location we can start moving the shipment."

"What's the location of the weapon?" van den Krijl demanded.

"Now, now, gentlemen, please," Enrique said.

Arkhipov spoke. "This is a delicate matter, Derek."

"Mister van den Krijl," Enrique said quietly.

"It's okay," the voice on the speakerphone said.

"Firstly, we cannot simply discuss such things on the phone. You know they are listening," Arkhipov said.

"This line is encoded, perfectly. No one is listening," van den Krijl said.

"Nevertheless, we can't be too careful with secrets like these. We have to be very careful to ensure it goes to plan."

"Yes, well, what I'm trying to work out is where exactly in the plan we are. Are the weapons safe? Are they accessible?"

"Yes," Isakov said. "The plan is solid as Siberian steel. The weapons are secure. We will use Mints' bank."

"Fine," van den Krijl said.

"Physical delivery is required," Isakov added.

"What do you mean?" van den Krijl asked.

"The bank is a vault. It requires physical delivery - gold, diamonds, silver, cash. Dollars only."

"Listen," van den Krijl said and sighed. "I can wire you cryptographically secure GaiaCoin in seconds. You can cash it out on your end for dollars. It's safe and accessible."

Arkhipov and Isakov glanced at one another. Arkhipov shook his head.

"No, Mister van den Krijl, that will not do," Isakov said. "We require delivery to Nebula Bank in *hard* currency. Much safer."

"And how do I get access to the weapons?"

"We understand you are in the market for a superyacht?" Enrique said. Van den Krijl was silent. "Is our information incorrect, Mister van den Krijl?"

"No, not incorrect."

"Where the missiles are, requires a submersible. It's the easiest way to ensure complete discretion for the handover. You will instruct your yacht broker to arrange a personal submarine to be included in the transaction or to modify your chosen yacht to accommodate such a vehicle. The Neyk Luxury L-1 or Phoenix 1000 would be best for their size and to accommodate the missiles."

"And how much is that going to set me back?"

Arkhipov said, "In comparison to what you will gain, the money is of little significance."

"How much?" van den Krijl demanded.

"Approximately two point three billion," Enrique said.

There was silence.

After fifteen seconds van den Krijl said, "Send me the deposit information for Nebula Bank. I will have my security team transport half the money there. Once you've sent the pickup information for the weapons systems, I will send you the location of the other half. This is non-negotiable. Enrique will handle the details on my side. Make sure I get the bank details as soon as possible. That is all —"

"Ah, Mister van den Krijl!" Isakov said. "Wait, wait—"

"That is my final offer —"

"You don't understand, sir. The location—the coordinates to the weapons—are in a safety deposit box in Mints' bank."

Van den Krijl sighed. "So how is this going to work?"

Arkhipov pulled out his smartphone and said, "Current value of GaiaCoin is two hundred and fifty-three dollars per coin. So let's agree on a spread of two hundred and fifty-five and you transfer half the balance to us in advance."

"This is not what we agreed," Isakov said to Arkhipov angrily in Russian. Arkhipov held up his hand to stop him and continued.

"We will wire you the location and account number for Nebula Bank. We will meet your convoy full of gold or cash at the bank and swap the passcode to the safety deposit box. Inside you will find the location of the missiles. We will take possession of the funds."

Isakov's face was a scowl. "Is there agreement?" he said gruffly.

"How will you deliver the bank details?"

"Mister Enrique will receive them after this call, as soon as the cryptocurrency is sent."

There was a moment of silence on the line.

"Mister van den Krijl?" Enrique said.

Arkhipov's phone buzzed.

"You should just have received it into your account gentlemen," van den Krijl said. The line went dead.

SEVENTEEN

HUNT OPENED THE BEDROOM DOOR AGAIN AND WENT inside. Raquelle was still there, lying on her back with her arms secured behind her. Her eyes were wide with rage. She was breathing deep, intense breaths from her nose. Hunt went to the bed and sat down on the edge of his. He leaned forward to remove her gag.

As he gently pulled it out, he said, "Sorry, I got a little distracted ..."

"Distracted! You left me here, what were you thinking? There is a toilet right here!" She sat forward and lifted her chin towards it.

"Turn around," Hunt said. "Let me untie you."

She scowled at him and twisted over on the bed.

"I can't believe you did that," she said as he loosened the tie.

"Something came up," he said. "Unavoidable."

"Like what, what could possibly be —"

"It's work," he said. "I fall too easily at people's feet."

She turned around and got on her knees and slapped him. It stung, but he didn't respond. Then she grabbed him by the lapel and kissed him hard on the lips.

"Sorry," she said. "That's the hot-blood Spanish in me. You make me crazy —"

"I need to —"

"I think you should leave," she said suddenly. "Though I hate to see you go," she said.

"I think you're right. I have a work emergency," he pursed his lips and looked at her.

"What?"

"Can I borrow your car?"

* * *

Hunt turned the key on the Maserati and the engine exploded to life. It was dark now and the headlights lit the path in front of him to a bright white. He revved the engine and pulled out onto the gravel drive and raced down the sharp, sloping turns toward Taormina. As he drove he passed security and called the operations room.

"Hunt?" she answered.

"Where are you?" he asked.

"At home, why?"

"Did you get the voice data?"

"Checking, one moment," she said.

He twisted the wheel full left and pulled the car close to the apex of the corner and accelerated.

"More to the point, where are you?" she asked.

"On my way to recover some intelligence," he said.

"How was your party?"

"Yeah," he said. "It was strange, thanks."

"Okay, I have a voice recording," she said. "Analysing it now."

"Isakov was there," Hunt said and swung the car to the right. "He was speaking with our corrupt lawyer and there was another guy. Gold incisors, tattoo up his neck, spoke with a Balkans accent. I think it was Dushku."

The line went static.

"Robin?"

Her voice was breaking up.

"Listen, if you can hear me, find out what they were discussing and tell me if there are any clues to the location of the intelligence. I'm going to look for it."

He hung up, gripped the steering wheel tightly, and put his foot down. He was pulled back into the chair as the GranTurismo accelerated through the bends.

HUNT PULLED INTO THE PARKING LOT AND SWITCHED off the ignition. He still felt the pulsing growl of the engine running through his hands and chest.

He made sure no one saw him enter and went straight to his room and dressed in black. He had a balaclava that he rolled up and put on his head. He put the Glock in the left, and suppressor in the right side of his dual shoulder holsters, and the VP9 he holstered around his waist. He put on a mid-length black coat that held his accessories, lock picking kit, head torch, and nitrile gloves. It also covered the weapons from view.

Hunt went out onto the balcony and checked over the pool and the garden below. The hotel was quiet and all he heard was the sound of waves moving against the cliff face below. He climbed over the metal and grabbed onto the lower rung of the railing and lowered himself. He shifted his hands to the terracotta tile so the length of his body was hanging down. Then he let go and landed in a crouch. He stayed like that for a moment. A quick mental check to make sure he wasn't physically compromised with a twisted ankle or broken bone in his foot. He felt fine. Just the residue of the jolt to his joints. He glanced left and right and stood and hurried to the southeast of the hotel's estate along the length of one of the hedged mazes. The Royal Suite's walled garden was at the far end. It had a tall hedge running around the inside of it for privacy. Hunt could have used the keycard to enter through the garden door, but for the sake of confusing any attempt to track his method of entry, he hoisted himself on top of the solid wooden slatted door and climbed over. He dropped down and faced a private apartment with a balcony and a single access door on the ground floor to his right.

He went to the solid steel door and pulled out the keycard. He checked the magnetic stripe and put it into the slot. He pulled it out and the light blinked red.

"Come on," Hunt said and tried it again. He could open the hotel door manually if required, but it would waste precious time. He knew the mark would be back that night. He put the keycard into the slot and waited a second. He pulled it out and heard the mechanism turn inside and pulled down on the handle. The door opened.

HUNT WAS ON HIS KNEES, IN THE DARK, USING THE LOW red light from his head torch to search through the contents of the bottom drawer under one of the built-in closets when he stopped and twisted his head towards the entrance hall. He thought he'd heard a noise.

He checked his watch, he'd already been in the suite for almost an hour. He'd searched everywhere. The first and most obvious place was the electronic safe. There was no point trying to guess the combination. Hotel safes were relatively simple to open. There were at least three methods that Hunt was shown at the Kill School which took seconds. The first one was a design error exploitation. As long as the bolts in a hotel safe were not under stress and free to move, but lifting them, they would unlock. He didn't need to try that one.

Every hotel safe has a universal passcode for those guests that forget their passwords and can't get their valuables out. Depending on the brand of electronic safe, certain settings allowed him to enter a manufacturer's override password. Very few hotels changed the default manufacturer settings, this one was no different. The safe was the first place he'd checked, but Isakov and his security were smart enough not to use it to store intelligence worth tens of millions of dollars.

Hunt put the clothes back and closed the drawer. He switched off the head torch and stood up silently. He went to the entrance to the room and put his back up against the wall and listened. He heard the front door close almost silently. No footsteps. No voices. Someone had entered the Royal Suite but didn't want to make any sound. A low light came on. To Hunt, it seemed like the lamp in the entrance hall. Hunt stalked back to the glass sliding doors which led from the bedroom to the terrace. He unlocked it silently and slid it open an inch as quietly as he could. His pulse was elevated. His breathing was measured. He was creeping around like a burglar in a sleeping house. His eyes saw a dissipating wisp of smoke. Then a white head of hair came into view. "Sh—," he swore silently. The admiral was walking around and smoking in the garden. He couldn't get down or get out. He left the balcony door open an inch and went back to the bedroom entrance.

EIGHTEEN

IF THE ADMIRAL WAS HAVING HIS NIGHTLY CIGARETTE outside, it could only be the bodyguard moving around the suite. It was good drills. The asset was in a protected outdoor space, out of the line of sight, while the security made sure the living space was clear of any threats. Hunt stalked into the master bedroom's en-suite. He pulled the balaclava down over his face and adjusted it so he could breathe and see properly. He always felt warm and suffocated with the cotton over his head.

He stayed in the dark with the door open and took out the Glock and the suppressor. As silently as he could he touched the barrel to the metal tube of the suppressor and started to screw it onto the barrel.

He held his breath and listened for sounds coming from the rest of the suite. It wouldn't take the Russian long to clear the place. Every turn of the suppressor onto the Glock sounded to him like a spade scraping on concrete. All the noises were exaggerated in his mind. As he turned the final thread and felt the suppressor lock tight, he saw the bedroom light flick on and heard the click of the switch. The bodyguard was in the room. Hunt held his breath. His heart rate was raised. He heard the swoosh of blood around his eardrums. He waited, expecting the guard to come into the bathroom. He heard his footsteps pad along the carpet. Hunt lifted the pistol and waited. Nothing came.

Then he heard the quick shuffle of footsteps towards the terrace and heavy breathing. Hunt leaned out of the bathroom door and looked left. The bedroom door was open wide, he didn't see anybody outside the room. There was a wall, halfway down the centre of the room, separating the bed from the entrance to the en-suite bathroom. Hunt could hear someone moving in the room. He sidestepped to his left and saw the dark suit and shape of the Russian's body. He was standing at the sliding door looking up at the top of the opening. Was he trying to work out if he was popped from the outside, or trying to remember whether they left it open? Hunt put himself in the bodyguard's shoes. If it were Hunt, he would be sure they didn't, but what were the options, housemaid? No, he'd left the *Do Not Disturb* out. The bodyguard pulled the sliding door shut and flicked the latch.

Hunt lifted his handgun. He saw the bodyguard glance to his right. He saw a shimmer of a movement in the reflection of the glass. Hunt fired. The sound of the suppressed gunshots was like a loud metallic tick. The sound of a doomsday clock. *Tick-tick-tick.*

Two rounds slammed into the wall where the bodyguard had stood. They left a tight grouping and two black holes in the wall that smoked. The third was a glancing shot that grazed the back of his tricep as he dived to his right. He'd moved with a split second to spare.

Hunt heard him grunt in pain and a thud as he hit the floor. Hunt charged forward. Just as the bodyguard raised his handgun, Hunt grabbed the side of the king-sized mattress and lifted it. The barrel of the bodyguard's handgun was on the edge of the mattress, before he could fire, the whole mattress bent and tilted the barrel upwards. Hunt drove forward with his legs and torso like a defensive lineman after the snap. He lifted the mattress and it bent in the middle. Hunt got underneath it and pushed it over onto the bodyguard lying on the floor. It made a loud thud against the glass and rattled the door. The bedside lamp crashed against the wall. Hunt kept pushing forward until he was on top of the mattress. The bodyguard shouted out in Russian and grunted. Hunt jumped on top of the mattress. The bodyguard was rolling around trying to get out from under the weight of it. Hunt felt like he was on a dinghy in choppy seas. The whole thing swayed as he tried to keep his footing. He dropped to his knees and lifted his elbow ninety degrees and held the Glock so the end of the suppressor pointed straight at the mattress. Hunt could feel the Russian moving under him. He pushed the tip of the suppressor into the foam and fired. Hunt's index finger pulled and released rapidly on the trigger. *Tick-tick-tick-tick-tick.* Rounds slapped into and penetrated the soft mattress. He heard the dull slapping thuds as the one-hundred-grain nine-millimetre rounds found their target. Hunt stopped firing. He was breathing heavily through the balaclava. The air was hot. He waited to see if the Russian was still moving. The back of his throat and nostrils were filled with the burned ammonia smell of gunpowder. He climbed off the mattress. He breathed heavily and was sweating. No movement came from underneath.

"Hell of a party trick," Hunt said.

Hunt glanced to his side and saw the wisp of white smoke floating up past the terrace. He lifted the balaclava over his face and breathed. Hunt heard the admiral say something from outside. He made sure to obscure his face and pulled the sliding door open a little. The admiral was standing in the garden looking back at the terrace. He said in Russian, "Come down and let me in Aleksandr, you have my key!"

Hunt tried to remember the tone and tenor of the bodyguard's voice from Enrique's villa and said, "*Da.*"

"Is everything okay? I heard a noise."

Hunt turned his head and tried to muffle his voice, "I fell," he said. Hunt slammed the sliding door shut and said out loud to the dead Russian, "Don't get up."

He put the bodyguard's keycard back in the dead man's wallet and quickly collected the brass casings he'd fired, when he was sure he had all of them, he left. Hunt pulled the balaclava down as he walked through the suite. The front door opened up to an external foyer. There was a service elevator, a set of stairs going down, and another door that led to the main part of the hotel. Hunt descended the staircase. As he did, still grasping the bullet casings in his right hand, he pulled the nitrate glove off, over his hand, and scooped up all of the loose brass. He tied it at the wrist and stuffed the glove and casings into his jacket. He made the Glock safe and unscrewed the suppressor and re-holstered the weapon and the attachment. Hunt pulled out the VP9. The single-shot, specialist weapon with its integrated suppressor wouldn't make any noise outside. Which meant it wouldn't attract any attention. Hunt pressed down on the handle and pushed the door open.

"Where the hell have you been —" Isakov stepped

forward and said. His eyes widened in horror as he saw the black-clad, balaclava-faced assassin standing in front of him. Hunt held the long handgun out and aimed directly into Isakov's eye. The old man put his hands up next to his head and said, "Please, don't shoot. I —, I'll give you whatever you want. Whoever you want —"

"Where's the data?" Hunt said in Russian.

Isakov glanced down and left and said, "I have no idea what you're talking about."

"Then what good are you?"

"No, no —"

Hunt pressed the trigger and there was a light kick from the VP9. There was a high-pitched hiss and Isakov's left eye exploded in a silent red spray of mushrooming blood and skin and his body crumpled to the ground. Hunt holstered the weapon and grabbed the admiral by the lapels and dragged his body prone on its back. He patted the body down. If the intelligence wasn't in the room, the only other place it could be was his person. Hunt felt his pockets. In the inside jacket pocket was a small, plastic box, about the size of a cigarette case. He took it out and unclipped it. Inside was a flash drive. Bingo, Hunt thought. And then realised he'd never actually played bingo. He felt the need to finish searching the admiral, just in case there was anything else of interest. There wasn't. He was certain he had what he needed. He used his left hand and reached into the coin pouch of his trousers and pulled out two silver coins. He placed them over the eyes of the departed. Payment for the ferryman. McKenna had said to send a message. That's exactly what Hunt intended to do.

He checked his watch. It was almost three in the morning. There was no way he would get any sleep. He'd need to inform the operations room that he needed an exfiltration, upload the contents of the flash drive to Robin, and get ready to leave. The VP9 didn't expel the fired round's casing, so he didn't need to worry about searching around in the grass. He exited the same way he'd come, only this time he went through the door and not over it.

NINETEEN

HUNT SPOTTED THEM AS SOON AS HE GOT DOWN THE
stairs and into the hotel's reception. He was carrying the
heavy cardboard box with his weapons and equipment in it.
He'd packed it so the handle protruded from the box as if it
were a suitcase. On a normal day, during a normal stay,
would he have noticed them? Hard to say. Probably. But
now he was on the lookout. Senses heightened. It was the
last part of the mission. The most dangerous part. Everyone
thinks about summiting Everest, but that is only half the
battle, you still need half the energy to get back down. The
bodies strewn on the face show the importance of thinking
through to the finish.

There was nothing to them. The short, bad haircuts,
cheap polyester shirts, the over-cologned scent, a silver and
black ring on the index finger tapping the side of the thigh
impatiently. They looked like they were on a mission. What
could you be so serious about at seven in the morning at a
Four Seasons? Hunt's sixth senses told him something was
off. They were too busy watching the numbers on top of the
lift to notice him. Hunt walked slowly and resisted the urge

to look over his shoulder. There was a large mirror behind the reception desk and he went to the side at an angle that he could watch them from, without them seeing him.

Hunt counted ten people in the large, open-plan hotel lobby, not including the two standing at the lift. Hunt hadn't decided exactly what to do. He was so close to getting exfiltrated that he didn't need to fight his way out, he could simply evade detection and slip the noose. He looked at them subtly in the mirror. They couldn't be police, could they? Italians have three main forces. State Police, an armed gendarme called the Carabinieri, and the Finance Police. They're all uniformed. What would these guys be, detectives? No, Hunt thought. Too unlikely. They were armed and not too worried about concealing it very well. The bulges under their nylon jackets made him doubt they could be intelligence operatives. No, not being paranoid, he thought. They were there to kill him. They had the same look as Dushku. That malnourished-Balkan look that said they'd do anything to survive.

The receptionist came over to him and said, "*Prego*, how may I be of assistance?"

"Good morning," Hunt said and kept his peripheral vision on the two at the lifts. "I have this case that I need you to keep for me."

"Of course, sir."

"And, I'm checking out. An associate of mine will collect it from you. Is there any chance of leaving it somewhere secure?"

"Yes, sir, we have secure luggage lockers that we can store it in."

She called the porter over and she explained to him in Italian. He nodded and took the case from Hunt's side.

"Fantastic, thanks," Hunt said. He watched the guys in

the mirror. Would these guys just walk up to him and shoot him in the head in the lobby? He couldn't put it past them.

The lift doors opened. They didn't wait for the people inside to step out, instead, they pushed impatiently past them. They turned around to face the open doors. The one on the right lifted his mobile phone to his ear. Hunt couldn't read his lips. If he'd been Slavic he could have. Russian was related to Slovak, Polish, and Yugoslavian. Albanian was not related to any of those languages. It was an ancient language spoken by the Illyrians. Hunt felt certain that these were Dushku's men.

There was a sudden recognition on the guy's face. His disinterested scowl turned, dropped away, and his eyes lit up. He nudged his colleague on the shoulder, and the lift doors started to close, he reached his arm out to stop them, but he was too late.

Hunt's adrenaline spiked. He hadn't slept. He hadn't eaten. He hadn't had a coffee. He should've been feeling tired, hungry, and lethargic. Instead, he was taking short, shallow breaths. His heart rate jumped. His pupils dilated. He was ready to react.

Of the ten people in the lobby, two were receptionists. A middle-aged man with a potbelly, open-collared shirt, gold chain, and curly salt-and-pepper hair was lounging on the phone while his bright red-lipsticked trophy wife looked at her nails. An older couple made their way through to breakfast. A mother with her young child. Two businessmen having a meeting. There were at least three viable exits, besides the front door, where Hunt assumed whoever the guy was talking to on the phone was waiting. They hadn't been watching his room. They expected him to be up there, possibly still asleep. Hunt had one problem. He was unarmed. They had a disadvantage too. Their plan, such as it was, had just been deleted. Hunt knew they'd be scrambling. They'd need to find him and corner him and put him down. The lift on the left was climbing, and the one on the right was lowering.

"Will there be anything else?" the receptionist asked him. Hunt realised he'd been staring into space and came back.

"Actually, I forgot something in my room," Hunt said and grabbed his key card back from the desk, "I'll be right back." Just then the right-hand lift *dinged* and the door opened. Hunt hurried away from the desk. He glanced up and saw that the left bank was descending fast. The woman was fighting with her child trying to get him into the lift. She was blocking Hunt's path to the open doors. The display above the left lift flashed one, then zero. Hunt said, "I'm so sorry," and stepped in front of the woman and brushed past her. He heard her scoff and puff as he stepped past her. He entered the lift just as one of the Albanians stepped out of the other side. Hunt put his back up against the sidewall. Come on, come on. Close.

The boy looked up at him amused. His mother glared but said nothing. Hunt gave her an awkward smile. Hunt saw the Albanian scanning the lobby. He walked forward towards the desk. The other guy must be coming down the staircase. Just then the Albanian turned and saw Hunt. The lift doors were closing. He started to run but pulled up when he realised he wouldn't make it. He swore and glared at Hunt as they shut.

TWENTY

As they rode the lift up in silence, Hunt did some breathing exercises. He wanted to stay alert, but he didn't want to panic. He needed his thoughts to be clear. He needed his mind operating without the brakes on. He wanted to be in the zone. Where things happened effortlessly and with precision. He inhaled two quick breaths through his nose and did one long exhale. The long exhale slowed his heart rate and forced his brain to release serotonin which made him calmer. Instinct was powerful, but by harnessing his autonomic nervous system, Hunt couldn't override his body's natural reactiveness, but he could manipulate it to his advantage.

Hunt's options were narrowing. If the two assassins had support, which Hunt had to assume they did, they would be standing them up as the lift climbed. They would be informed that the mark was on the run. That he'd headed back upstairs. Hunt's plans had just changed. Now he needed to alter them and adjust. He needed to be one step ahead, where he had been one step behind. Hunt saw a cleaner's room service trolley parked in the corridor and heard the sound of a vacuum cleaner. The door to the room was pegged open. Hunt saw the maid. She was swaying as she pushed the head of the vacuum cleaner over the carpet. Hunt went past the open door and saw what he was after. The maid's keycard sitting on the front of the trolley. He grabbed it and went to his room. He used his keycard to open the door to his room and put the latch on so it couldn't close. He turned around and used the maid's keycard to enter the room directly opposite his one. As he pushed it open he heard loud footsteps and heavy breathing coming down the corridor. He pulled the handle down and let the door shut silently and put his eye up to the spy hole. He saw the two figures emerge. They drew their weapons. One stood back and aimed, the other had his back against the wall with his weapon held in front of his face. Hunt took off his leather belt and wrapped the end of it around his fist. His heart was beating like was waiting for the starting gun. The guy behind lunged forward and kicked the bedroom door open and the guy on the wall swivelled around and raised his weapon and entered the room. He ducked into Hunt's room and as he did, the door bounced off the wall and started to close. The guy behind moved forward to follow his colleague. Hunt pulled open the door. Before the assassin in the corridor could enter the hotel room, Hunt lunged forward and wrapped his belt around the guy's neck. He used all of his force to pull back on it and lifted the guy's feet off the floor. Hunt pulled him backwards like a crocodile pulling an antelope into the water. The guy retched and clutched at the belt and tried to lift his handgun to shoot behind him. Hunt ducked to his left and pulled the guy into the room and down to the floor. As the weapon came up over the guy's shoulder, Hunt released the belt and grabbed the barrel of the gun. Hunt twisted it

towards the guy's head and used his thumb to press the trigger. The side of the guy's head popped open and the sound
of the gunshot right next to Hunt's head deafened him and
left his eardrums with a high-pitched whine. The guy in
Hunt's grip slumped and Hunt prised the weapon from his
hand. Hunt was lying on his back, his left leg under the
dead weight of the assassin, with the hotel room door held
open by the legs of the dead man. Hunt saw the bedroom
door opposite pull open. The other Albanian came out with
his gun raised. His eyes went wide when he saw Hunt. He
was too late to aim and fire. Hunt already had the sights
lined up with the gap between his thick eyebrows. Hunt
pressed the trigger on the Beretta 92 and the top of his nose
crumpled like a sinkhole and the assassin's head snapped
backwards. The Albanian's body followed the weight of his
head and continued in a slow arcing fall. He hit the ground
with a thud. A door slammed and a woman screamed. Hunt
scrambled to his feet and unwrapped his belt from the dead
guy's neck. He quickly looped it back around his trousers.
He bent down and pulled off the dead guy's jacket and
unclipped his shoulder holster. Hunt put it on under his
jacket and stowed the Beretta. He did a quick check down
each corridor. Doubtless, the police were on their way, but
Italian response times in Sicily weren't likely to be
anywhere near the best in the world. He was running out of
time. He checked his watch. Would the exfil team leave
without him?

Hunt stepped across the corridor and over the Albanian
lying in the open doorway of his hotel room. He went
through the room to the balcony and swung his legs over it.
He crouched and dropped down onto the paving stones
below. He stood up and straightened his jacket and tucked
in his shirt and walked calmly towards the reception.

Through the French windows, he saw guests hurrying along the corridors to the exit. Hunt opened one of the doors and heard people shouting and the sound of slapping footsteps as they ran for the exits. A uniformed hotel manager was yelling in a mixture of Italian and English and directing people through the reception and outside. Hunt went past him and slotted in behind a family hurrying for the exit. They went through the connecting doors and Hunt saw a stream of people heading outside. He breathed a sigh and relaxed a little. He was surrounded by people, he kept his head low and rubbed his eyebrows and looked through his fingers. He was about to step outside when he saw three people walking in the opposite direction. A big, square, bald guy in a black leather jacket was moving forward and pushing people aside as he rushed towards Hunt. Hunt didn't think he'd seen him, he was just fighting against the tide of people looking for gaps and trying to get into the hotel. Behind him, Hunt saw a short-haired, peroxide blonde, standing just where the mass of evacuees fanned out. Her eyes locked with his and she pouted. Natalia's red lipstick matched the glossy red of her long leather trench coat. Hunt and his half-sister stood and looked at one another for a second. Time seemed to slow down for him. He saw a taller, thinner man with straight shoulder-length blond hair and the same black leather jacket standing behind her. Their pause couldn't last more than one second, but for Hunt, it felt like ten. Suddenly, Natalia reached into her coat and lifted out her trademark Sig Sauer P250 with a long tubular suppressor attached. Hunt reacted instantly. He lunged forward and ducked down and grabbed the bald-headed guy coming at him. Hunt turned him and drew his weapon and wrapped his arm around his neck. People screamed. The mass of people went around him like a fast-flowing river around a stone. Hunt held his weapon to the bald guy's head. Natalia and the tall blond guy stepped apart in an arc with their weapons aimed at him. Hunt couldn't step back into the hotel because of the crowd of people pushing past him. He pushed back into the wall. He had a tall bush in a clay pot to his right. They were in a standoff.

"You can't win," Hunt said loudly over the crowd of people.

Natalia furrowed her eyebrows. There was a gap in the flow of people coming out. She lowered her aim from directly at Hunt's head to slightly down and right and fired two rounds. The rapid reports were suppressed into metallic clicks. *Click-click.* The guy in Hunt's arms went limp and his legs buckled. Hunt was holding onto dead weight. Natalia had shot him in the heart.

"Now *you* can't win," she said. The tall blond guy was looking sideways at her like she was insane. The look on his face was stuck between fear that she might do it to him and awe at her cold-bloodedness. Hunt tried to crouch with the body to keep some cover, but it wasn't sustainable. Hunt couldn't start a shootout with so many children and women around them.

"Cover him," Natalia said in Russian. The tall guy nodded and took a step to his left to widen the angle. Natalia stepped up to him and removed the Beretta from his hand. Hunt let her take it. He removed his arms from the dead guy's neck and let the body slump. Hunt went to stand and Natalia warned him and said, "Ah! Slowly. If you move too fast I'll kill you." Hunt put his hands up in front of his shoulders and stood. "Where is it?"

"Where's what?"

"Don't play games," Natalia said forcefully. Her eyes

were darting. She was aware of the predicament of her situation too. Lots of witnesses. Few escape routes. Security forces were on their way. She couldn't know if Hunt had a team or if he was alone. She was wary. "You know what," she said. "Don't move." She glanced at her colleague to make sure he had Hunt covered and holstered her weapon inside her coat. He pushed her hands into his chest. She was standing close to him. Hunt looked down at her. She felt in his pockets. She slid her hands down and felt along the inside of his waistband and ran her hands from his belt buckle around his back. Her body was pressed right up against his. Her lips close to his. She pushed her hands down the back pockets of his trousers. Hunt felt her grab the plastic box with the flash drive in it and pull it out. A satisfied smile spread on her sprayed-on lips. She brought her hands up to her front and clicked open the case. A police siren cut through the stilted silence. Hunt saw the thin blond guy glance at Natalia with a concerned look on his face. She looked up at him and she was about to shout out when Hunt reached to his right and grabbed the stem of the tall bush next to him. He pushed the plant towards the blonde guy and hit the case out of Natalia's hands. She immediately went after it like a kitten following a feather. "Shoot him," she screamed at the blond guy as Hunt darted back inside the hotel. He sprinted past the reception. The uniformed hotel manager stepped across and put his hands up and started to say, "Sir, you can't go that —" Hunt dropped his shoulder and barrelled into him. He felt the guy's ribs cave against his arm and Hunt knocked him back. Hunt burst through the door to the maze hedge garden and sprinted south towards the ocean. He ran past the shrubberies and hedges and into the outdoor pool area. He hopped over the fence and ran across the single-lane road at the southern end of the hotel's estate. Once across the street he ducked down and started bounding down the concrete stairs that took him down the steep cliff face. He could see the hotel's black and gold-trimmed Hacker-Craft runabout. The boat's captain was tying it to the dock. Hunt sprinted down the stairs. The captain was holding the mooring rope and looked up to see what the noise was. Hunt took big heavy strides on the wooden jetty. The captain said, "Sir, you can't —"

"Sorry," Hunt said as he pushed the captain towards the water. The guy's arms flailed and he tried to regain his footing. He tilted backwards and fell into the water. Hunt loosened the mooring line that the guy had just started tying and jumped into the cockpit. He heard the captain splashing in the water and shouting, "Hey!" behind him. Hunt fired up the engine and looked up at the top of the cliff. He could see Natalia in her red overcoat aiming at him. She held her forearm parallel to the ground and rested the suppressor against it. Hunt knew she could never make the shot. It didn't stop her from trying and a bullet kicked up some wood chips from the jetty. That was Hunt's cue to leave. He slammed the runabout into reverse and pulled away from the mooring. He shifted the lever backwards and powered away from the San Domenico Palace.

TWENTY-ONE

As Hunt steered the powerboat further from Sicily, and deeper into the Ionian Sea, he saw McKenna come into view. The Intelligence Director was standing on the top deck of a large Dreamline double-deck superyacht. He approached the black, one-hundred-and-eleven-foot motor yacht and slowed the runabout and turned it in a wide arc. McKenna was standing with his arms crossed in a smart suit and tie with dark sunglasses on. He didn't smile or wave. Hunt pulled in behind the superyacht and threw the mooring line to one of the deckhands standing on the stern. Hunt steered the powerboat carefully until it touched the stern. He switched the engine off and climbed out and jogged up the stairs leading to the upper deck.

McKenna wasn't outside anymore, so Hunt entered through glass sliding doors. It was a large living room with sofas on both walls and a large monitor at an angle on the wall. McKenna was standing behind a teak bar mixing a cocktail.

"Drink?" he asked as Hunt entered.

"No," Hunt shook his head. "What the hell happened?"

McKenna stirred fizzy clear liquid in a crystal tumbler with a black plastic straw. He lifted the drink to his mouth and took a sip and stepped out from behind the bar. He was still wearing his sunglasses. He came and stood next to Hunt and looked out to sea.

"Nothing like a gin and tonic on Her Majesty's dime," McKenna said and looked at Hunt. "Do you still have the drive?"

Hunt shook his head. "I was compromised, but I know who has it."

Hunt saw McKenna's jaw pulse, but he didn't say anything. He set his drink down without a coaster on the polished wooden side table and sat down on the white leather sofa. He crossed his leg over his knee and rested his arm along the top of the headrest.

"Why didn't we know that Natalia was involved in this?" Hunt asked.

"Take a seat," McKenna gestured to the armchair opposite him.

Hunt glanced at it and sat down and leaned forward with his elbows on his knees.

"Or did you know and that's why I'm involved?"

"We didn't know," McKenna said. "If we had the mission might've been different."

"Kill my own sister."

McKenna shrugged.

"They have the drive. What's on it?" Hunt asked.

"We're waiting for Robin," McKenna motioned to the television screen on the wall. "She should be joining us any moment. She's been analysing what you uploaded. It was encrypted from what I understand."

"You have no idea what the intelligence is?"

"We can make an educated guess, Stirling, but why guess when we could know for a demonstrable certainty?"

"Fine," Hunt said and sat back and looked out at the ocean. "But what brings all of the world's top arms dealers and an assassin connected to Anatoly Mints to a resort town in Sicily?"

McKenna pushed his lips together and gave a little nod. "Now, that is the question, isn't it?"

They sat in silence for a moment.

"How was it?" McKenna asked.

Hunt looked from the ocean at McKenna's sunglasses. "Isakov?" Hunt shrugged. "Fine. I mean, what do you want to know? He didn't beg if that's what you're asking."

Just then the screen flickered. McKenna uncrossed his legs and said, "Ah, Miss Adler," and stood up. "Robin's face came onto the screen."

"Can you hear me?" she asked.

"We can hear you," McKenna said. "Stirling is here too."

"You're safe," she said, then stopped herself. "Good to have you back."

Hunt didn't reply. He was too deep in his own head. Even though the mission was technically successful it felt like it wasn't. It felt messy. Unplanned. Contingencies weren't taken care of. It was too public. Too much attention.

"How'd I get made?" Hunt asked and stood up and went in front of the television.

"We believe Natalia Sukolova is with Dushku now. She could've been at the party —"

Hunt shook his head. "No, I would have made her."

"Maybe you didn't," McKenna said.

"Could have been Enrique's daughter," Robin said.

Hunt didn't respond. McKenna turned to look at him and took his sunglasses off.

"They could have got to her —"

"I doubt it," Hunt said.

"They found her hanging from a towel in a bathroom," McKenna said. "The coroner is ruling it a suicide. We don't think she killed herself —"

"No shit," Hunt said and flashed a look of disdain at McKenna. He was conscious of showing his emotions in front of the screen and his new boss. He bit his tongue. Tried to take a deep breath but his whole core of abdominal muscles was tight. His diaphragm couldn't move.

"She's a casualty of a war ..." McKenna said.

TWENTY-TWO

Hunt turned away and said, "Nothing good comes of this. Nothing."

McKenna looked up at Robin and said, "Continue."

He was dispassionate. Uncompromising.

"We've been analysing the data you sent," Robin said. "It's, erm, nothing."

"What'd you mean, nothing?"

"It's ... there's no data. It's—I think—it's a natural logarithm."

"A what?"

"A sequence of numbers. I think it's just Tau to infinity but it's only been partially decrypted. We're still working on it."

Hunt looked up at the screen. "Partially?"

"It doesn't even really make sense," Robin said. "It's a random string of numbers."

"Show me," Hunt said.

"Hold on," she said and her eyes moved down and out of shot, she pressed a few keys. In the left-hand corner of the screen, a white window opened. There was a long string of numbers.

"I need to run an analysis to see if there is anything hidden in there, maybe there is some code to reveal something but it looks like a decoy."

"You mean—"

"They were expecting to have it lifted and—"

"They let it happen," McKenna said. "Dammit!"

"Let me run this program I built, hold on ..." They waited in silence. McKenna was pacing. His brow furrowed, head bent, fist tight to his lips.

"Wait, I think—" Robin said. McKenna and Hunt looked up at the screen hopefully. "Look at this, numbers that don't fit the pattern! Hidden in the sequence." Robin highlighted a section of the number string and she zoomed in on them on the screen. "They're encrypted," she said. "I'm running a decryption on them now. It'll take time. The only exposed ones are—" she counted silently with her mouth. "We've only decrypted six of the possible seventeen characters."

"Those six are all numbers?" Hunt asked.

"Look," she said and zoomed in on the box. Hunt saw a string of numbers and letters.

556xVGtrK264PoLKa.

"It's only Hill Cypher with a key matrix, but it is proving more difficult than it should ..." she said and looked away.

Hunt could see that she was feeling self-conscious about not having solved it yet.

He studied the numbers.

"Why has it decrypted those six numbers, three at the beginning, and three in the middle?" Hunt asked.

She gave a slight shake of her head and said, "That's just

how the key matrix was set up, the deception software is working through it in order."

"And the letters don't mean anything?"

"No," Robin said, "Those are the covers or encrypted numbers. The ones we're trying to solve."

Hunt glanced at McKenna. He was unusually quiet. McKenna saw him looking.

"What?" McKenna asked.

"What was the admiral selling?" Hunt asked.

"That's what you were supposed to find out."

"We've got it," Hunt said and pointed at the numbers. "But what do they mean?" He stepped closer to the screen and peered at them. He counted them off on his fingers. "All of the world's top arms dealers and criminals. A defector from the top echelons of the Russian state. My half-sister. What do they all have in common?"

"Whatever is behind these numbers," Robin said.

"Is it only going to be digits when the decryption is finished?" Hunt asked.

"Looking at how the matrix is set up, yes, more than likely. It's really a simple cypher that is proving difficult to crack than a complicated cypher that is also hard to get at," she said.

Hunt lifted his hand to his chin. He looked at McKenna. Something in McKenna's face told him that there was more.

"Sir, seriously, tell us what you know," Hunt said.

"It's classified," McKenna said.

"So you're holding out on us?" Hunt asked. "I killed three people to get this code," Hunt held his hand up towards the screen.

"That's your job," McKenna said quietly.

"Come on, sir, a girl is dead because of this. The least

you can do is help us fill in the blanks. How did you know Isakov had something to trade? What was it that made you think British intelligence needed to stop it from getting out?"

"I can't, I'm sorry ..."

"Come on, Everett —"

McKenna shot him a look.

"— Sir, give us the background. Whatever it is, it's big. Big enough for people to die for. Is Enrique happy about his daughter dying for this secret?"

"Of course not," McKenna said.

"And yet he let it happen?"

McKenna shrugged. "I don't think he had a choice."

"Okay, so now we know that whoever is after this intelligence is not going to stop until they get their hands on it. Why?"

"We suspected that Admiral Isakov was selling Russian state secrets —"

"Yes, but what could be so important that they would have gathered all the top dealers to bid for it?"

"We don't know."

Hunt looked back at the screen and studied the numbers. His mind was working. "Get me a pen and paper," he said as he looked at the screen. McKenna went to the bar and found a notepad and pen.

"Write your order down, sir," McKenna said and handed Hunt the pen and pad. Hunt took it and copied the numbers from the screen.

"Five, five, six. Two, six, four," Hunt said and wrote them on the pad. "Fifty-five is an odd number, isn't it?"

"Yes," Robin said as if it was obvious.

"No, I mean, Fifty-five is strange. A strange number of numbers."

"Why?"

"Well, it can't be one long sequence," Hunt said.

"Why not?" McKenna asked.

"I don't know for sure, but wouldn't it be strange if it was one long sequence for the cypher to solve it from the middle?"

Robin thought about it. "Yes, it would be odd."

"So it is likely two sets of numbers?"

"Could be."

"So Fifty-five is strange, isn't it?"

Robin was silent for a moment. "Not if the middle letter, the ninth number was a gap."

"Is that possible? So two eight-digit strings of numbers."

"Possible," she said. "Likely, even."

Hunt looked at the notepad. "It's the location of something," he said.

"How do you figure that?" McKenna said.

"Well, it has to be. What were they buying ... arms dealers and terrorists?"

"A weapon," McKenna said.

"Or weapons," Robin added.

"Or, the location of those weapons."

"Okay, well, where is it?" McKenna asked.

"We have to wait until the programme has decrypted it," Robin said.

"And how long will that take," McKenna asked.

"I don't know," she admitted. "It could take a few days or a few weeks."

"We simply don't have that amount of time, Robin," McKenna said. "We have hours, not days, and the clock is ticking."

TWENTY-THREE

"WE DON'T NEED TO WAIT IF THEY ARE COORDINATES," Hunt said. "We can check the map. The fifty-fifth meridian east ..."

Robin tapped on the keyboard and brought up a new window. It showed a red line running north to south from the Arctic through central Russia, all the way to the Antarctic.

"Twenty-sixth parallel south," Hunt said. She typed again. Another red line running across the screen through Chile and Argentina, and then across the ocean, south of South Africa, through New Zealand."

"Middle of nowhere," McKenna said.

"Yeah," Hunt said. "But only if we use longitude and latitude in degrees, minutes, and seconds. What about if it's in decimal degrees?"

Hunt drew a small straight line in front of the number seventeen on the pad. "Try plus fifty-five, point six, comma," Hunt said, "And twenty-six point four."

Robin typed it in. The screen immediately went bright green.

"I don't know what happened," she said.

"Zoom out if you can," Hunt said.

He heard her clicking her mouse. As she zoomed out two patches of green appeared on either side of the screen.

"That's the middle of nowhere, eastern Lithuania," Hunt said and stared at the screen. "Literally in the middle."

McKenna turned and went and sat on one of the sofas facing the screen. He leaned forward and put his head in his hands. Hunt turned towards him. "What? What is it?"

McKenna took a deep breath through his nostrils and looked up at the ceiling.

"We can't do anything unless you tell us," Hunt said.

McKenna glanced at Hunt and then Robin in turn.

"You're going to have to trust us," Hunt said. "So we can fix this."

"This is highly classified," McKenna said.

"The Iranian, Russians and the Chinese were conducting joint naval exercises in the Indian Ocean last year. Their annual exercises. There were unconfirmed reports that one of their—the Russians—vessels was caught by surprise in the ferocity and intensity of the tropical storm, Idai. They deny it but we believe it sank."

"What kind of vessel?" Hunt asked.

"Well, that young Hunt is the problem. A *Kirov*-class nuclear-powered guided-missile cruiser. The *Lazarev* was carrying what the Russians hoped would be a chance to test-fire a brand-new hypersonic missile during the exercises. It never joined the rest of the fleet."

"The nuclear reactor?" Hunt asked.

"No sign that it was breached. Nothing that we can see from satellite anyway."

"We do believe, however, that a new, state-of-the-art

arsenal of nuclear-enabled, hypersonic cruise missiles went down with the ship."

"Somewhere in the Mozambique Channel," Hunt added.

"Based on the available data, it would appear that way," McKenna said.

"And all the world's terrorists and top arms dealers were at the table to line the pockets of one of the admirals who was in charge at the time to bid on the location of the sunken warheads."

They were all silent for a moment.

"How many missiles," Hunt asked.

"We don't know. One day the battlecruisers will be able to take between forty and eighty onboard. Right now, to test fire, we estimate between eight and ten were sunk."

"And now they're on the market to the highest bidder ..."

"These things travel at between Mach-8 and Mach-9; six to seven *thousand* miles per hour. They're manoeuvrable and fly too fast for radar systems to pick them up, which means they can't be defeated by missile defence systems. Do you know what a two hundred kiloton nuclear warhead fired from a thousand miles away would do to a city?"

"No," Hunt said. "And we don't want to find out."

"No, we don't ..." McKenna said, "But unless we stop whoever has those coordinates, we very well might be on the wrong end of that scenario. One of those missiles could be fired a thousand miles away and be in the centre of Washington, or London, or Paris, in less than nine minutes. You can't even make a decent coffee in less time than that."

"I've tasted your coffee," Hunt said to McKenna. "You couldn't make a decent cuppa in double that."

McKenna gave a single laugh and then turned serious again. "Quite," he said.

"There's no point going after whoever has the code. Theoretically, it could be the hands of a dozen different people by now."

"Then we go after them one by one," McKenna said. "Until it's over. That's what you signed up for, isn't it, Hunt?"

"Yes," Hunt said. "And if you decide that is the best course of action, that's what I'll do —"

"Damn right you will," McKenna said. "Isakov was in charge of the Pacific Fleet at the time the vessel sank and they lost their missiles ..."

"If they lost their missiles," Hunt said. "It could all be a grand plan, a big diversion. But there is another option."

"I'm listening," McKenna said.

"We go straight to the site of the coordinates ..." Hunt said.

"We don't know what the coordinates are yet," Robin said.

"We could see if we can at least find anything at the coordinates," Hunt said.

"They aren't anywhere near the site of the sunken Russian battlecruiser," McKenna said.

"Why would they go to such lengths to hide a location in Lithuania?" Hunt asked. "I feel like we are trying to twist facts to suit our hypothesis rather than interpret the facts based on their own merit. The only thing we know for sure is that Isakov had data with a string of numbers encrypted inside a logarithm," he glanced at Robin to make sure he got that right. "What if the purported sinking is a diversion? We don't have evidence, do we?" Hunt asked.

McKenna shook his head. "No," he said.

"So, what about it boss ... heads or tails?"

"You'd better be right, Hunt," McKenna said.

TWENTY-FOUR

HUNT ARRIVED IN VILNIUS. THE CAPITAL OF Lithuania was in the southwest of the country, close to the Russian border. Stern, round faces and narrow eyes of the watchful border guards. It reminded him of Cold War histories. To them, he was just another tourist. Hunt hadn't slept. His mind was focused on the perils of the task at hand. While he was travelling to the Baltic, Robin and McKenna were trying to connect the dots of intelligence. There were many unanswered questions. Was Natalia working for Dushku? The Russians had never acknowledged the loss of their battlecruiser or the missiles if they had indeed lost a ship. Western intelligence only had a hunch. It was a matter of state power and state secrets. The families of the sailors would have been paid off for their silence or killed. Isakov had stayed silent about it until he'd been turned. Possibly by Dushku, Hunt assessed. Whichever was the case, there was now a scramble from international arms dealers and terrorists to find the sunken weapons. Hunt knew he had his work cut out. He rubbed his eyes.

He didn't even bother getting involved as the new

arrivals rushed and scrimmaged to get one of the scarce immigration forms at passport control. It was cold and grey. Everyone was wrapped up in coats and jackets and which restricted movement. When they realised it was warm in the arrivals hall they started to undress.

Once the pushing and shoving had subsided into angry glances and tutting he bent down and picked up a crumpled and stood-on form off the dirty tiled floor. As he did, another hand came into view reaching for the same form. The smooth and thin fingers and elegantly manicured nails brushed against his. He hadn't seen her bending for the form. Hunt stood up and smoothed it out in his hand.

"Sorry," he said as he turned.

He heard a husky female voice say, "I have something none of these others does if you have a spare one of those for me."

Hunt saw a lightly made-up, smiling face looking up at him. She was radiant. With pulled-up black hair that curled at the ends and clear, coffee-coloured eyes. She held a pen up and looked ready to take on the world. Hunt admired her positivity and can-do attitude in the face of this rude arrivals hall. He felt unrested and sluggish after the flight. Small seats, restless sleep, weak coffee, and one too many Bloody Marys.

"Sure," Hunt said. "Take this one," and held it out for her.

"Oh, no. I couldn't do that," she said in as polite and prim and proper a manner as she could while at the same time half-reaching out for it. Hunt just grinned and gave it to her. She went to the counter to start filling it in. She wore black leggings and a grey sweater. Hunt glanced at the long queue waiting in front of the mostly unmanned border control booths.

"You may as well fill it in in the line," Hunt said. She looked at him and he gestured to the bulging mass waiting for entry. She picked up the form and her hand luggage and followed him. While they waited, he helped her fill in the details. She seemed grateful. The form had to be answered in triplicate and all of the instructions were in Lithuanian.

"Thank you," she said as Hunt started to sweat even without a jacket on.

"I'm Tabitha," she put the pen in her left hand and stuck out her right. "Tabitha Cougar-Rance," she said. "People call me Tibs or Racy. Mostly Tibs."

Hunt took her fingers lightly in his.

"Stirling," he said.

"Just Stirling?"

"Usually."

She gave a little curious smile.

"Stirling Hunt," he said.

"How do you do," she said.

"First time in Vilnius?" he asked.

She nodded. "Yes," she said. "By your smirk, I'm going to guess it's not yours?"

"No, I've been here once or twice."

"I see, and what do you do, Mister Hunt."

Hunt furrowed his eyebrows and surveyed the sprightly, forward, well-spoken young English woman in front of him.

"You're a journalist," he said.

Her lips parted a little and she glanced off to the left and creased her forehead.

"How did you know that?" she asked in surprise.

"You're good at it, I take it."

"What makes you say that?"

"Well, you ask a lot of questions and get people talking about themselves, so you must be good."

She hid her embarrassed smile by looking down and covering her mouth. Then she looked back up at him and flashed her shining white teeth. "It's my first real assignment, actually. Abroad, that is. Well spotted, Stirling. Are you a journalist by any chance?"

Hunt gave a single laugh. "No," he said.

"Well, what do you do?"

"I'm a bit of a jack of all trades," he said.

"And a master of none?"

"Maybe," he said. "Better than a master of one."

She studied his face.

"I'm a diver," he said. "I'm looking for a headquarters to start my rig dive company."

"Entrepreneur," she said and dropped the corners of her mouth and nodded. "I'm heading north too," she said as they stepped forward in the queue.

"Papers," the border guard said to her.

Tibs handed him her passport and the crumpled form. The guard looked at her passport and the crumpled document. He shook his head and threw it on the floor behind his desk. Tibs' jaw dropped. The guard reached for a stack of forms on his desk and said, "Call your husband forward."

"Oh! He's not my —"

Hunt stepped forward and said through gritted teeth and a plastered-on smile, "Just do as the man says, honey," and put his arm around her. She gave a little squeal of a laugh. The guard handed them each a new immigration form to fill in. While they did that, he checked and stamped their passports. Hunt handed the border guard their cards and he handed them back their passports. After they collected their luggage, Tibs scribbled her number in a notebook she had in her backpack and tore the page out and handed it to Hunt.

"In case you manage to think of an angle for a story," she said. Hunt folded it and put it in his pocket. "I'm hoping to break a story. There hasn't been much reporting here, so anything might help."

"Sure," Hunt said. "I'll see what I can do."

"Okay," she said. "Thanks. Bye! Nice to meet you." She walked off dragging her large suitcase. Hunt watched her go.

TWENTY-FIVE

As Hunt was coming down the stairs from his room in the Grand Hotel Kempinski in the fashionable old town of Vilnius, he heard some loud drunk voices over the top of the marble water fountain in the foyer.

"Bum like a peach, I tell you!"

Hunt saw two red-faced Englishmen stumble in together.

"The missus was so jealous when she caught me looking. Gave me one of those," the double-chin said and imitated him getting a slap. They laughed. "When I saw her climbing over the luggage carousel, well …"

"Neat backside," the other man agreed. "Snug in that tracksuit."

"They're called leggings," Hunt said and the two drunks glared at him and walked quietly to the bar. Hunt went through to the main reception. Everything was marble. The patterned floor was slick and shiny and tall, round columns held up the high ceiling. It was decadence in a desert of decay. He walked through to the dining room. He wanted to keep a low profile, but these were the places where prominent expatriates mingled. It would give him a sense of the place. The flow of current affairs and sentiment of the ruling class about what was going on in their vast and poor country.

Hunt saw about ten tables of people. Mostly couples. There was one clean-shaven, smart-suited, combed-over man with thick brown hair sitting alone with a cigarette in one hand and pretending to read the menu. Hunt also saw a pretty-looking younger woman in a lilac dress, teardrop pearl earrings, and matching eyeshadow. It was Tibs. She spooned at the food on her plate before pushing it away. She looked up and saw Hunt. Her face brightened and she lifted her hand to wave and then grew self-conscious. What the hell, Hunt thought. May as well.

He walked over.

"Hello, Stirling," Tibs said. She had a relieved smile on her face. "So nice to see a friendly face. Are you having dinner?" Before he could respond, her eyes pleaded and said, "Won't you join me?"

Hunt looked at her and then glanced around at the other diners. The smart-suited man at the adjacent table was trying to pretend like he wasn't watching or listening. Hunt pulled out the chair opposite her and sat down. He didn't like having his back to the exit, but he would make an exception.

"What's the matter, you're not hungry?" he asked her and looked at her untouched plate.

She sighed. "It's barely warm," she said. "And the meat has a strange taste."

"We should have gone to the local square for some traditional cuisine. Real food."

"Oh, I'd have loved that!" she said and looked down at

her outfit. "So much better than having to get dressed up to sit around in this stuffy hotel."

"Nothing to drink?" Hunt asked.

"I would have ordered, but the waiter seems to have disappeared, along with the wine list."

Hunt turned to see and put his hand up to call over one of the clump of uniformed waiters waiting beside a mirrored screen that led to the kitchens. One of the men spotted him and made his way over.

"I'm so pleased to see you," she said as he turned back to face her. "I was beginning to doubt myself. I'd said that, as a journalist abroad, I must get used to situations like this, eating alone. It's all part and parcel of being in a new country and a new culture and with no friends."

A man came to stand by the side of the table. Hunt glanced up. It was the smart-suited man who'd been smoking at the other table. He had his hand in the pocket of his pin-striped trousers and a broad, charming smile on his face.

"Well, you'll like it in here then," the man said and glanced up at the ceiling. "It gives you an impression of what Saint Petersburg was like under the Soviets." He then glanced down at Hunt and said, "Please excuse the intrusion, but I heard some friendly-sounding voices and my colleague is late in meeting me for dinner. Do you mind if I join you?" He looked to the waiter standing off from the table. "A bottle of the nineteen ninety-five *Petit Chablis*," he called to the waiter and pulled out the chair in front of him and sat down. Tibs flashed Hunt a look. "I'm afraid I saw you both at the airport this morning," he said. "Truth is I felt a bit of a prat sitting all by myself and thought we could share our woes as weary travellers," he said.

Barely a three-hour flight from London, Hunt thought.

The waiter came back with the cold bottle of white wine and showed the newcomer the label. He nodded and the waiter carefully poured a sip for him to taste. "Just pour, my good man, if it's corked, I'll be the first to let you know."

The waiter dutifully filled all of the glasses. "I'm Crook-shank. Albany Crookshank. Please call me Albie," he said and lifted the wine glass and the beading water ran down the sides of it.

Tibs reached for her glass and lifted it and said, "Tabitha Cougar-Rance."

Hunt didn't go in for all of this formality and fluff. He could've been just as happy sitting alone spooning through tepid beef stroganoff and sipping on a beer as sitting there trying to play the exiled expat in post-Soviet Europe lark. "Hunt," he said. "Stirling, Hunt."

"Well, how do you do. Thanks for having me at your table. I hope you don't mind me asking, but what brings you to Lithuania?" Crookshank asked.

His attention was focused on the attractive, dark-haired young woman. His shoulders turned slightly away from Hunt and his left leg crossed over his right to ease the slant away and create an invisible barrier. Hunt didn't mind. He would listen. Gather information. Make assessments. If it came to it, he could always snap this guy's neck. There is nothing quite in the world like an upper-middle-class Englishman's ability to be unabashedly polite and friendly and at the same time exceedingly rude. Most people never even notice. It's only a sensation they're left with once the interaction has ended and leaves them thinking something was wrong, without quite being able to put their finger on what it was. A sense of discomfort. Like being insulted but not realising it. Hunt preferred directness and plainness. It was a gift and a curse.

"I'm a journalist," Tibs said proudly.

Crookshank's eyes lit up. "Really! How fascinating," he glanced at Hunt and registered Hunt's displeasure as he took a sip of his wine. It tasted exquisite.

Hunt had to give him credit.

"And you, Mister Hunt?" Crookshank said and turned his attention.

"Stirling is starting a dive business," Tibs blurted out.

"Commercial dive business," Hunt clarified. "Lithuania is handing out oil exploration licences again ..."

"How marvellous," Crookshank said. "And you want one? Have you got a permit for that? For my sins, I happen to work for that splendidly stuffy government agency known as the Foreign and Commonwealth Office," he said. "My job is to make sure that the bottomless pit of international aid we send to this seedy and corrupt government is actually being spent on projects and not on lining pockets. So, if you need any assistance, I might know some of the people who can help you."

"Generous of you," Hunt said. "Thank you."

"Just the way things are in Eastern Europe," Crookshank said and waved his hand in dismissal of the thanks. He turned back to the damsel in distress. "You don't know much about the Baltics, I take it."

"I barely know anything outside of the Home Counties," she said and took an ashamed sip of her drink. "Oh! This wine is lovely," she said as she put it down.

"Lithuania seems a strange choice for your first assignment abroad if you don't mind me saying," Crookshank said. He was sitting forward now. Eyebrows pushed together, hands clasped under the table. Hunt watched him closely. He was open about being at the Foreign Office. That meant he was into something.

"Yes," Tibs agreed. "Well, it's partly personal and partly business. My mother was Lithuanian, you see, and I've never visited. I want to see the real Lithuania. I'm going to go north to report on the closed city network. Try and find a human interest story that will publicise the plight of ethnic Russians."

Crookshank sat back. "Oh, I'd hardly call it a *plight*," he said and smiled, but behind his eyes there was shade. "More of an uprising. Something for the locals to deal with."

Hunt could see Tibs begged to differ, but her public school education and inbuilt English reserve and restraint made her lean forward, look down, place her glass and bite her lip. She controlled her response and kept it light.

"Yes, I suppose you're right," she said and looked directly at Hunt with a blank stare. Crookshank smiled and said, "Well …" and topped up their glasses. Just then an older man in a cream-coloured linen suit walked up to the table and said, "Albie! A thousand, thousand apologies. I was on a call with London about this damn drama."

Crookshank stood and shook the newcomer's hand. "Oh, don't be silly, old stick, how's you, anyway?"

They shook hands forcefully.

"I see you've been putting the time to good use," the man said.

Crookshank turned back to the table. "Excuse me, Michael," he said. "This is the lovely Tabitha, and this is," his face went blank. "I'm so sorry I've forgotten your name."

"Stirling," Tibs said for him. Hunt grinned at the polite rudeness. It was exquisite.

"This is Michael Allen-Smith," Crookshank said. "He's second secretary or some high-up position at the British Embassy, isn't that right, Michael?"

"Something like that," Allen-Smith said.

"He's overseeing my work in the commercial section and making sure all the people dumped on him by London do and say the right things."

"Lovely to meet you both, I'm sure."

"We've just finished our wine," Crookshank said.

"That's okay. I actually can't stay. I'm meeting that dirty deputy minister at the discotheque. Care to join me?"

Crookshank looked at the two of them sitting at the table. "What do you think?" he asked. "Care to meet the who's who and see what the nightlife in Vilnius is like?"

TWENTY-SIX

THEY ARRIVED OUTSIDE THE LUMINOUS PINK AND green neon lights of the Pantera nightclub in Allen-Smith's chauffeur-driven Mercedes-Benz. Hunt stepped out and heard the thumping bass coming from inside the low-slung, colourfully lit building. Once they were inside, Crookshank leaned into both of them and pointed to a far corner of the room. He was pointing at a booth filled with smartly dressed men and women.

"That bald man, over there, is a deputy minister," Crookshank said loudly over the music. Hunt saw a smartly dressed middle-aged-looking man under a white light sitting in the middle of the horseshoe-shaped booth. "A couple of the girls are his daughters. Most of them aren't. The other men I don't know. Probably gangsters," Crookshank said.

Just then a song came on that the whole club seemed to like. The made-up girls, with big hair, and shimmering, reflective purple and blue dresses and high-heels started to slide out from the table. The deputy minister spotted Allen-Smith as the table dispersed and he raised his left arm and smiled and signalled him to come over.

"Right," Allen-Smith said and leaned in towards Crookshank, "I'm off to pour more oil on the fires that are already raging. Join me."

"This might be your lucky day," Crookshank said to Tibs and said, "Come on."

They all followed Allen-Smith to the table.

"Michael, come and join us," the Lithuanian man said.

"We don't want to interrupt your evening by talking business, minister."

"Nonsense," the Lithuanian laughed. "When has business ever interrupted my evening. Bring your friends and stop being so coy. You English! You act like you were too polite to ever have conquered half the world when that is exactly what you have done."

They all slid into the booth. Allen-Smith introduced them to Edmondus Mondleite, Deputy Minister for Foreign Affairs. Mondleite was a tall, imposing man, with a booming deep voice, bright eyes, and a quick wit. Hunt watched Tibs. He could see from her enthralment that she also thought Mondleite was handsome.

"Charmed, I'm sure," Mondleite said as he was introduced. He held Tibs's gaze and smiled warmly.

"Be careful what you say to this one, minister," Allen-Smith said loudly and turned to Tibs. "She's a journalist."

Mondleite smiled graciously. Allen-Smith turned to the rest of the table, "You'll excuse us for a moment if we talk business, you see, when the deputy minister isn't in Moscow making his case to the Russians, he's very rarely accessible to lowly bureaucrats like me and I have to take every chance I can get."

"Oh, you know you'll find me in Berlin more than in Moscow, Michael. Better nightlife! I know you love the disco as much as I do!" Mondleite said and the bass of his laugh kept time with the beat of the music.

"Hardly," Allen-Smith said.

"I am very passionate about making our case to the world," Mondleite said in seriousness. "People think the Russians weren't the worst colonialists, but they bled my country dry to feed their empire. The Russians still do even menial jobs here in Lithuania. How many foreign taxi drivers do you see in London or Edinburgh? The Russians destroyed all they could when they fled ..." His voice trailed off into the crescendo of another song and Hunt lost interest. Well-educated, a good taste in clothing, and the only jewellery he wore was a gold watch which remained concealed under the long double-cuff of his tailored shirt. Allen-Smith was leaning into Mondleite now and they were talking intimately about a serious topic. Hunt couldn't make out what. Crookshank leaned across the table towards Hunt. "If you need your licences," he pointed to Mondleite, "This is the man who can get them for you," he said. Hunt nodded and said, "Thanks."

"No problem," Crookshank said over the music. "You know, he's a real tough guy. You wouldn't think it. He missed out on the early struggles against the Russians and was among the one percent who prospered. But, he's missed out on the heroes of the struggle. He was studying abroad during the fighting. The plum jobs went to the families of the fighters. Now he's had to be patient and wait for his opportunity. A question of dead man's shoes in Lithuania. Unless you can commit murder." Crookshank leaned back and touched the side of his nose and gave Hunt a wink and knowing nod. Crookshank took a sip of his drink and watched Hunt over the top of his glass.

"What do you want with the closed city network?" Crookshank asked him.

Hunt furrowed his brow. "That was Tibs interested in that ... whatever it is," Hunt said and looked away and then back at Crookshank. A sly grin expanded on Crookshank's face.

"Right you are," Crookshank said. "My mistake. You don't know what they are?"

Hunt shook his head.

"The Soviets," Crookshank said loudly over the music. "Part social experiment, part security complex. All these countries, you see, were Russian satellites. They invested and built but they also sent ethnic Russians to live and work in the most important sites in the country. They created this network of secret, closed cities. They were industrially important towns. Nuclear power plants mostly. Western intelligence thought nuclear missile launch sites too. Never proven. Working theory. That's what little miss journalist is interested in ..." Crookshank waved his glass over at Tibs. She yawned.

Hunt leaned across the table and looked at her and said, "I'm going to get going. I have an early start."

Crookshank was leaning in and listening. His eyes were glassy from the alcohol. Tibs grabbed her clutch from next to her and lifted it onto her lap. She leaned into Crookshank's ear and said, "I think I'll go too, I'm so tired from the flight."

"No! Stay!" Crookshank shouted over the music. "I can take you home later, or you can sleep at mine ..."

Tibs smiled. Hunt knew she must have found it hard to be a single woman abroad and not give sexually frustrated men like Crookshank the wrong idea.

"Thanks, Albie," she said and put her hand on his

shoulder, "But I'm shattered and my head is swimming. I think I'm going to go home." She scooched over a bit and he relented and slid out of the booth and stood up. Hunt did the same. Crookshank put his hand out to Hunt and had a drunk smile on his face and said, "Well done. Well done, old man. You take care of her."

Hunt shook the man's hand and said nothing. Tibs climbed out of the booth. Allen-Smith and Mondleite were deep in conversation and didn't appear to notice, or didn't appear to care that they were leaving. Hunt and Tibs made their way through the crowd and stepped out into the cool night air.

"Ah! What a relief," Tibs said. "It was so hot. I was dying in there. How do we get a taxi?"

"We can walk back towards the hotel," Hunt said. "We can find a taxi on the way."

They set off down the quiet streets and walked through a nearby glass and tree lined park. It was a clear night and the stars were bright despite the city lights. They hailed a taxi and sat quietly in the back as they drove through the streets. When they got back to the hotel and walked into the lobby, Tibs stopped and looked in the direction of the bar. "Nightcap?" she suggested. Hunt shook his head.

"I think I'd rather go up to my room," he said. "We can have a coffee up there if you like?"

She thought about it. "Coffee?" she checked her watch. "It's a bit late for me, but I might have tea?"

———

IN THE MORNING, THE WINTER SUN WAS STREAMING through the open curtains and gleamed off the white sheets. Hunt half-sat up and with one eye open looked down at the sleeping naked figure beside him. Tibs was on her stomach, hugging the pillow, and her thick dark hair was in a bundle over the white cotton.

"Good morning," Hunt said and flopped back down and looked at the ceiling.

"Don't," she said, her voice muffled against the pillow. "Too early."

"I'm heading east today," Hunt said.

There was a moment's silence and she spun around and propped herself up on her elbow and said, "Can you give me a ride?"

Hunt was silent for a second and said, "Another one?"

She gasped in shock and then grinned and slapped him lightly on the shoulder.

"If you ask nicely," she said.

He smiled and turned his head to look at her and she bit her lip.

Robin Adler was alone. The light from her computer monitors glowed off her skin in the darkness of her small central London flat. Sponsored for her courtesy of McKenna and the Oberon programme. For how it made her feel, it may as well have been a prison cell. She sat looking at a wall of monitors. Her system was state of the art but she didn't have access to the Government Communications Headquarters (GCHQ) database and tools. For that, she'd need a favour. Priscilla, her fluffy white Persian cat was curled up on the sofa and purring as she slept. Robin reached for a cup of black coffee and grimaced as she gulped it down. It was cold.

This whole case was throwing up more questions than

answers. "Why didn't the Russians try to find the sunken vessel themselves?" she asked out loud.

HUNT HADN'T MANAGED TO RETRIEVE THE LISTENING device from Enrique's office. Robin had hacked into his wireless network and begun the slow process of uploading the voice data. Now she was analysing it. Removing the background noise, isolating the sounds, enhancing them, and running it through the GCHQ's voice recognition software program called Broad Oak. After Broad Oak analysed the data the only voice it recognised was Isakov. She updated the system to link Enrique and Dushku with the other two sound waves. Dushku seemed to be acting as a translator between Isakov who, through pride or simply ignorance, only spoke in a central Russian dialect. Dushku seemed to understand and could translate with brevity and heavily accented English for Enrique. It turned out that Isakov, sensing an opportunity and so close to his retirement, had lied in his report of the incident. He made it seem that the ship was unrecoverable, in the deepest part, far to the north of the Channel. Even if the Russians had sent a recovery team, they would have been searching the ocean floor hundreds of miles from the actual site of the sunken vessel. The three conspirators were discussing the likely condition and value of the supersonic missiles. Dushku seemed to grow more and more excited by the prospect. He stopped translating some of the more tasty information that Isakov was greedily sharing with the men. They all expected to grow rich from the recovery and subsequent sale of the weapons.

Robin had a sudden realisation. If the Russian intelligence services ever found out about the wreckage and its true location they would stop at nothing to stop those weapons from falling into the wrong hands.

"What if they already know?" she said to herself.

Priscilla stretched behind her and Robin looked back as her cat lifted her head and stuck out her pink tongue as she yawned. The cat got slowly to her feet and arched her spine and plopped down onto the floor. She padded over to Robin and rubbed the side of her body against Robin's shin. Robin reached down involuntarily and stroked her and the cat stopped moving and let her fur be compressed.

Robin's heart was beating faster. What were Dushku and Natalia going to do with it? Robin felt she had to warn McKenna. Maybe he had informants or access to wiretaps on his Russian Foreign Intelligence Service (SVR) counterparts. Robin bit the inside of her cheek. She hated McKenna. He'd threatened Hunt's life if she didn't cooperate. She'd betrayed Hunt once in her life, and she'd vowed that she would never do it again. Giving him up at the Kill School was one of the reasons she'd escaped. She felt it better to be on the run than subservient to one of the intelligence agencies that were all as corrupt and indiscriminate as one another. That was fine while she was alone. Not taking sides. Not caring about who it affected. Now she had to worry about Hunt. She couldn't just switch her feelings off. She knew that he was still in love with the memory of a dead girl. That he carried that burden with him wherever he was. She also knew that while they were both under the thumb of McKenna and Oberon they could never be together. If he even wanted to be with her. She had no idea. He never let on. She knew enough to know that he was keeping secrets from her. That he wasn't letting her help with the curvy, big-breasted contacts he was using to do his job and protect them both. If he only knew that she understood and even if it hurt her, she would be able to compart-mentalise it and crack on with the work.

McKenna couldn't be trusted. He'd told her that Hunt had sacrificed himself to save her life. That McKenna would terminate Hunt if she didn't comply. That she would be next if she so much as thought of skipping out on her sentence. What could be worse for a woman of her talents than being locked in a silent, glass cubicle for the rest of her life?

Priscilla sat on the floor and looked up at her. She flicked her tail from side to side and meowed and leapt into her lap. The cat settled on top of her thighs and Robin stroked her head. Priscilla flicked her ears and closed her eyes until they were narrow slits.

"How're we going to get out of this girl?" Robin said aloud as she stroked her cat's fine soft fur. She reached forward and left-clicked on her mouse and reached forward and tapped on her keyboard. She pulled up data on Hunt. Even if she wanted to warn him, she couldn't. He hadn't used his mobile phone in days. There was no data signal and no location. She crossed her arms and sat back. Had something happened to him?

TWENTY-SEVEN

Hunt had a map and compass in a clear folder around his neck and sat at the controls of a black EC120 Colibri five-seater, single-engine, utility helicopter. It occurred to him that the last time he was in a helicopter his mother had died. He suddenly felt anxious. He glanced over at Tibs not too sure why he'd let her come but glad she was there. He had his suspicions. She was very convincing and he was weak, he thought. He might have been thinking with something other than his brain. They'd flown north-east from Vilnius to the lake and forest district. Tibs nudged him on the shoulder and he glanced at her. She was wearing brown aviators and a big grin and she said into the headset microphone, "It's so beautiful, isn't it?"

It was. Hunt looked out at the frozen, flat water and tall, snow-covered forests.

"What're we looking for?" she asked.

"I'm not sure," Hunt said. "I got a tip-off that there was some good land around here for training and warehousing for the company."

"Right," she said. "What was it called again?"

"The company? Um, Pilgrim Diving Co."

She smiled. Hunt glanced down at the map, then up at the horizon. Tibs followed his eyes.

"What?" she asked.

"That's not meant to be here," Hunt said.

"What?" she asked again.

"That, those buildings, whatever it is. There's not meant to be anything here."

They looked down on an entire town. A town that wasn't on any maps. It was supposed to be forest and lakes but below them was a sprawling concrete mass. Hunt had heard of such places. The Russians had built towns and cities in their newly acquired Soviet republics. They shipped in entire populations of Russians to live and work in secret enclaves of their neighbouring countries. They mostly were home to secret military industrial factories or nuclear facilities. There were dozens of these closed cities, each guarded with perimeter wire and watchtowers. The watchtowers were gone but the Russian populations remained. Who knew what backroom deals were done to ensure their safety and protect their secrets after the Soviet Union collapsed.

"It's a closed city," Hunt said.

"A what?"

"It's what you were going north to find in Estonia," Hunt said. "Except we've stumbled upon one in the wilds of Lithuania. Your human interest story might be down there."

Just then his headset crackled. A heavy Eastern European accent came over the air.

"Unknown aircraft, unknown aircraft, this is Visaginas control tower. You are entering restricted military airspace. Identify yourself and land immediately. I repeat. This is restricted airspace. You are to identify yourself and land immediately."

"Control tower, this is Eurocopter four-five-six-echo-sierra. Position, five-five-six north, two-six-four east. One thousand feet, dropping to five hundred. Exiting airspace."

"Eurocopter four-five-six-echo-sierra, you will land. Do not exit the airspace. Air defence systems are armed. You will be destroyed."

Hunt glanced at Tibs. She looked scared.

"Roger," Hunt said. He had no choice but to set her down. He looked for a field, somewhere dry and flat.

"What's going on Stirling?"

"They want us to land. Seems we've strayed into restricted airspace."

She didn't look pleased.

"On the plus side," Hunt said. "This could be a good hook for your story?"

———

"IT'S A TRAP, STIRLING," TIBS SAID AND RUBBED HER arms and blew into her hands as they stood beside the helicopter and watched a row of blacked-out Range Rovers speeding towards them.

Hunt dialled Robin. It was an unsecured line but he had no choice. She answered after one ring.

"What can you find out about Visaginas, Lithuania," Hunt said.

"Why has your phone been off?" Robin asked.

"Hurry," Hunt said as he watched the vehicles approaching them. "It wasn't off, I've been trying to avoid detection by the authorities."

Tibs gave him a curious look and Hunt held up his hand to placate her.

"Here's the thing, Stirling, I've been doing some digging. We've found some more Easter eggs hidden in the data from Isakov's USB. I don't know what it means yet but McKenna and I have been connecting the dots. We think it's a closed city linked to Anatoly Mints."

Hunt swore.

"Mints, through his shell companies, owns a private bank called Nebula."

"How're we getting out of this, Robin?"

"Who's we?"

Hunt paused and glanced at Tibs.

"Us. You and me. How am I getting out of this?"

"Whoever Isakov was selling weapons to was required to travel to that location to access the intel, right?"

"Right," Hunt said.

"I can send you the data we've pulled from the disk."

"Okay?" Hunt said. The drivers of the Range Rovers were visible now.

"Well, think, Stirling. You think whoever was buying weapons would go there themselves to collect whatever it was Isakov has left for them?"

"Probably not."

"No," Robin said. "The admiral has left information on the drive and how to access it. I assume this is linked to Mints' private bank, don't you?"

"Pretty big assumption, lady."

"Lady?" she scoffed. "Do you have any better ideas?"

"Not really," Hunt said as the vehicles skidded to a halt beside the helicopter.

"Think of it like a criminal's Swiss bank account. The people in charge don't do their own laundry. They have biometrics and data to access their accounts. Who they are is not part of the equation like it is for regular people, it's all about who has access to the account information."

Hunt hung up as the doors opened and large men carrying automatic weapons stepped out.

TWENTY-EIGHT

"What's the plan here, Stirling?" Tibs asked in a forceful whisper. Hunt glanced at her as the six men in black combat gear stepped out of the vehicles.

Hunt lifted his chin towards the forest and the lakes that surrounded them.

"Geography," Hunt said.

Tibs cursed. "What the hell does that mean? We're in real trouble!"

"It's all about proximity," Hunt said. He had a glint in his eye. "If this really is a bank, its biggest strength might also be its biggest weakness." He said it with confidence he didn't feel.

A tall man with dark features and buzzed black hair walked towards them. He was serious and annoyed.

"This is a restricted area," the man said in heavily accented English. He spoke well though, Hunt thought. Hunt lifted his chin and took a deep breath and rose to his full height. He saw at least two modern, black AK-style assault rifles with the men in the vehicles. These were the latest AK-12s used by the Russian special forces. The symbolism was clear. There was no one around. No need to be quiet with their weapons. There was no escape. He and Tibs would be executed with their hands behind their heads and left to rot in a swamp, or maybe just under a tree in the forest. No one would ever know what happened to them. He told himself to forget it. Deal with that problem when it happened. Right now, he needed to pull off a pretentious lackey to some billionaire whose business meant that not even a Swiss or Luxembourgish private bank account was safe enough to keep the authorities out of his business. A billionaire so criminally minded that they had to pay Anatoly Mints an ungodly amount of money just to keep theirs away from government hands.

"Yes, I understand," Hunt said. "And I'm here to take advantage of the security for my employer."

The man stopped and eyed him up. Hunt saw his mind working. Hunt could see that he was realising he might need to tone down the interrogation.

"I see," the man said. "And you are?"

Hunt shook his head. "That's not how this works, Mister ...?"

"I'm going to need to search you and your aircraft."

"And who are you?"

"Head of security," the man said. It was blunt and told Hunt more than the title. He was finished speaking.

"Search," Hunt said and stepped away from the helicopter and gestured an invite to the square-jawed security guard.

"Come here," Hunt said to Tibs. He shut her door and hurried over to him. She stood close to Hunt's side.

The guy shouted to one of his men and spoke rapidly to him in Russian. He told him to search them thoroughly. Hunt waved his index finger in the guy's face.

"*Uh-uh*," Hunt said. "No, no, no. There is no chance of this gorilla searching this woman. If you want her searched you can get a female out here and they can do it in private. How dare you! You think I am going to stand here and be okay with these men watching as she's searched. You have another thing coming ..."

The guard didn't understand. He ignored Hunt and reached out an arm for Tibs. Hunt grabbed the guard's thumb and twisted it in the wrong direction and over the guy's shoulder. He yelped and bulked under the pain and pressure. His colleagues lifted their weapons and shouted to let him go.

"Let him go!" the head of security shouted.

"I think you mean 'let him go, sir'," Hunt said.

There was a second of puzzlement on the head of securities face and then he relented.

"Let him go, sir!"

Hunt threw the guy's hand away from his and the guard crumpled to the ground holding his damaged hand. It was purple and white patched where the blood had been cut off and Hunt'd been squeezing.

"Take him away," the head of security said to two of his men. They came over to lift their colleague up by his armpits and half dragged him back to the vehicles.

"Let's start again, shall we?" Hunt suggested.

The man was silent. "Are you unarmed?" he asked. It was a simple question. Hunt nodded that they were.

"I'm Gregor Milosevic," he said.

"Head of security," Hunt said.

"Yes," Gregor said. "You are correct that you are not required to identify yourself. So that is fine but you have the credentials?"

"Yes," Hunt lied.

"Vault or safety deposit box?"

"Box," Hunt said.

"You didn't think to call ahead and notify us of your arrival?"

Hunt stared blankly at the head of security. Undoubtedly a former special forces operator. Chechen name. Probably fought for Russia against his own people in the Chechen war.

"Is that a requirement?" Hunt asked knowing it probably wasn't. The men who needed to use the facilities that Mints had to offer were unlikely to make the trip to the wilderness themselves. Hunt wondered what sort of deviant art, videos, and contraband was hiding beneath the surface in Mints' vaults.

Milosevic shrugged. "Okay," he said. "You drive with us. We go."

———

Hunt saw guards lift a barrier ahead of them and the convoy sped past. There was a concrete dome ahead of them. It looked like something they'd cover a leaking nuclear reactor with to stop the radiation from spreading. The SUVs pulled up outside the dome. Hunt's phone buzzed in his pocket. He glanced at it. A text from an unknown number. Just a series of digits. Hunt and Tibs climbed out of the vehicle. She still looked worried. A man in a smart blue suit came out of the glass sliding doors and skipped down the concrete steps towards them.

"This is Pavel," Milosevic said. "He will escort you."

Hunt nodded.

Pavel was tall and wiry. He looked like someone had applied his skin with a meat hook this morning. He was gaunt and pale. He had his arms behind his back and leaned forward to speak like he was trying to see over a small fence.

"Do you have your account number, sir?" he asked in a German-foreign-exchange-student kind of way.

"Yes," Hunt said and felt the sheen of sweat on his forehead. He felt warm. His breathing was shallow. Tibs looked at him and pulled a face. She stood close to him and squeezed his arm.

"Pull yourself together," she whispered.

Hunt glanced down at her, he was surprised at how well she was handling this whole situation. They were in mortal danger. Did she not realise it? Perhaps she did. If it didn't work Hunt wasn't sure they could escape. As if from thin air Pavel produced a handheld computer. "Code, sir," he said.

Everyone stood around watching him. "Ah, yes," he said. "One sec." He had no option. This had better work. Without knowing where the digits had come from or who sent them to him, he read them out. They could have been a tracking number for a parcel or the code that Robin had managed to decrypt from the dump of numbers on the flash drive he'd acquired from Isakov. Hunt read them out in batches of four like he was reading off his bank card. Pavel punched them in with a serious look on his face. His lips were turning blue from the cold. Tibs shivered next to him. Hunt hoped it would work just so they could get out of the cold. It was like being on the tundra.

The machine in Pavel's hand beeped and he smiled. Hunt saw his overlapping front teeth.

"Your account number is confirmed," Pavel said. "Follow me."

They walked up the stairs and the green glass doors

opened with a satisfying whoosh. Hunt felt the warm, dry air from inside. Tibs rubbed her arms, "Oh, thank God," she said.

Pavel half turned and addressed Tibs directly, "We have a comfortable waiting area just over here," he held out a long arm and extended it towards some brown leather sofas and chairs. "There is a coffee machine you can use," Pavel said.

"Oh," Tibs said.

"Yes," Pavel nodded gravely. "I am afraid only, sir, will be permitted into the bank's vault."

Hunt wasn't going to question it. Tibs went over to sit down with a coffee and a magazine. Remarkably calm, Hunt thought.

"Follow me, sir," Pavel said and gave Hunt a polite smile and nod of the head before he led him down some stairs. It was dark below them. As they descended the floor lights at the edges of the stairs turned on and glowed one after the other. Hunt saw the lights extend far down a concrete tunnel in front of them.

"It might look industrial," Pavel said. "But it is state of the art, I can assure you. Is this your first visit to the bank?"

"Yes," Hunt said and kept quiet. Pavel's breath smelled of pickled onion and he preferred if the living Lurch kept his mouth shut.

"This used to be an underground laboratory," Pavel said. "You can see the similarities between Soviet state security for biowarfare and a gilt-edged private bank like Nebula, can't you, sir?"

Hunt didn't answer. It sounded like a rhetorical question. If it wasn't meant like that it was simply redundant.

"We have several large vaults here, sir. I will take you to the secure wing for the safety deposit box you require. As in

Switzerland, we use fire-red burn bags for any contents you wish to be incinerated. I will take care of that personally. It looked truly impenetrable, Hunt thought. He glanced behind him down the long concrete corridor. "We simply require your password, sir," Pavel said and gestured to a screen in front of a huge steel vault door. Hunt swallowed.

He pulled out his mobile. Pavel had a straight smile planted on his face. He waited with his hands behind his back and leaned awkwardly to the side again. *Password*, Hunt typed and pressed send. He waited awkwardly and glanced at Pavel. Hunt wondered if he could strangle him and get away. It wouldn't take much. He could probably wrap his hand around the man's turkey-like neck. No, he thought. I'd never get away. Plus Tibs was up there. Come on Robin, he thought.

"I hope you're not struggling for signal?" Pavel said through half-closed eyes, swaying to the side as he waited calmly. "We've installed the latest Five-gee relay system. Some of our clientele are very discerning, you see," Pavel said.

Bars on his phone weren't Hunt's problem right now. He didn't have the password to access the vault. What if Robin hadn't found it yet. Did she even know she was looking for it?

TWENTY-NINE

Hunt's head popped up. He stared right at Pavel. Lurch was taken aback and opened his mouth to speak. "Don't," Hunt said in the middle of his idea. For some reason the night he shot Isakov was in his mind's eye. He remembered being on his knees in front of the hotel safe flipping through black and white images from the folder. The number twenty-one, looked like it was a random closeup of a photograph taken of a house number. There was the name of the ship. It was in Cyrillic. Hunt realised now it was backwards. An image taken on the surface of the water. He closed his eyes. It looked like яиргелла but if it was a reflection it was backwards. So аллегори.

"What does *allegoriya* mean in Russian, Pavel?" Hunt said and smiled.

"Why, allegory, sir," Pavel said and looked confused.

"That's right," Hunt said and stepped to the screen.

He punched in 2-1-2-4-4 3-4-5-6-9. The machine buzzed bright red. Wrong code. He cursed silently. Last chance. He put the 27 at the end.

2-4-4-3-4-5-6-9-2-7. Come on, Hunt silently wished. A

delicate tinkle on the piano. It flashed green. Oh, thank God, he thought and exhaled. Pavel smiled.

"I presume your employer wouldn't have been happy if you'd forgotten your code after such a long journey here," Pavel said.

"No, I suspect not," Hunt said and still felt the tightness in his chest. He's done it. He didn't know how he'd done it. Only, the pictures made no sense by themselves. Standing here now though, thinking back, they were with the flash drive. They were a code hidden in plain sight. Obscure enough to mean nothing alone, but to Hunt, too odd to make sense alone. Crucially they were in Cyrillic. The keypad on the screen had given him the idea. The keypad denoted both Latin and Cyrillic alphabets beside each number. Allegory twenty-seven. Isakov was making a joke and Hunt had spent too many years at Catholic boarding schools to not have had some of the Old Testament seep into his brain. Galatians 4:21-27 was an allegory. *Tell me who you want to be under the law, do you not listen to the law?* Whoever was supposed to be retrieving whatever Hunt was about to find in the safety deposit box probably wouldn't have got the joke. Isakov was explaining how they were above the law. The large value door opened and a long room full of safety deposit boxes opened.

"Please wait in the private room over here," Pavel showed Hunt to some offices behind frosted glass. "I will be with you shortly with your box, number twenty-one."

Pavel came back wearing white gloves carrying the safety deposit box and placed it on the desk.

He gave a slight nod. "I will be outside when you are finished, sir," Pavel said. "Simply leave the burn bag, should you require it, behind the curtain and I will dispose of it immediately in our incinerator. You may also use one of the

Louis Vuitton weekenders for your personal items should you require them."

Robin would love that, Hunt thought. Then he remembered Tibs upstairs too. He didn't know if she liked Louis Vuitton. Safe assumption that she did. Pavel checked his watch.

"Please, sir, I have just been informed that we are expecting a very important person imminently. He has asked for perfect privacy so I am required to ask you to take no longer than five full minutes to conclude your business."

"And then?" Hunt asked.

Pavel tutted. "Let's not go down this route, sir. Please take no longer than your allowed five minutes. I do not wish to be rude ..."

"Of course," Hunt said. Even though he was a blatant thief, breaking into someone else's safety deposit box, he still felt the sting of inconsiderate customer service. He shook it off and smiled internally. He really believed he was who he said he was here. Pavel left him alone with the shining metal box and Hunt heard the vacuum suction of the frosted glass door close tightly shut. Hunt checked the box for booby traps. Such a strange name for a harmful device triggered by the unsuspecting victim. You'd feel more than a 'booby' if you stood on a landmine, Hunt thought and grunted at the idea. He couldn't see any concealed wires or alarms that he might trigger by opening it. Hunt opened the drawer. There was a pale blue folder in there. He took it out and examined it. Documents. Pictures. He set it aside. He checked the rest of the box. It looked empty but there was a slight bump in the felt underlay. He ran his hands over the top of the felt. There was a hard lump there. It was shaped like a wire. He lifted the felt and the tiny single eye of a camera was looking at him. Hunt pulled the camera out and looked closely into it. Whoever was watching or being alerted to the feed would have seen the close-up of his eye looking into the android-like face of the pinhole video camera. Hunt pulled it out and dropped it to the floor. He stomped on it and heard the plastic crunch under his boot. He'd have to move faster. Now he had no idea what was waiting for him when he left this place.

Under the felt, there were several official-looking Russian ID cards. Some underwater maps. Blueprints of a subsurface structure. Hunt took it all and stuffed it into the Louis Vuitton bag. Hunt had no idea what he'd uncovered here but whatever it was, Isakov had sold something big. He needed to get out of here. He closed the safety deposit box and put the broken video camera in a burn bag. He gave the room a quick scan and pressed the door release button. It slid silently open. He hurried alone, down the concrete corridor. The lights came on as he moved. His mobile phone buzzed again. He grabbed it as he hurried out.

"Sir! Sir! Wait, I must escort you," Hunt heard Pavel yell from behind him. Hunt waved him away over his shoulder and checked the phone.

Nebula is a trap. You've been made. Get out now.

Hunt deleted the message. As he did, another appeared.

PARADISE LOST.

Hunt had no idea what it meant. As he got to the top of the steps he saw Milosevic waiting near the entrance holding a tablet computer. Tibs saw him and threw down her magazine and pouted and stood up. Hunt beckoned her over.

"Come on," he said with urgency, "We've got to go."

"What's the matter?"

Milosevic was coming towards them as Pavel caught up from behind.

"Sir, I must escort you, always."

"Okay. Sorry." Hunt said. "I need you to arrange to take us back to our helicopter."

"Not possible," Milosevic said.

"Excuse me," Hunt said.

"Security protocol," the head of security said. "We have been notified of a potential breach.

"Oh, my," Pavel exclaimed. "If we believe there has been a breach you must provide the requisite codeword."

Hunt felt like Milosevic was about to quiz him. A simple verification check, in case he'd somehow gained access to the passcode data fraudulently.

"What is the account emergency passcode?" Milosevic asked.

Pavel and Tibs both looked at him. Hunt pretended to think.

"Paradise lost," Hunt said. He heard the tablet beep.

"Incorrect," Milosevic said. Hunt felt his heart rate jump. Milosevic said something into his shoulder radio. Tibs watched Hunt's face in confusion.

"There must be some mistake —" Hunt started to say. Tibs lunged forward. Hunt instinctively stepped aside. Milosevic had his hand on the pressel calling for security. Tibs grabbed the hard rectangular tablet computer from his grip and spun. She held the tablet and spun like she was about to throw the discus. As she twirled she extended her arm and instead of releasing the computer, she hit the Nebula head of security just below his cheekbone. His head whipped backwards and he raised his hand to his face as blood sprayed through his fingers. At the end of the movement, she ducked towards him and pulled his handgun from the holster on his hip. She threw the gun to Hunt. He was surprised by the toss but managed to grab it with wide eyes and his cinder block-sized hands. She kneed Milosevic in the groin and tripped him to the ground. He hit the floor hard as Hunt cocked the weapon. Pavel was in a crouch with his hands up above his head.

"Please don't shoot me, please, but you will never get out of here."

"Stay there," Hunt said to him.

"Come on, Stirling, hurry!" Tibs yelled. Milosevic was on the ground holding his face. She bent over him and pulled off his two-way radio system. She clipped it onto her belt and stuck the earpiece in her ear. Good thinking, Hunt thought. Now he knew she wasn't a mere journalist. As they headed for the front door Hunt said, "I really wish you wouldn't use my name while we're still in an enemy compound."

"Fair enough," she said. "Sorry."

A convoy of black SUVs was racing towards them.

"It's like *déjà vu* all over again," Tibs said.

"This is a VIP they're expecting," Hunt said. "We could surprise them and nick their vehicles?"

"Are we expecting security?" Hunt asked.

"They're asking him to repeat the message," Tibs said and held her finger to her ear to press the mic from the receiver further in. "The chatter is all about the convoy.

"So we quietly hijack the front vehicle and get the driver to drive us out?"

The convoy of cars pulled up to the entrance. Immediately the doors opened and black sunglasses-wearing bodyguards jumped out to hold the doors open for their primaries.

"We need Pavel," Hunt said and went back for him. As

he walked past Milosevic he double-stepped and put his boot through the Chechen's jaw. He heard it crunch and the head of security's body slumped. He bent down and took Milosevic's tactical black sunglasses out of the Velcro top pocket of his combat shirt. Hunt put them on and bent and grabbed the shaking Pavel by the back of his collar and lifted him.

"Come on pretty boy, you're walking out with us. If you say anything, I will put a hole in your lung." Hunt pressed the barrel of the MP-443 Grach pistol into Pavel's ribs. He whimpered and nodded.

Hunt concealed the pistol in his trousers as they walked down the steps. He saw the bodyguards holding the doors open. The VIPs were waiting for privacy, he thought. Hunt followed close behind Pavel as he went to the window of the driver of the first vehicle. They exchanged words and Pavel gestured towards Hunt and Tibs. The driver nodded.

"He will take you," Pavel said. "Now please leave." Hunt could see he was terrified. "Please I don't want a shoot out at the OK Corral," Pavel said. Hunt couldn't help but give a single laugh. "Please let me go," Pavel said.

Hunt and Tibs went to climb into the black SUV. As he passed one of the other vehicles, Hunt glanced up. He saw a man's face with two black eyes and wearing a cast on his arm. Hunt looked away as an expression of recognition registered on the man's face. It can't be, Hunt thought. He daren't look back again. He and Tibs climbed into the vehicle and told the driver to go. Hunt held the handgun low right at the driver's back. As they drove to the front gate Hunt looked back.

"What?" Tibs asked and followed his eyes. The driver was trying not to look at them in the rearview mirror.

"I thought I saw someone I recognised," Hunt said. "But he was supposed to be dead."

"How do you know he was dead?"

Hunt glanced at her. "Because I killed him."

Hunt felt the driver's eyes on him.

"Face the road," Hunt said in badly accented Russian. The driver didn't respond. The barrier in front of them lifted. "Keep going," Hunt said, "And we'll leave you somewhere you can call for a lift, rather. Or you can try something and they'll be lifting you into a hearse. Understand?"

THIRTY

They decided it was too risky to go for the helicopter. They decided to hightail it through the forest roads and avoid the motorways until they found a car they could switch to. Hunt adjusted the rearview mirror. He still wasn't feeling safe. They'd left the driver by the side of the road in some abandoned-looking field. Hunt'd taken a picture of the driver's ID.

"Now we know who you are and where you live. Keep your mouth shut and we won't come after your family," Hunt had said. While he still had his phone in his hand he'd managed to get a picture of Tibs and send it to the unknown number in his messages. He had to assume it was Robin. Find out who this is, he'd typed.

Tibs was unusually quiet.

"Those were some moves for a journalist," Hunt said.

"I did karate as a kid and —" she said and stopped talking abruptly. Hunt could see that she knew the lie was finished. He wasn't going to ask her who she was working for. They'd find out soon enough.

His phone buzzed.

"Hello," he answered and then cursed. An electronic voice asked him to key in. He glanced at the road and at his phone while he punched in his clearance number.

"How the hell did you get away?" McKenna asked.

"You've got to get us out of here," Hunt said.

"Who is 'we'?"

Hunt glanced across at Tibs. "You tell me," Hunt said, and then, "A civilian."

"A woman?"

"Yes."

"Oh, Stirling," McKenna said. It was an admonishment.

"You sound like a disappointed father. Why don't you bugger off? Can you do it or not?"

McKenna paused.

"I'll send you the details of a safe house and an extraction plan now. Did you get anything?"

Hunt was wary of Tibs listening again.

"Yes, I don't know what it is yet, but it is something big."

"How did you get out?" McKenna asked.

"Tell, Rob—" Hunt caught himself. "I thought I saw the bodyguard from the San Domenico."

"I thought you neutralised him."

"So did I," Hunt said.

"Well that's a pretty big fu—"

Hunt hung up.

"Everything okay?" Tibs asked. Her voice was sweet and the question light, like she was asking if the dinner reservations had changed.

Hunt didn't respond. He checked the phone as the location of the safe house came through and accelerated hard into the corners.

THE DIRECTOR OF INTELLIGENCE SAT BACK AND CLOSED his eyes. After a few seconds, he opened them and leaned forward and dialled the number. After a few rings that sounded like the engaged tone of a foreign number, his operative answered.

"Concierge."

"We have a last-minute reservation."

McKenna heard Marco Mykolas pause and digest the information. It was likely that he'd been sitting on his hands with nothing to do for months. Maybe years. He would be keen. On edge. Possibly a liability. McKenna wanted him calm. Hunt was one unpredictable operative himself. He needed Hunt calm, patient, and to not feel threatened.

"How many guests, sir?"

"Two."

"ETA to check in?"

"Sometime tonight. Five Spire Advisory."

"Roger that, sir."

McKenna stayed on the line. He could hear his operative breathing on the other end.

"Anything else, sir?" Mykolas asked.

"One thing. The field agent. It's Stirling Hunt. You know him?"

"I know of him."

"So then you know how dangerous he can be?"

"I've heard the rumours, sir."

"They're more than rumours. He has some intelligence on him. Make sure we get copies of it, all right? All of it. And —"

"Yes, sir?"

"He has a guest with him. She could compromise the mission. I want her interrogated. Find out what she knows. My guess is, too much. Hunt might need to be restrained.

So restrain him. Keep him alive if you can, if you can't, dead is just as good. We need that intelligence though."

"Yes, sir."

"One more thing ... the girl needs to be neutralised. Do you understand?"

"I understand," Mykolas said.

"Was there something else?" McKenna asked.

"When I do this, sir, we'll talk again about my posting?"

"Yes. Paris, wasn't it?"

"Yes, sir, my fiancée —"

"I remember," McKenna said. He was being purposefully blunt. He was unsure about how correct the current decision he was making was. He'd played his hand, however. Hunt might have outlasted his usefulness. He was compromised. He knew too much. If anyone could extract what McKenna needed to know it was Mykolas. McKenna had kept him like an underfed dog straining at the end of the chain for his food bowl which was just out of reach.

"One slot and twenty-seven applications, Marco. You see what I'm saying? You need more field experience. Do what I ask and you will get what you want," McKenna said.

"Yes, sir."

McKenna hung up and took his jacket from the back of his chair. He went into the basement to the situation room for Op Zambezi Dawn. He walked into a buzzing operations centre. Telephones ringing. People huddling over maps and running analysis on data.

"Listen up! Everybody off the phone, I have an update for you on the situation in Lithuania. Stirling Hunt is accompanied and has highly sensitive intelligence — national security level intel —he is headed, now, to a safe house outside Vilnius. I want an extraction team stood up and ready to go in the next five minutes. Get ready to accept and analyse the intelligence once it comes through."

A female analyst hung up her desk phone and leaned back, "Extraction team will be airborne within the hour, sir, and on the ground in approximately three hours."

"I want them in and out within six hours," McKenna said. "Any communications about Hunt's location — from now— are eyes only. Strictly need to know."

"Yes, sir," the analyst said.

"I also want the concierge briefed. Hunt is coming in with a high-priority target. We want the safe house quiet. I don't want any communication—from anyone—until the extraction team has left. Is that understood?" McKenna was met with a wall of blank faces. "Did you hear what I said?" They nodded. "Then get on it!" Immediately phones were picked up and the chatter started. McKenna walked out to the rapid tip-tapping of typing.

MYKOLAS SAT IN THE CONTROL ROOM WATCHING THE monitors for movement. He was in the countryside just outside the Lithuanian capital. Mostly all he got was stray deer and the occasional fox looking for scraps. He's been in post for over a year and it was driving him insane. His computer beeped a notification. Encrypted message from operations command. He opened it. McKenna had briefed the team, he thought.

Incoming: high-profile asset. Package is hostile and dangerous. Restrain if possible. Use all necessary force. Proceed with extreme caution. Danger to life. They certainly knew how to get their point across. Everyone had heard of Stirling Hunt. Could be that his reputation preceded him. Mykolas would give him the benefit of the doubt. Safety protocols needed to be extreme. After all, McKenna needed cover for when Mykolas had to defend himself from the dangerous asset.

Mykolas saw the glow of headlights on the screen from the video feed. Two passengers in an estate car. The car stopped and a big man stepped out. He checked his surroundings and waited. Mykolas watched in silence. The guy went to the intercom on the wall and pressed the button. Mykolas pressed a pressel on the desk.

"Yeah?"

"Do you have a room?" the man said.

"Name?" Mykolas asked.

"Hunt. Hotel. Uniform. November. Tango. Five Spire Advisory."

Mykolas picked up his desk phone and called the operations centre at the River House. "Hunt, Five Spire Advisory," Mykolas said.

"Confirmed," the voice on the other end said and clicked dead.

Mykolas pressed the pressel again. "We have a room available, sir. I'll buzz you in now."

He saw Hunt signal for the woman to step out of the vehicle. She did and rubbed her hands on her arms. It was cold. They both looked tired. He didn't think two tired and lost travellers were going to be much of a problem. He was already dreaming of Paris in the spring.

THIRTY-ONE

"C'MON, C'MON," ROBIN SAID AS SHE HELD HER PHONE to her ear and bit the cuticle of her thumb. Everett McKenna was always supposed to be available to her. Now she was feeling locked out. Stirling had been more or less alone during the operation in Lithuania.

She wasn't happy with the level of the equipment and the processing power they'd left her with. Now she'd decoded the flash drive and finally had some luck with getting the voices analysed through Broad Oak. Now she really needed to speak to McKenna.

"Screw it," she said and hung up the phone. "I'll go to him." She grabbed her coat, scarf, and MI6 pass.

She passed security and hurried into the large marble-floored foyer. It was busy with colleagues and visitors in business dress. There was a hum of conversation and the clatter of leather shoes on the slick stone surface. She walked briskly past the long desk of receptionists and went to the electronic barriers. She put her card on the biometric scanner and the lights flashed red.

"Bugger it," she said and tried again. Red flash. One of

the uniformed security guards walked slowly up to her and gestured towards the waiting row of receptionists. She gave him a weak smile and walked up to them uneasily.

"Hi, I'm Robin Adler to see Everett McKenna. He's an intelligence director but my ID card isn't working for some reason."

"Right," said the stern-looking middle-aged woman. "Who did you say you work for?"

"MI6, just like you."

"Can I see your ID?"

Robin took the lanyard off from around her neck and handed it to the woman. She snatched it and typed with one hand while looking at the card. Robin watched her face and she frowned.

"I'm sorry but you'll have to be issued with a visitor pass to see Mister McKenna. Also, you'll require an escort."

"That can't be right, I work here ..."

"I'm sorry that's what the system says. Your place of work is registered at an undisclosed location off of SIS property. Protocol states you'll require an escort and a visitor badge."

Robin sighed. "Fine," she said, impatient. "Whatever, I just ... it's an emergency."

The woman pouted and put a blank card into the printer, "It always is, dear. It always is." Robin scoffed. "Look into the camera please."

"Which one?" Robin asked around her terminal for the webcam.

"Thank you," the woman said and she reached her hand out to wait for the printer. Rather than look at Robin she inspected the nails on her right hand. Robin never took her eyes off her and made no attempt to hide her contempt. The printer whirred and spun and then shot the card out of the slot. The woman placed it into Robin's lanyard and held it out for her.

"You'll have to take a seat over there and wait while I call your escort," the receptionist said. Robin followed her gaze to a black faux leather bench along the far wall. She'd have to sit next to the entrance and watch as people entered the building. She took her ID card and said, "Thanks," without meaning it.

McKenna was in his office. He was staring at the paper calendar on his desk and not really thinking. He sometimes had some self-awareness of what he might look like, hands held in prayer touching his mouth, staring into space. Anyone who saw him would think he was deep in concentration with a hundred thoughts swarming one after the other into his mind. This was more of an overwhelmed inertia. He had so much to worry about that his mind just went into a kind of procrastination-induced stupor. Then he was aware of someone standing at his ajar office door. He moved only his eyes and the shape and head of Gerald D. Soames was looking at him. McKenna thought about imme-diately sitting bolt upright and shuffling his papers like he should if he was caught daydreaming but he decided to stay as he was. Bugger giving Soames the satisfaction of such a basic human tendency. The play-act at businesses that they'd both recognise, not comment on, and would form the tone and content of their resultant conversation: 'working hard or hardly working' Soames might feel obliged to say, McKenna thought.

Instead, McKenna lowered his hands from his mouth slightly and said, "What do you want, Gerald?"

Soames was a large man. In many different ways. He used his long forearm and the side of his hand to sweep McKenna's office door open and strode in. Soames had that public schoolboy arrogance practically radiating out of him creating some kind of invisible forcefield, you couldn't see it but you could feel it.

"Is that any way to greet an old friend, Evie"

McKenna sighed and sat forward.

"I thought you were —"

"Kicked to the curb? Yes, me too for a while there but it seems your old chum has found favour from friends in faraway places. And by faraway, I mean high-up in the clouds."

"I see," McKenna said. "Mind if I ask?"

The little game of who is more senior than whom unfolded.

"Of course," Soames said graciously. "The queen bee's little messenger-consort-commissar-*confidante* combo," Soames grinned.

McKenna shook his head no the wiser about what the hell Soames was doing at the minute.

"I'm sitting on the National Security Council," Soames said and watched McKenna waiting for his response with slightly raised bushy eyebrows.

"Like hell you are!" McKenna said.

"Fine, the National Security Secretariat," Soames conceded.

"Doing what?"

"I told you, my boy, deputy national security advisor to the PM."

Now it was time for McKenna to raise his eyebrows. Maybe he *had* been too busy. That was usually the kind of appointment he kept abreast of or, at least, would have thought someone would mention to him.

"You kept that on the down low," McKenna said through slitted eyes.

"Despite your scepticism—"

"So *you're* shaping security and defence policy," McKenna said and shook his head. It was somewhere between astonishment and disbelief sprinkled with a hint of lack of respect.

Soames dropped the corners of his mouth and shrugged. There was the privately educated forcefield again. "Not only that, dear Evie, I have the ear of—for all intents and purposes—your Lord and saviour, Angela Langdon."

McKenna waited in silence. The game had been played and he had been severely beaten. He wasn't going to give Soames the satisfaction of now asking what he could do for him. It was all a bit of a grovel and lacked tact. Both men stood in silence. Soames with the wisp of a smile spread on his thick pink lips.

"Mind if I sit?" Soames said finally and indicated the chair.

Did he mind? Yes, he minded. Too close and I'll feel the need for a shower, McKenna thought. He conceded with a wave of his hand. Soames pulled the chair out and sat down with a heavy flop. He unbuttoned his jacket and flapped it over his gut and crossed his legs.

"I understand you and I both share the same problem," Soames said.

McKenna suddenly felt very tired. His shoulders slumped and he asked, "Which is?"

"Stirling Hunt aka The Boatman."

"And what problem is that exactly?"

"He's still breathing ..."

McKenna stood up and closed the door.

ROBIN WALKED AHEAD OF THE SECURITY ESCORT hurrying between the offices and turning her head to read the nameplates on the doors as they rushed along. The stiff leather heels and tight business skirt of the escort held her back. Robin saw McKenna's door and stopped. She lifted her crooked index finger to knock and as she dropped it to the wood, the door pulled open. A large man with a sagging double chin was standing in front of her. He started to do up his jacket and turned to McKenna who was standing behind his desk looking ashen-faced.

"Don't forget what we talked about," the large man said and then turned back to Robin. "Excuse me," he said as he pushed past her and the escort.

For a moment it appeared as though McKenna hadn't seen her. He had a faraway look on his face.

"Sir?" Robin said.

McKenna looked up glassy-eyed. His forehead creased in the middle as he pushed his eyebrows together.

"What're you doing here?" McKenna asked.

Robin went into the office and rested her hands on the back of the chair. "What do you mean, what am I doing here? I've been trying to call you all day. I had no other choice. And," she grabbed her lanyard and lifted it towards McKenna, "why do I need a visitor permit and a bloody escort?" Robin turned to the security escort standing in the doorway. McKenna waved her away, and she turned and left in a huff.

"Shut the door," McKenna said.

"You shut it," Robin said. "And answer my question!" She followed him as he went to close the door. "Why doesn't my pass work? What aren't you telling me, Everett? Do I even work for MI6? Does Stirling?"

"What? Of course you do. You are part of Oberon. You have to work for MI6."

"So why can't I get into the building? Why was Stirling left alone in Lithuania?"

"He knew the risks," McKenna said and went to stand behind his desk.

"You really don't care what happens to him, do you?"

McKenna didn't respond.

"Look, Robin, what is it? I'm busy and you claim it's important, so please ..."

She pushed her lips together and looked at the floor and took a second to compose herself.

"It's a couple of things, actually," she said. "It's Isakov's bodyguard, well, the man we thought was his bodyguard. I ran the voices from Stirling's surveillance recording and we got a hit from the NSA database ..."

"The NSA? How did you get access—never mind."

"It's not his bodyguard, sir, it's Aleksandr Arkhipov."

"Who is Aleksandr Arkhipov?"

"The name sounds familiar though, doesn't it? He captained the *Severomorsk*."

"The Russian sub—"

"Yes, the one that caught fire and had to be rescued. There were fourteen fatalities among the crew. Most survived. The sub broke the surface in the Arctic and the crew were rescued before she sank."

"It was a major embarrassment," McKenna agreed. "But so what?"

"We've been looking in the wrong place. Isakov wasn't

the one selling the missiles. It was Arkhipov. Isakov probably facilitated the whole operation—disaster—at the higher ups but Arkhipov carried out the plan."

"What plan?" McKenna asked.

"Don't you see! The fire was a cover. They manufactured the fire onboard and evacuated the crew. While they floated about in the Arctic Sea, Arkhipov unloaded the weapons systems—"

"What were they carrying?"

"Shkval-2 nuclear torpedoes."

"Too big to unload at sea, surely?"

"Maybe," Robin said, "But the warheads weren't."

"No way Arkhipov did that himself."

"Well, he didn't, did he? Fourteen dead bodies. All posthumous Heroes of Russia. That was the crew he'd either bribed or coerced into helping him. Think about it, he and Isakov hatch the plan. Isakov is in charge of their missions. He puts Arkhipov somewhere he'll be able to carry out the deception. They light a fire, evacuate the crew, and then the submarine 'sinks'. Right?"

"They found the wreckage though," McKenna said quietly with his hand on his chin.

"Sure but did they recover any bodies?" Robin asked.

"They never said any weapons were missing either," McKenna said.

"No shit! When has Russia ever said anything truthful? Either they didn't tell the world that they lost nuclear warheads and have no idea where they are, or Isakov covered it up. That's if they were able to recover the weapons. The vessel broke in half, who knows what is left down there or where the weapons systems scattered."

"All right," McKenna said, staring at his desk again. "So what did he do with the warheads?"

"He left them."

"Where?"

Robin shrugged and looked up at the ceiling. "Some place they could dock underwater, unload, kill the crew, and scuttle the ship," she said.

"Research station," McKenna said.

"But where, aren't there dozens?"

"That we know of ..." McKenna said. "That has to be the intelligence that Hunt is sending."

"Hunt? Then he's alive?" Robin asked. She was genuinely surprised.

"Yes, didn't you know?"

"No, I didn't know. I haven't had contact with him," she checked her watch, "in hours. I thought he was captured, possibly dead."

"He's alive."

"And he's sending what he found in the safety deposit box?"

"As far as I understand," McKenna said. He was quieter now. More subdued. It made Robin suspicious.

"Who is the buyer?" Robin asked him. She stood waiting for an answer.

"I thought you were going to tell me ..."

She debated whether or not to give McKenna what she'd found. It could be useful information later on. They might need it to trade. On the other hand, if she didn't give it to him, there might not be a later on.

"There was another voice," Robin said. "No hits on our database. I used XKEYSCORE—"

McKenna's eyebrows furrowed again. "You don't have access—"

"Jesus, sir, do you really care how I got what we needed or do you want to know what I've got?" She was enraged.

Bits of spittle on her lip which she wiped away with the back of her wrist. McKenna didn't say anything else. She calmed down.

"I got a hit on a slight voice recording from an archive. A Canadian kid named Maximilian Wiltord."

McKenna shook his head. "Never heard of him."

"You wouldn't. No one has. He doesn't exist. At least not anymore."

"Who is he?"

She shrugged. "I can tell you who he was …. A young communist in Canada. A few minor felonies. Arrested for marches and destruction of property. In the late nineties, just eighteen, he was arrested for a plot to hack into the Bank of Canada attempting to cancel the debt."

"That sounds serious."

"It was but ultimately a failure, he was released."

"What then?"

"He disappeared. Until his voice popped up on a recording in a lawyer's Italian mansion which included a dead Russian naval officer, a known Albanian arms dealer, and the former head of the Russian pacific fleet."

McKenna was staring at his desk again.

"Sir?" Robin said. He didn't respond. She put her hand in his line of sight and snapped her fingers. "Sir," she said. McKenna looked at her. "What are we going to do?"

"We're going to wait for the intelligence from Hunt and then—God willing—if your theory matches the data we'll find the warheads before the enemy does."

And if we don't, Robin thought. She stood silent for a moment studying McKenna's face. He'd been picking at his lip.

"Anything else?" McKenna asked.

"One thing, sir, who was that man? The one leaving as I was coming in?"

McKenna shook his head. "Never mind. Now, if there is nothing else," he said and picked up the phone. He pressed a button and set it down again. "You really should be getting back to your station."

There was a light tap on the door and it opened a crack. Robin turned to look. It was the same security escort as before. She turned back to McKenna and he gave her a polite smile and gestured to the door. She walked out feeling trodden on. She brought him the key piece of the puzzle and he reacted as though she'd just dropped his ice cream cone in the grass. I'm done with this, she thought. I'm out of here. She stormed ahead of the escort again and slammed her visitor pass down in front of the receptionist on her way out.

THIRTY-TWO

MYKOLAS STARED AT THE CCTV FEED. THE WOMAN. Just standing out there in the cold. This wasn't right. Maybe he could just finish this here now. He unlocked the gun rack in the control room and took out a 12-gauge shotgun. He checked it and racked it and headed for the front door. When he got there he took a deep breath and snatched the door open. As he did he lifted the shotgun into his shoulder. The woman got a fright and she jumped and shivered.

"Who are you?" Mykolas demanded. Her eyes darted to the side. Before he could turn he felt the hard, cold steel of a pistol barrel pressing into his temple.

"Thank you," a man's voice said and took the shotgun out of his hands. "Who're you?"

"I'm Mykolas, safe house keeper. Authorisation Oscar, Bravo, India, Whiskey, seven. You can call and ask." Mykolas looked out of the corner of his eye at the guest.

"I'm Hunt, this is," Hunt said and looked at Tibs, "Doesn't matter who this is." He flicked the gun barrel towards the door. "Inside. Let's go."

Tibs hurried past Mykolas and into the house. He turned and Hunt followed him in. The passages were painted a dark green. There were few windows and mostly LED lights. Tibs rubbed her arms to warm up and then waited for Mykolas and Hunt to move past her. Hunt kept the pistol trained on the base of the safe house keeper's skull.

"You're not exactly following protocol," Mykolas said to him. This guy was calm, Hunt thought.

"Just tell me where the guest rooms are," Hunt said.

Mykolas lifted his arm and pointed, "Over there, to the left. Make yourself at home."

"Go and get warm," Hunt said to Tibs and she walked past them the way Mykolas had shown them.

"Control room?" Hunt asked.

Mykolas started walking. He got a steel door and flipped open a panel and entered a code. The door's lock popped and Mykolas pulled it open. "After you," he said to Hunt.

"I insist," Hunt said. Mykolas went into the control room. It had a wall of television screens and the glow of stacked computer monitors.

"Call it in," Hunt said. "Let me hear it." Mykolas sighed and lifted the telephone. He pressed zero and dialled a number. It rang.

"Manager," the voice on the other end answered.

"My guest is *here*," Mykolas said.

There was a pause.

"Account?" the voice said.

"Five Spires Advisory," Hunt said.

"With a guest?"

"Confirmed," Mykolas said. "Luggage included."

Silence again.

"Scan the passports."

"He wants the intel," Mykolas said.

"I know what it means."

Hunt took the documents out of the leather 'weekender' and pulled all of the staples and clips off of the sheets.

"Give it to me," Mykolas said. Hunt looked hesitant. "I will put it on the scanner and send them," the Lithuanian said. He took the papers and put them into the load tray. The machine started working, sliding one piece in, scanning it, and sending it out the other side.

"Confirmed," the voice said. "One night stay, airport transfer scheduled. Pick up ETA zero two hundred."

Hunt checked his watch. A few hours from now.

"You see?" Mykolas said. "Nothing to worry about. They're on their way." He pressed a button to end the phone call. Mykolas stood looking at Hunt. "Please stop pointing that gun at me now."

Hunt held it there for a second longer and then lowered it reluctantly. He made it safe and put it away.

"Why've you got this?" Hunt asked and looked at the shotgun.

"It's late at night. I need to protect myself. I am suspicious, just like you, no? You hungry? We leave document scanner and we make food," Mykolas said.

Hunt thought about it. He hadn't thought of food in seven hours. His stomach felt like it had shrunk. Just a small knot of pain the size of an acorn. He made the shotgun safe. "Put it away," Hunt said and watched Mykolas return the weapon to the gun case. While he did that Hunt asked, "What'd you have?"

Mykolas shrugged. "To eat? Lithuania food. Something like a pierogi."

"Okay," Hunt said. "Thanks."

Hunt followed the safe house keeper to the kitchen. "Please," Mykolas said and pulled a chair for him. Hunt put the pistol on the table and sat down. He watched the Lithuanian closely. The guy went to the stove and turned on the gas flame underneath a large pot. He took out a chopping board and pulled a long carving knife from a wooden block. He put it down next to the chopping board. He then took a large bottle of thick, green gherkins from the shelf. Hunt watched him closely. You can take your eyes off a human being but you can't take your eyes off an agent. Mykolas went to the fridge and took out two beers and said, "Do you mind?" and came and sat down opposite Hunt. They looked at one another for a moment. Mykolas opened his beer and took a big gulp.

"You don't like beer?" Mykolas asked. Hunt looked at it and shrugged. He was just tired. "You know, I been here eight months. Eight. My wife is away. This is the most exciting thing that is happening to me." Mykolas laughed and leaned back and patted his belly. "Just getting fat and lazy." Hunt smiled politely. Mykolas took out his mobile phone and put it on the table.

"You first guest I have in eight months. Eight." He held up the fingers on both hands.

"*Uh-huh*," Hunt grunted. He was being polite but felt like he might not be able to keep it up for much longer.

"You know, you guys, I'm jealous of you ... flying all over the world, women, cars, extravagant life."

"It's not all it's cracked up to be," Hunt said.

Mykolas looked confused. "Sure it is," he said. "Two women, one in London, one over here."

Now it was Hunt's turn to be confused. How did this safe house keeper who claimed to not know who he was, know about him and Robin? He stayed quiet. Watched him. Tried to keep his face relaxed. Tried to keep his finger from sliding onto the trigger of the handgun.

Mykolas' mobile phone buzzed. His eyes glanced down at it and back up at Hunt. His expression had changed, Hunt thought.

"What you want instead? Coffee?"

Hunt nodded unconsciously. "Sure, coffee. Good."

Mykolas stood and went to the cupboard. As he reached up for a cup he half turned to Hunt and asked, "Could you boil water? Is there on stove."

Hunt went to stand. As he did, Mykolas swung a heavy pewter mug in an arcing backhand. The hard mug clipped Hunt on the side of the head and it immediately stung. Hunt went to raise the gun but Mykolas jumped across at him and swung Hunt's arm across his body. He slammed Hunt into the kitchen cabinets and the crockery crashed around inside. Hunt was hit with force and had a moment of surprise at the stocky strength of the Lithuanian.

"The hell are you doing!" Hunt grunted as Mykolas tried to pin him against the cabinets. He pulled Hunt down and tried to run him into the opposite wall. Hunt stumbled forward and onto the countertop. He twisted to raise the handgun again. As he did, Mykolas grabbed the kettle from the stove and swung it at Hunt's hand. He knocked the gun out and it skidded across the floor. Mykolas was on Hunt like a fighting dog. Teeth bared in a snarl. Grunting. Gasping for air. He charged and knocked Hunt's arms away again and got inside him. He slammed him back against the countertop and had his hands around Hunt's throat. Hunt grabbed Mykolas back on the throat and the Lithuanian lifted Hunt's head and slammed him back down. He lifted and slammed, lifted and slammed trying to subdue him. Hunt wasn't going anywhere. As Mykolas lifted his head again Hunt managed to create space between them and raised his knee to his chest. Hunt shot out a boot and caught the Lithuanian right in the sternum. The wind knocked out of him and Hunt's size twelves sent the operative reeling backwards into the kitchen table. He yelled out in pain as his lower back smacked into the edge of the table. Mykolas reached backwards and grabbed a carving knife from the chopping board. He swung it wildly at Hunt's face and neck. Hunt leaned back and ducked and grabbed the Lithuanian by the elbow. Hunt drove him hard and fast back into the cabinets. One of the doors flew open and plates and dishes fell out of the cupboard and crashed to the floor. Hunt swung heavy right hands into Mykolas' side and head and held the arm with the knife pinned under his chin. The Lithuanian grunted and snorted and tried to get free. He dropped the knife. Hunt's knuckles were bloody and sore from slamming into the Lithuanian's skull and ribs. Hunt grabbed him and threw him onto the ground. He hit the deck with a heavy thud and gasped for the air that was knocked out of his lungs. Hunt dropped down. Knees either side of him and pressed his fist into the operative's throat and jaw as he threw overhand punches into anywhere there was a gap. Hunt's nose was running. Every punch smeared more blood on Mykolas face, neck, and chest. Spit and saliva were coming out of both men. They were running out of steam. Mykolas looked around desperately for something to get him out of the pinned position. His hand fumbled next to him as he stretched out. Hunt continued to land heavy punches. Mykolas balled up his extended fist and plunged a punch into Hunt's side. It caught him right under the ribs and Hunt let out a low moan. The Lithuanian scrambled and grasped a sharp piece of broken plate. Hunt moved to stop him but the Lithuanian wriggled out and managed to get on top of Hunt. He was holding the broken shard in both hands, blood dripping through his fingers and onto Hunt's face, as he pressed down with all his weight to try and sink the pointy end into Hunt's throat. Hunt held up the man's weight and tried to hold him there. His energy was sapping away. The sharp point inching closer to his skin. Just then Hunt used his knees to rock Mykolas in the back. It forced the Lithuanian forward and changed the angle. He unbalanced and Hunt grabbed a washing-up cloth hanging from the oven. He wrapped it quickly around Mykolas' wrists and twisted his body to get out from under him. The Lithuanian dropped the shard and tried to get himself free. Hunt loosened the towel and wrapped it around Mykolas' neck. Hunt was behind him now. The tea towel around the operative's neck. Both men were smeared and caked in blood. Hunt was pulling hard on Mykolas' neck. He strained and let out a whimper as he did. He was fighting for his life. He pulled and held on. Mykolas' rasped and gargled as he flayed, grabbing at the towel, trying to scratch Hunt's face, kicking out for any kind of purchase. His energy started to drop. His writhing became less intense. His eyes were bulging out of his head and the purple colour of his skin shone through the smears and streaks of blood.

Hunt glanced up. Tibs was standing there. Watching him. She had a look of horror on her face. It was disgust mixed with hate. She was pointing the handgun at him. She cocked it and aimed for his head. Hunt couldn't stop.

"Let him go," she said. It was barely above a whisper. Then, "I said, let him go!"

Hunt kept holding on. Mykolas' body went limp. His head lolled to the side. Hunt heard his windpipe crunch as his muscles gave way. Tibs fired. The round smashed into the wooden cabinet door just to the side of his head.

"Okay," Hunt said and let go of the tea towel and lifted his hands beside his head. "He's dead," Hunt rasped. "He's dead."

HUNT FELT EXHAUSTED. HIS BODY ACHED. HIS HANDS were swollen. Tibs sat opposite him at the same kitchen table with the gun pointed directly at him.

"We have to get out of here, Tibs," Hunt said.

"Don't call me that."

"I see ... okay. Well, what do I call you?"

She shook her head. Hunt put his hands on the table in front of himself.

"I said, don't move," she said and lifted the barrel. "Shut up. Put these on," she said and slid some cable ties across the table.

"We've got to go, you know they're coming for us."

"For you—"

"It's not an extraction team, Tibs! Sorry. *Errr*, lady. It's not an extraction team. It's a kill team and they're coming to kill whoever is in this house."

"You don't know that ..."

"Who're you working for?" Hunt asked.

She glanced away.

"Tell me," Hunt said. "I might be able to help you."

"Like you helped Tom Holland?" Hunt was stunned into silence. "I said shut up and put those on."

Hunt furrowed his brow and looked at the cable ties around his wrists and pulled them tight with his teeth.

"Fine. Happy now?" he said. She nodded. "What're you talking about, Tom Holland?"

"Don't play dumb. I know you too well now to know you can't pull it off. You know exactly what I'm talking about."

"I didn't murder Tom Holland. I wasn't even in the country at the time of his death."

"Our intelligence says different," Tibs said. "It's plausible, likely even, that you were in the country at the time and used Robin to create a false *alibi*."

"You can ask my old head of section, Gerry Soames," Hunt said. "He can tell you."

Tibs didn't reply. She pursed her lips. Hunt studied her face.

"So you're working for Soames? I thought he was demoted or kicked out of the service."

She didn't respond, just looked away.

"Why would I kill Tom? What possible motive could I have for murdering him?" Hunt asked.

"Perhaps he was onto you. Your play with the Russians —"

"My play!? What play. You think I have something to do with them?"

"Your sister certainly does. Your mother certainly did."

"You don't know what you're talking about. You think you can read a file and get fed a shovel of shit and understand me?"

"Stop talking now," Tibs said.

"Or what? You'll shoot me. Are you going to tell them you could have saved your precious safe house keeper's life, except you couldn't because you couldn't shoot me then?

And you expect me to believe you'd kill me now? They want me alive. Whoever they are."

Tibs was silent.

"Who are you working for? MI5? The Met? Is this about the murder?"

"This is about treason," Tibs said.

"Listen to me," Hunt said. He took a deep breath and calmed down. He lifted his hands slightly off the table.

"Keep them down. On the surface," Tibs said.

"Fine. Listen to me. Whatever you think this is about, it isn't, okay? Whatever is going on, Mints, the Russians, the Albanians, whoever is buying and selling nuclear weapons."

"Yes, or you are the one selling it for them. How do I know you aren't in on it and playing both sides from the inside."

Hunt shook his head. "I can't believe this."

"Believe it. It's happening. You're coming back with me and you'll be investigated and put on trial."

"You mean tortured and found to have suffered a heart attack in my flat."

"It's Soames, isn't it?" Hunt asked. "That's who you're working for."

Just then there was a buzzing sound. Someone was riding the buzzer incessantly. Tibs started to rise.

"Come on, get up, you walk ahead. Go to the control room."

Hunt did as he was told. She kept the gun pointed at him all the way. Hunt walked into the control room with his hands up. It was grainy black-and-white footage. It was snowing outside. White flecks of snow jumped in front of the camera. Tibs walked in behind him.

"I'm telling you, that is not an extraction team," Hunt said. "That is a kill team."

The guy on the monitor had a hooked nose. Long black hair parted in the middle. Well-groomed facial hair. Black leather jacket. He looked Middle Eastern. Tibs hesitated, unsure. Then pressed the intercom.

"Yes?"

"Parcel collection," the Arabic-looking man said.

Tibs glanced at Hunt. "Authentication?"

"Sure, *ah*," the guy looked at a slip of paper in his hand. "Blue Orchid Insurance."

Tibs pressed zero and dialled the number for the command centre.

"Management."

"Authentication."

"Send."

"Blue Orchid Insurance," Tibs said.

There was a long pause.

"Confirmed," the voice came back.

"Come on, it's cold out here," the guy on the intercom said.

"Okay, you're cleared, come in."

"This is a mistake," Hunt said as he watched Tibs hand hover above the keypad. She pressed the buzzer. As soon as she did Hunt watched the Middle Eastern guy push the door open and wave in a team that's been lurking in the shadows. They were in full black tactical gear and they weren't westerners.

They burst into the safe house. Hunt heard the clink and thuds of flash bangs and gas being thrown. Men were shouting and running down the corridors. Tibs looked scared. Hunt went to close the door and lock them in.

"No!" she yelled and fired. Hunt's ears were ringing. She'd fired right next to his head. He could smell the smoke from the discharge all around him. He went to push the control room door shut again and as he did a submachine gun and an arm came through. Hunt rammed against it and the guy attached to the arm screamed out. Hunt pushed but he couldn't get it shut. Just then a canister came bouncing in through the gap and exploded. The gas stung Hunt's eyes and throat. His skin felt like it was being ripped off. Tibs was coughing violently. There was nowhere for the smoke to go. It was useless. Hunt let the door fall open and collapsed to the ground coughing and wrenching in the cloud of gas. The last thing he saw was the heavy butt of a shotgun coming down and connecting with his cheekbone and knocking him out.

THIRTY-THREE

McKenna stood in the European Command Centre listening to the radio communications coming from *HMS Entrenchment*. The room was engaged with what was happening on the radio channel. McKenna's phone buzzed. He took it out of his pocket to check who it was and then looked up and signalled to Sabrina Rocca, his second-in-command to take over the headquarters. She nodded and moved to where he was standing in the centre of the room. McKenna made his way to the rear and answered his phone.

"Any sign of her?" he asked.

There was a one-second pause. "No, sir," Dennison said. He was one Mastiffs. MI6 internal security. He was used to cleaning up other people's messes.

"What do you mean, Neil?"

"No sign of her, sir."

"You've been to the apartment?"

"My men are combing through it now."

"And tech? I need whatever she has on her system."

"That's going to be tough, sir. We've got two signals

guys here now. They're really struggling to get into her system."

McKenna heard someone in the background say 'bloody impossible'. Dennison covered the speaker with his hand and told whoever it was to 'shut it' with an added expletive.

"Sorry 'bout that, sir."

McKenna massaged his temples and tried to think.

"What about the cat?" McKenna asked.

"Cat's here, in fact, she's circling my shin as we speak."

"She wouldn't leave the cat, would she?" McKenna said. Dennison didn't respond. "Course you wouldn't know, Neil. You'd waterboard your own mother, wouldn't you?"

"Only if she spoke ill of the country, sir."

"Yes ..." McKenna agreed.

"We've got all ports covered, sir. She's not leaving the country without us knowing about it. She'll turn up, sir."

Yes, McKenna thought. You would think that unless you knew the kind of individual you were dealing with. He needed time to think.

"Call me if you turn anything up. Whatever you do, Neil, I need access to her system. I need to know what she was up to. Understood?"

"Roger that, sir."

McKenna hung up. He found another number on his mobile and dialled it. It rang. McKenna waited. He thought it was going to ring out. He was about to hang up when the ringtone stopped. He heard breathing and wind rush in the background.

"Mykolas you bloody soviet spy, is that you? Where's Hunt?"

McKenna waited. It was silent on the line.

"Where's Hunt?" McKenna asked, this time quieter, more sombre.

"He's out of the game," a female voice said.

The line went dead. They weren't supposed to kill him, McKenna thought. He was suddenly very hot. He wiped his brow with the back of his wrist and then wiped it on his trousers. Mykolas was supposed to bring Hunt in. Who was that woman? He was losing control of the situation. If I ever had any, McKenna thought. He went back into the control room. A few heads turned towards him and then back at the monitors when they saw it was him. He stood next to Rocca who didn't look at him.

"Where are we?" McKenna asked.

"Submarine nearly on target," Rocca said.

McKenna glanced at her face. She didn't look at him.

THE HMS ENTRENCHMENT GLIDED SILENTLY BENEATH the polar ice cap. The submarine's twin screws turned noiselessly pushing the Royal Navy's newest research sub along under the roof of ice above her. A proximity warning buzzed loudly and a silent red bulb flashed.

"Turn off that bloody noise," Captain Pierre Gregory-White said while standing in the periscope stand. The light stopped flashing and the buzzer was silenced. The control room was still again. His eyes were focused on the optical piece and he studied the waters around the subs titanium and plate-carbon steel double hull. Above him, there were stalactites of sharp ice plunging eighty feet or more. They were all around the sub. Ridges caused by pressure as the Arctic ice pressed and moved and twisted itself below the surface. He was captaining a research class of British submarines, and the last thing he wanted was to crash into one of these mountains of ice. Right now, all he knew was, they'd been sent on a top-secret mission. Co-ordinates, looking for an installation of some kind. He had little more to go on than that. And, he knew 'they' were listening.

"*Mein Gott*," Gregory-White heard from behind him and saw Doctor Erika Mueller, a NATO-imbedded researcher there to assist in their primary mission, a study of the floating mountains carving off the Arctic polar cap. Gregory-White stepped away from the periscope.

"Commander Brink," Gregory-White said. "You have the conn." He joined Doctor Mueller.

"Fancy checking it out from the observation bubble?" Gregory-White asked. He was formal with her in front of the men and women on the bridge but the forward observation bubble was called the *fobble* by the crew. "Come on," he said. "Come and see it with your own eyes."

She nodded and turned to follow him. This submarine had been modified specifically for research. As such, forward of the bridge were research labs and beyond the labs was a cavernous section at the front of the sub. Gregory-White shut the hatch behind them.

Designers had been thinking of ways to create more visibility from inside a submarine for decades. Different kinds of materials had been used to try and create safe, useful viewing platforms. None had worked but new technology was changing the possibilities.

Captain Gregory-White handed Doctor Mueller a virtual reality headset. She put the white, skiing goggle-like headset over his eyes. Gregory-White did the same. They stood at the front of the sub with open space around them.

"We're ready," the captain said to the technical staff in the room.

After a few seconds of looking out into the jet-black water and the submarine's xenon headlights shining against the eery, glassy ice, Mueller said, "It feels like I'm flying. It's everything I dreamed it would be!"

Gregory-White had to resist the urge to crouch down. Standing inside the bubble felt like the entire weight of the ice continent would come bearing down on them. He tried to control his breathing and stay in the moment. The view was so realistic and clear that it was as if they were in the freezing water. The high-definition cameras installed all around the submarine gave them a perfect three-hundred-and-sixty-degree view of their surroundings in real time. While the technology was still in the test phase, it had the potential to change the game for submarines. Connected to satellites or long-range drones, submarine captains could get a view of exactly what was around them at all times without exposing themselves to the enemy.

"We're testing the new LIDAR system," he said.

"What're we looking for?" Mueller asked.

"Something in the ice." She furrowed her brow. "I'm told there *may* be an old ice station down here," Gregory-White said.

LIDAR (Light Detection and Ranging) was new technology for submarines employing lasers to give heat signals back to the system. This, in turn, allowed users to map a picture of what a target looked like beyond the surface. Traditionally difficult to penetrate water, *HMS Entrenchment* was one of the first in a new class of submarines equipped with the technology to allow submarines to 'see' underground and into ice.

"We're hoping to prove a use case for the SightLine system by surveying the ice and seeing if we can find any non-natural matter inside," Gregory-White said.

As SightLine fired invisible lasers at the huge column of

ice a luminous red, green, and yellow image started to appear in their headsets.

"What *is* that?" Mueller asked and put her hands on the sides of the headset as if she was trying to peer further into it.

"Could you zoom in please," Gregory-White asked the technicians.

"What is that?" Mueller asked again.

Gregory-White looked at the thick disk-shaped caverns which showed up black on his screen against a field of bright green. There were five of them each with a connecting tube. They grew bigger the deeper they went into the ice.

"It's an abandoned ice base built into the side of the ice shelf. Seems like rooms connected by corridors. Definitely not a natural formation," Gregory-White said.

"What about these things?" Mueller asked and waved her finger in front of her face indicating things on the screen that nobody else could see.

"Sully," Gregory-White said, speaking to one of the technicians. "Is that what I think they are?"

The technician zeroed in on darker objects scattered around in the lowest level.

"Bodies, sir. I think. Those are dead bodies."

Mueller gasped.

"Give me a count," Gregory-White said.

"I count twelve, no, thirteen, sir," Sully said.

"Same as me," Gregory-White confirmed. "Radiation?"

"We're picking up traces, sir."

"Give me some decent close-ups of what we see, I need to make a report," Gregory-White said.

EVERETT MCKENNA AND SABRINA ROCCA LISTENED patiently to Captain Gregory-White's report over secure comms.

"And you're sure?" McKenna asked. Rocca furrowed her brow and shook her head.

"Sir, as the captain of a Royal Navy submarine, I am as sure as I can be. We could try to dock and gain access to the ice base but I believe we'd be in a sketchy area, legally speaking, if we boarded an enemy country's polar base without the proper authority."

"There's no radiation, you say, captain?" Rocca said.

"That's correct ma'am. There is a residue. A lingering quantity, like a fingerprint, of where nuclear components may have recently been but there is no sign of anything there at the moment."

"Damn it!" McKenna said into his balled-up fist.

"Sorry it's not better news, sir," Gregory-White said.

"You and your team have done a great job," Rocca said and slapped McKenna lightly on the shoulder telling him to get a hold of himself.

"Thank you, ma'am, I'll pass it on."

"Out," Rocca said and ended the communications.

"So no nuclear warheads, an AWOL cyber criminal, one Oberon operative missing presumed dead, thirteen dead Russians," McKenna said. "And, what the hell are we going to do now?"

THIRTY-FOUR

THE HELICOPTER SHOOK AND GYRATED AND HUNT twisted uncomfortably trying to get into a better position. The cable ties on his wrists had been replaced with steel handcuffs locked to a chain connected to his ankles. The chain was too short and he was forced to sit forward to relieve the tight pressure on his wrists and ankles.

"What'd you do with her?" Hunt asked. He spoke into the microphone attached to the radio headset he was wearing. His mouth hurt from where his cheek had impacted against his teeth. The butt of the rifle made him bite his tongue. His words came out sounding like he'd had a local anaesthetic in his gum. He looked up and saw Natalia Sukolova sitting opposite him. Her ice-coloured eyes were burning into him. He'd never felt someone radiate so much hate for him as he felt from her. It made him want to explain. Give his side. The only issue was that it would be like trying to explain how a deer feels to a tiger. Natalia was like a wild animal. Her bloodlust for him was like a predator in the wild. She ran on instincts and didn't bother with motive. She didn't need any. Shoot first, don't ask any questions later. That was her. Shoot first, and never think about them again.

"Hey," Hunt said and caught her eye. Natalia looked at him. "Did mum ever talk to you about her time with us—with me—in Africa?" Hunt asked her.

She was silent. All he could hear was the hardworking engines fighting the cold and the wind outside. He couldn't see anything through the windows. It was pitch black.

Hunt tried again, "Talk to me sis, where are we going?"

"Hush now, little Stirling. Save your strength. You're going to need it," Natalia said. It was full of menace and filled him with angst.

Finally, she spoke, he thought.

"I didn't do it, you know," Hunt said and tried to give her a warm, brotherly-like smile. She gave a single, inaudible laugh. He could see her thinking it over. Then her face relaxed as if to say, 'fine, I'll bite.'

"Do what, exactly?"

"Whatever it is you think I did. Whatever your reasons for this vendetta against me are."

Now she scoffed. She rolled her eyes and looked out of the window.

"Be quiet," Natalia said again. This time it was stern like she was scolding a child. "They've promised me time alone in a room with you once we get where we're going. I promise we can talk then."

The hiss of her voice through the headset and her perfect red lipstick against the bottle blonde hair pulled back in a ponytail made it all the more sinister. Hunt was sure by 'talk' she meant 'torture'.

"I didn't do it, you know. Kill mom," Hunt said. This time he was pleading with his sister to understand. She shook her head and avoided looking at him. "We tried to get you."

Suddenly she snapped.

"You tried!? You tried to do what? You were flying—"

"You ran off!"

"—You didn't try! You left me there and then you killed her."

"Natalia—"

"Don't call me that, don't you dare speak my name," she spat.

"Okay, sorry, but you must try to understand. We were in danger—"

"I was in danger too—"

"We tried to get you, we did—"

"You left, you didn't come back. Now she's dead. You were flying. It's your fault."

"How do you think we crashed?" Hunt asked her. "You think it just malfunctioned."

"You were flying. Incompetent, entitled ..." she swore violently in Russian.

"Is that what he told you?" She stopped and glared at him. "Is that what Mints told you?" Her forehead creased. "He obviously wouldn't tell you that we were shot down, would he?"

She gave a slight shake of her head like she was trying to get him out of there.

"Stop talking, now," she said.

"We were shot down by your father figure, Natalia!"

"I said stop talking, or I'll have them shut you up," she said and indicated one of the rough-looking mercenaries beside her. They didn't have headsets on but they could sense the tension, Hunt thought.

"We were shot down—" Hunt started to say.

"But you're alive," Natalia said. "You're sitting here, alive. Where is my mother? How could you survive and she died?"

Hunt closed his eyes and bowed his head. He didn't want to relive that moment. He didn't want to feel the freezing water around him again while trying to resuscitate his asphyxiated mother.

"She drowned," Hunt said. Natalia said nothing. She watched him with scorn on her face. "She drowned," Hunt said again. "I tried to save her, but we hit the water too hard. There was no time. It was like hitting concrete," Hunt said. "I drowned too but some kids found me. I couldn't save her." Hunt started to cry. It was an uncontrollable sob. It started in his throat and rushed up his head to his eyes. He blinked away the tears because he couldn't wipe them on his arms.

"You're pathetic," Natalia said.

Hunt sniffed. "Yeah, maybe I am. But I know the truth. I know you've been lied to. I know what really happened. Ask your precious Anatoly. Look into his eyes and see if those eyes can convince you. I looked into her eyes when she died. She wanted to get away from him. She wanted to get you away from him. And he killed her."

Natalia leaned forward and grabbed a cable plugged into the wall beside Hunt. She yanked it out and the hissing in his ears stopped. Now all he could hear was the loud wind rush and droning engine and propeller noise. Natalia looked out of the window.

THIRTY-FIVE

"You know," a quiet voice echoed behind him, "with the sea ice receding here, billionaires wanted to mine Greenland for her rare Earth metals to power their batteries. It could be part of a climate solution, they said; I said it could be the perfect symbol for our dystopian times."

Hunt heard footsteps behind him and turned his head to listen. He flinched at the cold touch to his shoulder. He was underground. He could feel the cold on his naked torso. He could hear the steady drip-drip-drip of melting ice around him. Hunt heard someone crouch down in front of him. He pulled his head back and away as hands touched the eye mask they'd put around his head.

"Let's get a look at you," the voice said. Hunt blinked in the dim light. He saw a slender, young, well-dressed man on his haunches in front of him. "You know," the man said. "I wasn't sure if I wanted to come and see you. The thought of it, a man down here, chained against his will like some crazed predator. I didn't know if it was the right thing to do … to come and see you. But then I thought, I need to see him. I need to see the face of the people who would stop me

—sent like white blood cells protecting the host, fan out and scour the body for infection. They call us a virus, don't they Mister Hunt? But what is a virus really? Sometimes it is a cure for evil. Sometimes —"

Hunt tried to get his tongue around his swollen lips and cheeks to speak. He just made a garbled noise and then swallowed and cleared his throat and said, "Yes, the only thing you're missing is that I have no idea who you are."

The man laughed and stood up. He had a glint in his blue eye and showed Hunt a perfectly straight set of whitened teeth. He had dimples on the side of his grinning mouth and Hunt imagined how satisfying it would be to wipe that smirk off his face.

"Tell me, how often does a body know the name of the invader? Your blood simply seeks out anything that it feels doesn't belong. It's the same with the system. Anything that doesn't conform is a threat. It was the same with the preachings of Jesus. A man with a single idea brought down an entire empire. Look it up," the man said, seeing the quizzical look on Hunt's face. "The early Christians were the only conquered people who refused to amalgamate with the rest of the dysphoria of people in the Roman Empire by refusing to acknowledge the existence of any God but theirs. That seed. That tiny implanted concept eventually overthrew the whole system. So, tell me, when is a virus, and when is it progress or a saviour?"

Hunt coughed. He was cold but he felt like he coughed to avoid having to entertain the grandiose ravings of someone so clearly unhinged.

"So what does one do?" the man mused. He put his hand on his chin enjoying the attention. Forced or otherwise. Hunt wondered who else was in the crowd in the shadows behind him.

"Sorry, but who the hell are you?" Hunt asked.

The man tutted. "Now, now, silly Stirling. Never you mind. There is no time for that, we won't have long now."

"Heard it all before mate, believe me. If you're expecting to trade me, you're wasting your time. I'm the most dispensable person you've ever met. To them, sure, but to myself too. Do whatever you like."

"Oh, I intend to. You see, I'd like to know exactly what they know. And, when the time is right, I believe one of the billionaires who was sniffing around the treasure hunt for nickel and cobalt has a special request for what should happen with you."

"There's nothing you can offer me," Hunt said.

"Oh, really?" the man looked amused. "I think your nephew would disagree ..." The look on Hunt's face had told his prison warden everything he needed to know. "Ah, you didn't know? Why yes young Hunt, your sister has a boy. Don't worry, he's very well looked after. For now. He has the best of everything. Boarding school in Switzerland. A nanny. He doesn't get to his mommy very often, that is true, but surely she would rather him be alive, no?"

Hunt shook his head. He strained at the hard wire tying his hands.

"What do you intend to do?" Hunt asked.

"Have you heard of Gaia?" the man asked.

"Mother Nature," Hunt said.

"Yes but the cryptocurrency?" Hunt shook his head no. "Pity, so you are so very far behind me. This almost seems like a waste of my time. Gaia is what funded all of this," the man said looking around the room. "We use the naturally cold climate underground in Greenland's used and abused mines to store our servers. No air conditioning required. Gaia is a global currency now. It is everywhere. And, we've used the proceeds to enact our singular mission. We have to save the Earth before it is too late. We need to give her time to renew herself. How do we do that?"

"Nuclear war," Hunt said.

The man in front of him pulled a face like Hunt had just told the punchline to the joke before he'd finished.

"Not just any nuclear war, Field Agent Hunt, Oberon Project. Military Intelligence Six, winner of the Conspicuous Gallantry Cross ... Global nuclear annihilation." His captor's voice crescendoed as he spoke the words. He looked down at Hunt and said, "You look dubious."

"Wouldn't you? It's not possible."

"So they say—but just for the sake of argument—explain the British nuclear deterrent to me."

"Second strike weapon. Guaranteed nuclear threat fired from an untraceable submarine immediately after an attack on the UK."

"It's a bingo! This man knows his stuff. Now for a moment, imagine that Trident became a first stole weapon —"

"As I said, impossible," Hunt said.

The man laughed. "I know, right! Well, what if someone launched nuclear missiles at the UK and they appeared—very convincingly—to come from Kaliningrad. Say, London, or Edinburgh was hit, what do you suppose those submarine commanders would do? Not fire?"

Hunt thought about it. This person, with the funds, the know-how, and the influence, attacks the United Kingdom with the express wish that Her Majesty's Government respond in kind.

"You want a nuclear war," Hunt said. He couldn't hide his incredulity. "You're a climate extremist," Hunt said. The man didn't respond. He waited. Watching. "Isn't there a conflict of interest between destroying the world in a mush-room cloud?"

"Do you know how many nuclear weapons America has?"

Hunt shook his head. "Not exactly."

"Several thousand. Same with Russia. The Chinese are catching up. India, Pakistan. Mutually assured destruction Mister Hunt. We're too smart for Gaia. We're the virus, don't you see? We're killing her."

Hunt thought he might break down in tears. The cracking voice and damp eyes were replaced with clenched jaw and angry eyes. "This is her revenge. Someone from the inside. You see we can use our own human hubris against ourselves. We'd rather all die for revenge than live together for peacefulness."

"Poetic," Hunt said.

"No. True poetry will be watching the western human race destroy itself in a global nuclear war."

"You're hoping to make the very place you want to save uninhabitable," Hunt said.

"Tut-tut, Mister Hunt. On the contrary. You hear that quiet hum?" His captor lifted his hand and cupped his ear and listened. Hunt heard it. "Those are my servers. Enor-mous computing power. We feed it data and it feeds us scenarios. The safest place to be in the case of global ther-monuclear war—"

"Africa," Hunt said.

"You beat me to it again. Yes, indeed. Sub-Saharan Africa. Specifically Mozambique. You see, the land is cheap there. Life is cheap. After the fallout, which we will spend below ground near the coldest part of the planet, we will venture south in my specially designed yachts, submarines if we have to, and we will start a new colony there."

"You're insane."

"Perhaps. My question always is, so what? Ask yourself, what if you're the insane one and we're the sane ones?"

Hunt didn't have an answer. What was sanity? He didn't know.

"You see, we've cultivated a group of like-minded people. They live on my ecological estates and are at one with the planet they serve."

"A cult," Hunt said. "You're talking about a cult."

"Just a label, Mister Hunt. Just a label. It doesn't mean anything. People scream their heads off at athletes and wear the same colour shirts, are they in a cult? You worry about some imaginary monetary system and how much money you owe some imaginary corporation. Is that a cult?" Hunt didn't respond. "We're no more a cult than—"

"Scientology," Hunt said.

"Christianity," the man countered.

"Christians aren't trying to end the world," Hunt countered.

"Oh, contraire, that's exactly what they want. Haven't you read the book of Revelations? That's exactly what they want and exactly what they get and I hope they meet their God. You've certainly just had the pleasure of meeting yours ..." The man looked to the back of the room and signalled. Hunt heard two sets of footsteps.

"Natalia, I want to know everything he knows. Everything. I want to know what he got for his eighth birthday. Everything, understand." He checked his watch and looked down at Hunt. "Don't skip any juicy details now, you hear? I need those answers in fifty-six minutes and counting. That's when we fire our missiles at London."

THIRTY-SIX

VAN DEN KRIJL LEFT THEM ALONE IN THE CAVERNOUS rock-walled room. Hunt heard a heavy metal door slam. There was the constant running and dripping of water. It was damp and very cold. He sat naked on a freezing cold metal chair. His hands and arms were strung together behind his back. He was fading. Adrenaline kept him awake but he felt he was slipping into delirium.

"Did you hear her scream?" Hunt's eyes snapped open. He looked up at his sister standing before him. She looked warm in a white mink scarf and heavy cashmere jersey under her leather coat. "You did hear her scream, didn't you?" Natalia asked.

Hunt had. He'd kept his granite features motionless in front of the crypto billionaire terrorist. He'd know those anguished cries anywhere. They had Robin. The only question now was, did someone give her up, or were they smart enough to catch her on their own. Hunt couldn't believe Robin had left anything to chance. He assumed someone had given her up but whom? Hunt felt another presence in the room. Back, over his right shoulder, standing in the shadows. One of Natalia's goons.

"I really wanted to know every juicy little detail." Natalia's heavy Muscovite accent was laced with venom. Hunt knew she had the fangs to back it up too. Hunt shivered. He was freezing but the thought of Natalia going to work on soft, delicate, beautiful Robin froze him to his core. "I made her tell me everything. Everything. Most curious how you met," Natalia said, switching out the English words she didn't know for Russian ones. Hunt knew enough to understand her meaning.

"What did you do to her?" Hunt asked. Natalia nodded to the man behind him. Hunt heard the figure step forward before he could glance to the side he was hit by a fist wrapped in a leather strap. It caught him flush on his right cheekbone and his head snapped to the side. He felt the blood trickle into his mouth. He leaned forward and spat. Natalia grabbed him under the chin and twisted his head to look at the man standing over him.

"This is Ivan. His father was one of the men you killed at Mints' compound. He asked me specifically if he could be present for your questioning."

Hunt groaned. "You mean torture," Hunt said. Nothing worse than being at the mercy of someone out for revenge. Ivan stepped forward to hit him again. Hunt flinched but Natalia held up her hand and Ivan postured as if he intended to hit him. Hunt had seen that move a thousand times by young, drunk, angry men who had more interest in showing dominance without resorting to actual violence. Weak men. Men who would rather have a loud bark than a sharp bite. The type of man who would hit someone sitting in a chair. Hunt ignored Ivan. He wasn't afraid of the pain anymore. How could he care about such a weak man hurting him? Hunt would always be a better man than that and he knew it. His disdain for his torturer meant the pain inflicted immediately felt less poignant.

"What'd she tell you?" Hunt asked.

"All about the two of you, actually. How very sweet. Unrequited love." Hunt furrowed his brow. "Oh! You thought she was in love with you. No ... not this time, my dear. In fact the opposite. She has been using you. In other words, she told me everything." Natalia nodded and out of nowhere Hunt felt the stern snap of leather against his cheek. Hunt's head shot to the side and blood dribbled out of his mouth. "He's very accurate, isn't he, our Ivan," Natalia said and glanced up at the huge Cossack.

Hunt'd had enough. If he was dead anyway they may as well get it over with.

"That's enough, Ivan, thank you."

"Get back in your box, coward," Hunt spat.

"That's enough, Stirling," Natalia warned him. Her tone was different now but Hunt ignored it.

"What did you say," Ivan said in Russian.

Hunt replied to him in his own language. "I said, you— and your miserable father—are cowards. He died as a coward. His miserable son will have the same fate. I'll gut you like a—"

Ivan was on him instantly. Hunt barrelled over and Natalia jumped out of the way. The Cossack rushed him. Ivan was on top of Hunt and pummelling him with his balled-up fists. The rage tore out of the Russian in a high-pitched whine that tore from his throat like a fox at the mercy of a pack of hounds. Hunt's face was completely exposed. The Russian's swings were wild and inaccurate. His anger made it so he couldn't concentrate on inflicting the most amount of pain, just that he would tear Hunt apart

If he could. Hunt did his best to move and wriggle to avoid the shots. To Hunt, it seemed like an eternity. He was sure he was going to die. It suited him. Deep under the freezing earth in some godforsaken country he'd never been to. Beaten to death by a Russian whose father Hunt had murdered. Getting pretty much what he deserved, was his only thought.

Ivan's dinner plate-sized hands went to Hunt's throat. Hunt felt his cable-like fingers wrap around his neck and throat and begin to squeeze. He was in a death grip. Unable to move. Unable to get away. The Russian strained as he squeezed. Hunt felt his neck shrinking and compressing to the size of his spine. The world started to go. He heard only the whoosh of blood in his ears. It sounded like a faraway waterfall. It was over.

Just as he was resigning himself to his fate, he heard the unmistakable sound of a suppressed 9 mm bullet being fired. The suppressed gunshot thumped in the underground cavern. Hunt's face was turned to the side. There were a further two shots. Hunt felt the warm viscous spray of blood as it hit him in the cheek and on the side of his neck and chest. The massive Russian's body went limp and his dead weight lay on top of Hunt and crushed him.

"Argh, get him off!" Hunt said. He was panicking. He thought he was going to die. What'd happened? Someone saved him. Where was Natalia? Hunt struggled and tried to get out from under the Russian. His head ached. It was no use. Then he saw Natalia's face. She crouched to get under the Russian's limp shoulder. As she lifted and rolled the dead body, Hunt asked, "Why'd you do that? Why'd you save me?" Natalia heaved the body with some effort and managed to roll it off her brother. She pulled a knife from her coat and flicked it open. Hunt saw the blade glint. She'd killed her own comrade just so she could finish her brother off herself. Hunt turned away and closed his eyes as the blade came near his throat.

"Hold still," she said and reached down and cut his binds. Hunt rolled out of the chair and onto his front and coughed violently holding his throat.

"Miss Adler tells me they're planning to destroy Moscow," Natalia said. Hunt writhed and coughed and sat up.

"He nearly bloody killed me," Hunt said.

"You deserved it," Natalia said and folded and put her knife away.

"So why didn't you let him?"

"Is it true?"

"Is what true?" Hunt asked and massaged his throat.

"About the plan to bomb Moscow?"

"Why would she lie?"

"Just answer the question, bastard."

"You're the bastard as far as I remember," Hunt said. Natalia raised her handgun and pointed it at Hunt.

"Tell me," she said.

Hunt looked out of one eye at the gun in her hand. It was still. She was certain. She would kill him.

"Okay," Hunt said. "Yes. Our intelligence says he plans to hit London in an attempt to provoke a reaction. A retaliatory strike against Moscow."

"But the weapons are flying from Greenland," Natalia said.

"I've seen a military installation. Owned by your pal Mints, as far as I can tell, where they have bunkers and silos. I expect they'll create a diversion to make it appear as if the missile was fired from there ..." Natalia shook her head.

"You're lying."

"Why would I lie? You're in with a dangerous crowd, sis," Hunt said.

"Don't call me that."

"Fine. But it's true."

They both heard Robin scream.

"Get her in here and she can explain it. Maybe you trust her more than me."

"Why would I?"

"If you didn't know Moscow was the true target then someone lied to you. Was it Mints?"

Natalia didn't respond. Robin screamed again.

"For God's sake! Before they kill her. Ask her yourself."

"I have," she said. "Now I'm asking you. Tell me what you know ..."

"Get Robin in here and I'll spill the beans. Until then ... you can just kill me."

"Urgh!" Natalia vented. "You're insufferable." She pulled out her firearm and headed towards the steel door. "Put some clothes on for Christ's sake," she said.

Hunt looked down at Ivan and groaned as he stooped to undress the dead Russian.

THIRTY-SEVEN

"I'm telling you," Robin said as she watched Natalia's expression showing her dubiousness. Hunt finished buttoning his new jacket. Ivan's naked corpse lay at his feet and he tapped it with the tip of his new desert boots to test the fit. He dropped the corners of his mouth and nodded, *not bad, not bad*. Hunt glanced up and caught Natalia staring at him. Cold blue eyes, like the blood in her veins, he thought. She was listening to Robin but watching Hunt. Her desire for revenge against him had clouded her judgement. She couldn't see all of the permutations of her role in helping secure the warheads.

It seemed an insane scheme because it was. Ingenious. In a genocidal-criminal kind of way. The whole concept that underpinned the United Kingdom's Trident defence system was that of mutually assured destruction. It was a way of guaranteeing that if the UK was attacked by a nuclear weapon—or any weapon for that matter—Her Majesty's Government had a second strike capability no matter how dialled the country was. If Moscow fired nuclear weapons at the UK they were guaranteed to receive a nuclear strike in retaliation. And, as far as nuclear war theory went, this should ensure that no one was ever gung-ho enough to attack the UK. The possibility that eluded strategists was the exact loophole that van den Krijl was trying to take advantage of to bring about his group's extremist prophecy. As far as he was concerned, they didn't need to bring down the western capitalist system themselves, all he had to do was give the system a reason to destroy itself. His unregulated cryptocurrency backed by individual investors and venture capitalist billions gave him unchecked power to operate in the shadows. He was untraceable. He and his devout followers would start a new world, while the northern hemisphere regenerated. He saw himself like a piece of genetic code that seeks out and allows the body's natural defences to recognise and remove cancerous cells before they could replicate themselves into a tumour. He saw the human race as the tumour on earth's body. Robin was explaining this to Natalia who was listening intently while watching Hunt.

Fully dressed, he stepped forward and cleared his throat and said, "I'm sorry, I really don't mean to interrupt ..." he tapped his wrist, "but if I'm not mistaken we are on the cusp of nuclear war if van den Krijl is able to launch those missiles."

"How do you know I will help you?" Natalia asked Hunt. Robin answered for him, "Because we know about your son."

"How?" Natalia said. She seemed like she didn't want to believe it but their knowing meant it was true.

"There were signs. Strange payments from Mints' shell companies to private schools in Switzerland. We followed it up. He is Mints' child, isn't he?"

Natalia turned away. "He is in Moscow," she said quietly. It was barely audible.

"I have a nephew?" Hunt asked.

"We've got no time to waste," Robin said.

"We have to stop the launch," Hunt said.

Natalia swept her hair from her eyes and dabbed her eye with the finger of her glove. "I can delay the guards," she said. "I know most of them. We recruited soldiers on van den Krijl's behalf. They know me."

"How many are there?" Hunt asked.

"Not many. This is a secret location. It is meant to be uninhabited, except for the servers and the computers."

Hunt glanced at Robin and she at him. Had they thought the same thing at the same moment?

"It's only twenty minutes to launch now," Hunt said.

"What?" Natalia asked.

Robin turned to her. "I need access to the server room."

"This whole place is servers. They stretch down the old mine, huge rows of them blinking and buzzing," Natalia said.

"If I can get access to the servers I can get inside his system and make changes to the code from within."

"What will you do?" Natalia asked.

"Crash his cryptocurrency."

"I will do something else," Natalia said.

"Which is?"

"I will disable the nuclear warheads," Natalia said. "We were taught this method called pit-stuffing. If I can stuff a wire down the tube I can permanently disable the warheads."

"I've read about this," Robin said, "Every modern, boosted nuclear weapon has at its core a 'pit'—a hollow sphere of plutonium or highly-enriched uranium—with a tiny tube through it that allows the tritium to be fed into the hollow inside the sphere. If a steel wire is fed in through this small tube until the inside of the pit is 'stuffed' with tangled wire, the pit can no longer be compressed enough by the explosives surrounding it to sustain a nuclear chain reaction —the weapon is physically incapable of going off—"

"Listen, I'm sorry, that's very interesting but we don't have time for a science lesson here, we'll go to the server room and try to hack the system, you head to the silo and try to disable the weapons," Hunt said. "Let's go."

THIRTY-EIGHT

In London, Soames was on the phone with McKenna who wanted to know what happened to his agent and why he was hearing about missile silos being fired up near the Russian border at a site linked to Anatoly Mints.

"I'm actually just about to step in with the Prime Minister, McKenna," Soames said. "Got to go."

Soames hangs up the phone and steps into the Prime Minister's office in Downing Street.

"What the hell do you want Gerald?"

"Yes, Prime Minister. Glorious isn't it?"

"What?"

"Never mind, ma'am. I have something you should see. We are seeing activity near the Russian border."

"What sort? Forced marches?"

"Actually something more sinister. It seems someone in Russia is preparing to fire two nuclear-capable missiles."

"Dear God! What is the target?"

"We don't know ma'am but I have it on good intelligence that Everett McKenna was running a blacklisted agent called Stirling Hunt. He was in the vicinity of that bunker and military complex mere days ago. He has known ties to Russian FSB agents and is wanted for the murder of one of my own men, Thomas Holland."

The Prime Minister shook her head. "This sounds like something for Special Branch or MI5," she said.

"Yes, ma'am, indeed, forget the circumstance. What will we do if these missiles are fired at the UK?"

"Get me COBRA convened, now, and find out who has my actions-on in case of nuclear weapons are targeted at the UK."

"That would be—"

"Yes, I know—thank you—Gerald, you waste of human skin, the UK Nuclear Weapon Command Control and Communications—UK NC3—," the Prime Minister turned back to the phone.

"Were you talking to me, ma'am?"

"Not unless you're a waste of human skin, Margaret."

"No, ma'am," the voice said.

"Then I wasn't. Get me Chief of the Defence Staff for CBRN."

"C.B.R ..."

"Chemical, biological, and nuclear," the Prime Minister said.

"I see, yes ma'am."

"And get me a lawyer ... who knows about Prime Ministerial powers for a nuclear strike. And prepare to use my letters of last resort."

Van den Krijl is in his control room with his team of scientists, engineers, and technicians. This team will know all things nuclear work on a simple principle: when a heavy nucleus of an atom splits, it converts a tiny amount of mass into pure energy. That energy can be used to treat cancer, generate electricity, or level a city. There were only two things van den Krijl cared about during the design of the control room. The ability to monitor and track the strike price of his precious cryptocurrency, GaiaCoin, and the NASA-like design and layout of his rocket launch system. There was a large stock ticker running across the top of the screens at the front of the room showing the price of the cryptocurrency.

Something van den Krijl had come to understand was that nuclear blasts are triggered through an uncontrolled chain reaction in a large block of material, where each new split causes more splits, releasing more energy. It reminded him of a virus, each victim infecting the next until an exponential contagion—whether that be thoughts, an idea, or a movement—explodes. He felt tense, nervous even. He wanted it to work. He was one of the only people who knew the extent of what they were doing. The extent of it, the surprise of it, the intensity of it. His name would live on in history as the 'first man', the re-creator of the world. He could feel the power. He could see the potential of this new and improved vision for life on planet Earth.

"What's that?" van den Krijl said and leaned closer to the monitors. He was watching a feed of the missile silos. His workers were preparing the missiles for launch. He'd seen something. A woman. Natalia? No. She was downstairs extracting the last drop of information and the last drop of blood from Stirling Hunt. Partly, van den Krijl felt good that the authorities were on to him. He was not afraid. There was nothing they—or anyone else— could do to stop what was about to happen. All he needed was a few strategically placed chess pieces moved into position at the right times and he was practically assured of mutually assured destruction. Only a race like human beings could come up with something so violent, so exposed, and so evil, he thought. He was right. They needed to be eradicated. We need to start again.

"I'm doing the right thing," van den Krijl said.

"Sir?"

Van den Krijl looked across at a white-coated engineer. "Sir?" the technician said again. "Did you say something?"

"Find out what the hell she's doing in the missile silo," van den Krijl said.

"Yes, sir."

Van den Krijl watched her closely. She was walking along one of the steel walkways connected to the rocket. Van den Krijl couldn't have been the only one concentrating on the closed-circuit television screens. Natalia pulled out a suppressed 9mm handgun and lifted it towards one of the security guards on the platform. The control room collectively held their breath. There were two short sharp muzzle flashes and the guard dropped. The control room gasped collectively. A lone engineer with round glasses and a clipboard was left standing, frozen to the spot behind where the guard fell. Van den Krijl instinctively grabbed the handheld microphone. He pressed the button and shouted down the line in a frenzy.

"What the hell do you think you are doing!? Stop this instant! Have you lost your mind?"

Natalia flinched at the sudden loudspeaker echoing around the silo but as van den Krijl watched, she didn't deviate.

"Sound the alarm!" van den Krijl yelled. "Don't just stand there! Bloody do something!"

The room of quiet rocket scientists and engineers tried to look busy and avoid his rage. He was staring wide-eyed and unblinking at the screen. Natalia carried a balled-up knot of wire.

"What the hell is she doing? What the hell is she doing!" van den Krijl screamed.

Suddenly a general alarm started blaring. The light in the control room went from white to red. The scientists' lab coats glowed under the red light.

HUNT WAS DEEP IN THE SERVER ROOM LOOKING OVER Robin's shoulder. Her fingers were moving so fast over the keyboard that Hunt couldn't follow them. The code seemed to be printing itself automatically on the screen.

"How do you —" Hunt started to say and stopped himself.

She glanced over her shoulder and said, "Could you not?"

"Not what?"

"Not stand there looking over my shoulder. It's really distracting," Robin said.

"Sorry," Hunt said. "I just want to know what you're doing."

"Go and wonder somewhere else, shouldn't you be guarding me in case they find us."

"They'd have triggered an alarm," Hunt said. Just then sirens started sounding around them and red lights flashed.

"Right on cue," Robin said. Hunt heard shouts in the distance and heavy boots hitting cold steel as they ran.

"Okay," Hunt said. "I'll cover the entrance."

"Got it!" Robin yelled.

"*Shhh*," Hunt said and shushed her.

"Sorry."

"What is it?" Hunt asked.

"Van den Krijl stores everything—and I mean everything—on these servers. The firewalls and encryption are astounding. From the outside, unbreakable," she said. "But from the inside ..."

"You got in," Hunt said.

Robin raised her index finger high about the keyboard and dropped it onto the 'enter' key. "Not only did I get in," she said. "I have the code base for van den Krijl's cryptocurrency. He controls the supply of coins, which keeps their price high."

Hunt smirked. "What did you do?"

Robin turned and smiled that smile at him. "I might just have increased the supply of his GaiaCoin by several billion."

"From how many?"

"Around two hundred million," Robin said cheekily.

"So you've—"

"Crashed the price," she said. "Yep."

"Smart girl ..." Hunt said. He was about to head over to the entrance and stopped. "Hey, if you're in his system ... what else could you have access to?"

"Depends on what you want?"

"What about the code or backend—whatever you call it —for his navigation system."

"For the rockets?" Robin asked.

Hunt nodded.

"Let's see," she said and started typing again.

NATALIA FLINCHED AS THE ALARM STARTED BLARING. She kept her weapon raised and pointed it vaguely in the direction of the technician. He dropped his clipboard and put his hands up beside his head.

"P-p-p-p-please d-d-d-d-don't shoot, don't shoot me," the technician stuttered.

"You speak Russian?" Natalia asked.

He nodded swiftly.

"Where are you from?" she asked.

"Moscow," he said.

"Me too," Natalia said. She held up the balled-up wire in her hand. "You know what this is?"

The technician looked blankly at her.

"Do you know what this is!" she repeated, shouting over the siren. She heard footnotes and shouting behind her. "Answer me!"

"W-w-w-w-wire?"

"Do you know how to 'pit stuff' this warhead?" she asked.

"W-w-w-w-warhead?"

"What's your name?" Natalia asked him and glanced behind her to see how close the security guards were.

"It's Stenli."

A guard was holding on either side of the metal ladder and popped his head above the steel walkway. Natalia dropped to her knee, dropped the wire, held her weapon in both hands, aimed with one eye, and depressed the trigger. The suppressor kicked up and a look of shock hit the guard's face. A red hole opened in his forehead and he hung in suspended animation for a second before plunging backwards off the high ladder. Natalia turned back to the technician. Stenli was cowering.

"Stop shaking, Stenli." He nodded and glanced up at her. "You don't know this is a nuclear warhead?"

"I-i-i-it's inert," Stenli said.

"No," Natalia said. "It's live and they're firing it at Moscow."

"N-n-n—"

"Yes," Natalia said. "I'm FSB dear Stenli. You think I would be here otherwise?" Stenli dutifully shook his head. "They've kept you in the dark. Yes?" Stenli nodded and mouthed the word, 'yes'. "Okay. Now, do you know how to 'pit stuff' a nuclear warhead?"

Stenli nodded. "Y-y-y-yes."

There was a sudden, loud, hydraulic clank and a hiss of steam.

"What was that?" Natalia asked.

"T-t-t-they're preparing to launch," Stenli said.

VAN DEN KRIJL'S FACE WAS A DEEP PURPLE UNDER THE red lights in the control room. A vein looked like it would pop out of his face.

"What in the name of every loving God is going on! Get me London! Get me my head of trading!" Van den Krijl watched the price of GaiaCoin plunge from $17,567 a coin to under $100 in seconds. It kept going down. His mobile phone started buzzing and the screen lit up. Messages were piling onto the screen one after the other. Hundreds of them. He received so many alerts from his mobile that it danced its way to the edge of the table and fell onto the floor. He left it.

"Get me my head of—Oh! Bugger it I'll do it myself should I!?" Van den Krijl yelled and grabbed a landline phone off the desk. He held the phone close to his chest and punched in the numbers. As he did that he watched as Natalia shot and killed another of his guards. Van den Krijl stopped what he was doing. He had a sudden calmness to him. He hung up the receiver and placed the phone gently down on the desk.

"Prepare to launch," he said. It was so quiet as to be barely audible.

"Excuse me, sir?" the bald-headed lab coat asked.

Van den Krijl cleared his throat and stood to his full height. He lifted his chain and said, "Prepare the rocket to launch."

"But, sir, we—"

Van den Krijl fixed the bald lab coat with a look.

"I am not here to argue with you. You are not here to argue with me! You are here to fulfil my mission! Now, if you value your lungs filling with air on a regular basis you should do what I say—exactly what I say—right bloody now!"

Suddenly van den Krijl's mind clicked. The server halls. If Natalia Sukolova was in his missile silo then no one was with the prisoners.

"Get a security team to clear the server rooms. Now!" Van den Krijl yelled.

Robin called out for Hunt. He was being lookout.

"Stirling!"

"Coming," Hunt shouted back. "What?" he said as he jogged up to her.

"It's strange, his whole launch sequence and rocket control system is on a different system."

"What does that mean?"

"He was very careful to keep the missile controls air-gapped from the rest of the servers and the rest of the Gaia system."

"Okay ..." Hunt said. "Can you break it or not?"

"Of course," Robin said.

"Well stop talking and get it done," Hunt said.

She shook her head and clicked her tongue. They both heard it at the same time and glanced at one another. A heavy thud of metal doors slamming.

"They're coming," Hunt said.

"I know," Robin said. "I'm nearly there."

"I'll hold them off for as long as I can ..." Hunt said. He kept looking at her. She glanced up at him again from her laptop screen. He leaned in and kissed her. She kept typing for a moment and then stopped. Hunt kept kissing her. Her hand lifted and touched the side of his face. He pulled back. They were quiet.

"Okay," Hunt said. "Hurry up," and turned back to where the noises were echoing from. He heard Robin scoff behind him and he smiled.

"Wait!" Robin yelled from behind him.

"What is it?"

"They're launching! They're getting ready to launch. They're— they've started the launch cycle."

"Can you stop it?"

She shook her head. "No, I—"

"What is it? You can't stop it? Why—"

"It's too late," Robin said as she battered away at the keys. "I can't do anything! We're too late."

"Christ, what're we going to do?" Just then Hunt heard footsteps running in their direction. "Hold on," Hunt said and pulled out the dead Russian's weapon. He cocked it and walked silently to the end of the servers.

"I have an idea," Hunt heard Robin say from behind him.

. . .

Natalia had meanwhile killed another two guards. They were now firing sporadically at her from below. Stenli was fidgeting with the wire against the neck of the missile. A small aperture on the side of the rocket was open and he was feeding the wire in.

"I-I-I-c-c-c can't do it in time!" Stenli cried as he fed it in. A bullet ricocheted around them and he ducked. "A-a-a-and t-t-t-tell them to stop firing at a nuclear weapon!"

Natalia fired a round from a crouch position and went to the control panel next to where Stenli stood on a stepladder. She picked up the phone-style receiver.

"Hello?" Natalia said as another bullet pinged off the metal around them. She flinched instinctively and continued, "There is a live warhead here, idiots! Do you want to be responsible for damaging the weapon? Tell your goons to stop firing and we will leave your precious missile in peace." She hung up.

"Do you have it?" Natalia asked Stenli. Another shot was fired and pinged off the walkway. Then the shots ceased.

"I c-c-c-can't believe that worked," Stenli said.

"Yes, but has what you're doing worked?"

"Nearly," Stenli said. He was leaning at a precarious angle, his elbow up at ninety degrees trying to force the mangled bit of metal into the side of a nuclear warhead.

Hunt leaned around the side of a server mounting and fired. He heard someone scream out. Got another one, he thought.

"Stirling!"

Robin was shouting for him. He turned his cheek towards her and yelled back, "What?"

"Come here!"

"I'm a little busy right now," Hunt replied and turned back to fire another shot.

"I think I got it!"

"That's great," Hunt said to himself.

THINGS STARTED HAPPENING ON THE WALKWAY. IT WAS vibrating violently. There were lots of hissing and pipes clunking.

"We have to go now," Stenli said.

His stutter was gone, Natalia thought.

"You go, Stenli, get down and get away."

"You have to come with me," Stenli said. "They're going to launch and you'll be fried like an onion ring."

"We'll have to shoot our way out," Natalia said.

"After you," Stenli said and motioned for her to lead.

VAN DEN KRIJL WATCHED THE SCREENS. IT DIDN'T matter now if Natalia died or not. Nothing could stop him now. He bent down to pick up his phone. He wasn't interested in the hundreds of alerts about the crypto coin price, or the news outlets seeking comment on the spectacular collapse of his invention. He was only interested in one person. A lab coat with a headset started the countdown.

Ten.

Van den Krijl scrolled through his messages to the one he was waiting for.

Nine.

He opened it and checked what it said.

Eight.

With her now in the bunker. NC3 conveyed. Ready when you are. No signal from now.

Seven.

Van den Krijl put his phone away. The ever-reliable Gerald D. Soames. He was the crucial piece on the chessboard. He was right there, the King next to the Queen. Whispering in her ear.

Six.

The UK Prime Minister would have to make the decision. Soames was the silent spy who would influence the outcome of any emergency meetings. If she was holed up in a bunker then she was taking it seriously.

Five.

All eyes in the room turned to look at him. Van den Krijl's eyes stayed fixed on the screen.

Four.

He felt his heart rate leap. He squeezed his hands hard into fists and lifted them to his mouth.

Three.

The whole control room started to shake. The thruster's immense power made the desks and monitors gyrate.

Two.

He couldn't believe this was actually about to happen.

One.

It was like a moment of ecstasy. The roar was unbelievable. The power coursed like adrenaline in his veins. The control room clapped and whooped as the rocket went airborne and the noise and rumbling died down.

Not one of these poor fools even realises what they've just done, van den Krijl thought.

.   .   .

HUNT STOPPED FIRING AND LISTENED AS THE MISSILE launched into the atmosphere. I thought she was going to stop it, Hunt thought. Just then he heard the dull thud of suppressed rounds fired in double taps. Natalia, he thought and flicked the safety on.

"It's us," Hunt heard Natalia yell.

"Over here," Hunt said. "Who's this?"

Natalia turned to look at the technician following her.

"Stenli," she said. "Where is she?"

"Back there," Hunt said. "What about the guards?"

"Took care of it," Natalia said. They followed her back to Robin's station.

"What the hell happened?" Hunt asked. "I thought you were going to stop it?"

Robin was concentrating on the screen. "No, I told you I was too late."

"You said you had a plan."

"I do, kind of ..."

"Kind of?"

"Kind of, yes. It's a partial plan ..." Robin said as she kept hitting the keys.

"Go on," Hunt said and looked around anxiously. "I'm sure we're all very eager to hear it." He glanced at Natalia and Stenli and encouraged them to offer him moral support. They both nodded and Stenli said, "I-I-I-I—"

"Stenli would very much like to hear the plan," Natalia said dryly, interrupting him.

"My plan relies on your part of the mission working," Robin said and glanced at Natalia. "Well?"

"Well, what?" Natalia said in her sharp Russian tone.

"Well, did you manage to disable the device?" Robin asked.

Natalia looked at Stenli. "Well? Did you?" Natalia asked him.

"Oh!" Hunt said. Stenli's presence suddenly made sense.

Stenli shrugged.

"What do you mean?" Natalia said and shrugged back at him. "Did you do it or not?"

"I-I-I-I-I—" Stenli stuttered.

Natalia looked back at Robin. "He thinks he did it," she said.

"Okay," Robin said. "Well then ..." she entered some more information and hit 'enter'.

"Well then, what?" Hunt asked. They all looked at her.

"Well then I guess my plan is worth a try," Robin said.

"And that is?" Stenli asked.

"I've hacked the guidance system and overridden the controls—"

Stenli scoffed. "Impossible," he said. "I wrote that code myself." Robin spun the laptop to him. Stenli studied it.

"Where've you sent the missile?" Hunt asked.

Robin waited. Stenli studied the code.

"H-h-h-h-h—" Stenli stuttered but couldn't get it out.

"Come on," Natalia said and checked her weapons as she walked towards the exit. "I know a way out of here."

VAN DEN KRIJL STOOD ADMIRING HIS MISSILE AS IT blasted towards the stratosphere. The lab coats started fussing and talking amongst themselves. One of them called up to him.

"Sir? Sir. We have a slight problem. When I say slight, I mean, we have a problem."

"What is it?" van den Krijl asked.

"Well, sir, the—the—"

"Spit it out, man."

"The guidance system, sir."

"What about it?"

"The course is correcting drastically and we—"

"So course correct and it back on—"

"We've tried, sir. We've lost control. The missile won't respond to our commands!"

Van den Krijl looked up at the monitor. The missile was making an arc.

"Where is it going?" van den Krijl asked.

"Here, sir. It's been redirected to return to the launch site. It will make landfall in—" the lab coat checked his watch, "—seven minutes and seventeen seconds."

Van den Krijl lifted a red button cap on the desk in front of him. It was a self-destruct override. Van den Krijl glanced at the technician.

"And you're sure you have no way to regain control?" van den Krijl asked.

"No, sir. We have no way. Not in—" he checked his watch again.

"Yes, yes. I understand," van den Krijl said and scowled at him. "Someone is going to pay for this."

Van den Krijl flicked the self-destruct button. He watched the missile. Nothing happened. He furrowed his brow and flicked the button again. Nothing.

"Sir?" the lab coat said.

Van den Krijl started flicking the button up and down trying to get it to work. Nothing did.

"It won't work," van den Krijl said. The panic in his voice made the rest of the room glance at one another. Then they scrambled to try and get out.

. . .

"OVER HERE!" NATALIA CALLED OUT.

They'd been running down tunnel-like server rooms. She'd led them down a set of stairs and into what felt like an old sewer system.

"What is this?" Robin asked.

"A way out," Natalia replied. "Through there." She pointed at a double door and handed Robin her security pass. Robin scanned it and the hydraulic mechanism opened the doors.

"What is it?" Robin asked.

"Submarine," Natalia said. "*Private* submarine."

THIRTY-NINE

HUNT WAS AT THE CONTROLS AS THEY PULLED OUT OF the cave on the side of the sheer cliff face.

He was working out how to submerge van den Krijl's Phoenix 1000 private submarine on the touchscreen control panel. He'd set the engine to full power and headed out to sea. Above water, the submarine looked much like a superyacht. They were on the bridge looking back through the glass at the Greenland coast as they pulled away.

"There," Stenli said and pointed up to his right.

They could see the missile moving in.

"Christ, here we go," Hunt said and lifted his fingers to his ears. Before he did, he asked, "What about radiation?"

"What do you mean?" Robin asked.

"From the second warhead," Hunt said. "There were two nuclear warheads right?"

Robin shook her head. "If Stenli and Natalia managed to *pit stuff* the warhead properly then it won't result in a nuclear reaction. For the other warhead to go off requires fission, and that can't happen if it gets destroyed, or, we destroy the compound."

"D-d-d-dive!" Stenli said.

"Okay," Hunt said and programmed the dive sequence.

The missile disappeared into the earth. For a second there was no sound, no explosion. Then a bright flash and a fireball followed by a plume of black smoke erupted like a volcano above them.

Everyone was stunned.

"Let's get out of here," Robin said.

"Do as he says!" Natalia instructed him.

"We're diving," Hunt said. "Hold on!"

GERALD D. SOAMES SAT TO THE RIGHT HAND OF THE Prime Minister in a boardroom-style meeting room deep below 10 Downing Street. He knew his presence wasn't welcomed by most of the top brass sitting at the table with the PM. She was receiving an intelligence briefing—that Soames had planted—about an old Soviet-era closed city that UK spy satellites had been monitoring based on an anonymous tip-off from an informant close to Soames.

One of the generals was briefing the PM. Soames was listening but watching her closely. His heart was racing and he was employing all of his many years of experience keeping a straight and—indeed—the bored-looking expression he'd practised and cultivated during decades of service to Her Majesty's Government. He casually checked his watch. Not long now, he thought. Soon, he'd be part of the biggest shake-up the world had ever seen. A new beginning. Finally, he would have his way out of the spider web of deceit and lies he'd been both knitting and unpicking for so many years. He would wipe his guilt away and start fresh. No shame. No prison. No contemptful stares—just then there was a commotion outside the secure steel door. It broke his concentration and everyone looked towards it.

The door burst open. It was McKenna. What the hell was he doing here? Soames immediately thought. He's going to ruin the whole thing!

"Stop, sir! Please, stop!" One of the inadequate Specialist Protection policemen from the Met was saying.

McKenna strode it.

"What is the meaning of this!?" the Prime Minister blurted and stood as McKenna spoke over her.

"Ma'am, excuse the interruption," McKenna said waving a folded piece of paper. He pointed it right at Soames. "We've just learned about a—foiled—imminent attack on the United Kingdom."

"Yes, I know, I was just hearing about it from General —"

"No, ma'am, excuse me but this was not from some disused Soviet compound—this was an attack launched from Greenland—"

A murmur went around the room.

"Greenland? Come now, Mister ..."

"McKenna, ma'am, intelligence director, MI6," McKenna glanced at Soames. Soames closed his mouth and hid his nervous expression. It was replaced by the oft-practised slack-jawed flabbiness from before. "And, yes, Greenland. Save to say that the missile and the nuclear warheads have been destroyed by my operatives—"

"Nuclear missiles! Why weren't we made aware of this? " the Prime Minister asked.

"Ma'am—" McKenna started to say but before he could, Soames cut him off by pushing his chair back and standing up and saying quickly, "Come now, Evie!" He used his public schoolboy nickname to undermine McKenna in front of a group of high-ranking officials of the United Kingdom. McKenna's expression told him he'd inflicted a cut. Just a thousand more and Soames might still have a chance.

"You mean to tell the Prime Minister and her security council that one of your rogue—compromised—burned agents know more about it than the executive branch of the UK government? Please!"

"Come now, Gerald ..." McKenna was saying.

Soames turned to the PM, "If you please, ma'am. Evie here is a bit above his station. He's in charge of a—small— ragtag bunch of has been spies who —"

"Now, now, Gerald," the PM said. "Hold on now. I'd like to hear what Mister McKenna has to say, so, if you please ..." she indicated the seat Soames had leapt out of. He glanced at it and then sat heavily.

"You've been fed a pack of lies, ma'am," McKenna said. He looked around the room. "You all have. We've been infiltrated by a rogue group bent on destroying London and the United Kingdom."

"That is an exceptional allegation, Mister McKenna ..." the PM said.

"I have proof, ma'am," McKenna said and waved the paper. "It wasn't the Russians. It was an eco-terrorist billionaire who wanted you to think it was the Russians so we could fire back in response, leading to an apocalypse."

Hunt had managed to contact the European Task Force command centre with a SITREP. They'd contacted one of the UK's polar patrol vessels. They were to dock in Iceland and rendezvous with the UK vessel before being flown back to the UK. Seems Natalia had other plans. Hunt was below deck and she approached him quietly from behind. He flinched as she spoke.

"Stirling —" she said.

"Jesus! You scared me," Hunt said.

She smiled. "You scare easily for a big man," she said. She was amused.

"Lately I do," he said. "Have you come to kill me again?"

She laughed. "No, not this time."

"What is it then?"

"I still have a problem," Natalia said.

"Your son?" Hunt asked.

She nodded. "Yes, my son. The problem is Anatoly. As long as he is alive, Frederick cannot be safe and neither can I ..." Hunt lifted his hand to his chin and thought about it. Natalia continued, "But the problem is also Soames. He is very close to Anatoly. He has access to a lot of information detrimental to me. Access to powerful people, detrimental to—"

"Us," Hunt said finishing her sentence.

"Yes," Natalia agreed. "We need to —"

"Get rid of them."

"Yes," she agreed.

"So how do we do it?" Hunt asked.

"I can take care of Anatoly," Natalia said. "I know him. I have his trust. I can get close enough to him before anybody realises."

"... And you want me to do the same with Soames?" Hunt asked.

Natalia dipped her head indicating that that was the obvious compromise to the situation.

"So I take care of your problem with Soames, and you take care of my problem with Mints, and we call it quits?"

"We help each other out of the other's pickle and we are finished," Natalia said. "No more killing. No more vendetta. We can leave this world behind."

"So what happens when we get to Iceland?" Hunt asked.

Natalia shrugged. "You can give Stenli to them. Robin too, if you so wish, but I will disappear. Mints will wonder what went wrong but he won't question it ..."

"He'd have to be able to speak to question it, right?" Hunt said with a glint in his eye.

"*Da,*" Natalia said.

FORTY

One time Director of Intelligence at the Secret Intelligence Service, Gerald D. Soames, hurried up his garden path and to the front door of his house in Richmond-upon-Thames. The wind stung his cheeks and fragments of frozen raindrops pelted his coat and hat. He pulled off a glove and fumbled for his house keys and unlocked the door. He stepped in and sighed and stamped his feet. He was glad to be inside.

"Reverend!" he called as he dumped his keys in a brass bowl and dropped his hat on the table in the entrance hall and removed his coat. His Parsons Russell terrier was usually waiting for him when he got home wagging his tail and excited for his supper. Soames removed his coat and scarf and hung them on a wooden coat stand.

"Where's this damn dog," he muttered to himself as he turned on the lights. It was a habit he'd formed in the past year. Soames was a man who'd always preferred soft light or even darkness. He liked the stillness and the cloak of the dark. Now, he preferred the light. He'd gotten into the habit of sleeping with the bedroom lights on. When he could sleep. He told himself that, like Churchill during the war, he had perfected the art of short naps. He never truly slept. He preferred to stay awake.

Soames went into his library and office. It led onto the sunroom at the back of the house and overlooked his wide and mature garden. He'd also cocooned himself on his property. Security had been tightened. Access to his property was restricted. Landscapers were employed to build a maze of hedges and paths he could walk. Unless he was travelling to the office, he rarely left the confines of his space.

He flicked the switch next to the door. The chandelier on the ceiling should have lit up and revealed his floor-to-ceiling library. The mantelpiece and fireplace. He liked to sit in his armchair in front of the fire and read. He felt safest there.

"Blast it," he said and stepped into the room. He walked to the end and flipped a switch on the far wall. Round yellow lights lit up the paths in the garden and the ambient light filtered into the library. He pulled on a copper chain on his desk lamp and soft yellow light came from under a jade lampshade.

Soames pulled open the desk drawer and reached into it. He quickly spun and lifted a handgun and aimed into the darkness behind him. his eyes darted around the shadows against the far wall. His voice was shaky, and his hand was too.

"Who's —" he started to say.

He sounded fearful. His tone hardened and deepened.

"Step out," he said. "Reveal yourself."

Slowly, out of the shadow, a figure emerged. The face of Stirling Hunt, his protege, the Boatman, his most effective field agent—and the man he'd framed for murder—moved silently out of the darkness.

Soames stood with his pistol aimed directly at Hunt. For a second, Soames wasn't sure whether to drop the weapon and greet Hunt like a long-lost son, or pull the trigger and put him down.

He didn't know what Hunt knew, or what he suspected him of.

"Stirling," Soames said in recognition. "What're you doing in my house, goddamnit! How'd you get in here?"

He decided to try and sound cheerful and nonplussed. To him, Hunt was like a wild animal. If you showed fear, he would be more likely to attack. If you were calm and cheerful, he'd leave you alone. That's what Soames thought, anyway.

Hunt didn't say anything, instead, he slowly raised his right hand out in front of him. As he did, flustered and scared, Soames pulled on the trigger. Click. He looked at the shining black weapon in his hand. As he did, Hunt opened his fist and turned his palm towards Soames. The bullets clinked together as he opened his fingers.

"It's empty," Hunt said.

It wasn't much above a whisper. Soames' body seemed to instantly deflate. His arm swung down by his side and his shoulders slumped. He turned back to the desk and, still holding the handgun, placed his hands on the surface and leaned on them. His body seemed heavy. Weighed down by some invisible burden.

There was a long silence before Soames spoke. "Where's my dog?" Soames asked.

Hunt didn't respond. Soames heard him step forward a few steps. He glanced over his shoulder and saw the figure there, dressed in black, blank-faced, calm.

"You put a contract out on me," Hunt said.

Soames gave a single guffaw.

"You did, didn't you?" Hunt asked again.

"I don't suppose it'd do much good for m help ..." Soames said, thinking out loud, t anything other than what Hunt wanted to know.

"Tell me the truth, Gerry. You owe me that much."

Soames felt a surge of rage. "Owe you? *Me*, owe *you*. Don't make me laugh. On top of it all, I think you'll find you murdered poor old Tom," Soames said and looked at Hunt's reflection in the window.

"Excuse me?" Hunt said.

"He was in your kitchen with your fingerprints on the murder weapon. Face all crushed into mush like some mannequin."

"Is Tom Holland dead?" Hunt asked. Soames closed his mouth and glared at Hunt in the reflection in the glass.

"You know damn well," Soames said. It was unconvincing.

"I wasn't in the country though, you know that. And I haven't been. I tried to leave it all behind, but you won't let me."

"*Ha*! Go and try and prove that one. Your prints are all over the murder weapon."

"That's not possible," Hunt said.

"Maybe you should look after your whisky more carefully in future."

"The only person with access to my prints was you," he said quietly. Soames' face scrunched and he shook his head. "No, your prints are everywhere."

"No," Hunt said. "The bar, the glass, the drink. After the general was killed, you needed insurance. Isn't that right? You came to find me to buy yourself time and to buy yourself an alibi. You used me like you used Holland —"

Soames spun around. The pressure was building. He

elt cornered. He exploded. "Oh, Holland was a fool! He stumbled onto something he shouldn't have. Something you had all the incentive in the world to want to silence. He should have left it to me," Soames shouted and jabbed his finger out at Hunt.

Soames shut his mouth. He sucked in air through his nose. He was thrown by Hunt's calmness. He was blank-faced and business-like. Soames felt a surge of fear. He realised he was now on the working end of an assassin he'd created.

"Just do it!" Soames shouted.

"I'm not going to kill you, Director. I don't murder my colleagues. My friends. I don't let my partners die. I don't let liars win."

"Oh, mister morals, *excuse me*," Soames jibed. "And, it's not Director Soames anymore. They took it away from me. Everything I worked for." Soames looked at the ground and said quietly, "I did what needed to be done. I did what no one else wanted to do. I protected this country against all enemies, both foreign, and domestic."

"Enemies like Tom Holland ..."

"Holland was in a position to compromise the whole operation," Soames said and then checked himself. "That's why you —"

Hunt pulled a handgun from behind his belt and moved forward. Soames recoiled and leaned back against the desk. Hunt stuck the barrel in his temple and grabbed Soames' wrist and twisted it behind him. His body rolled and Soames was on his chest, head forced down into the desk by the warm steel pushing against his skull.

"Don't kill me," Soames said, begging. "I can bring you in, I can protect you. We'll say it was part of the operation."

Hunt pressed the barrel harder into Soames head and he grunted at the pressure and the pain.

"Okay," Soames said. "What do you want, money, freedom? I can give it to you."

"They demoted you, didn't they?" Hunt asked.

Soames tried to nod and then said, "Yes."

"You're powerless now. Why'd they do it?"

Soames was silent.

"Because of Holland?"

"They think you killed Holland. They demoted me because of you. Rogue agent. Missing in action. Creating a war on the establishment. You're their worst nightmare."

"No," Hunt said.

"Who sent you?" Soames asked. "Was it McKenna? It was Evie, wasn't it?"

"What makes you say that?" Hunt asked.

"You're working for him now."

"I'm not. Not since he made a Faustian bargain with you. He sold me out like you did —"

"I never!"

"Shut up!" Hunt said. "I was gone," Hunt said through gritted teeth. "I'd disappeared. I was out."

Soames scoffed. "You'll never be out of this, my boy."

"Don't you dare call me that."

"You are this. It's inside you. I didn't create a monster. I just saw what was already there and harnessed it."

"You used me —"

"You aren't innocent in all this. You were there. Just because you were unwilling, or unable to see what was going on in front of your own eyes doesn't mean you aren't culpable. You were involved in this as much as I was."

"How did you do it," Hunt said. "How did you lure Tom to the flat?"

"You and Tom were in on it together, weren't you?" Soames asked.

Hunt lifted the barrel off of Soames' temple and fired it at the wall. Soames cried out at the gunshot and heard his dog yelping from upstairs.

"Reverend!" he shouted above the ringing in his ears. "What've you done with my dog?"

"Tell me the truth," Hunt leaned in and said in a jaw-clenched whisper and pushed the barrel back into the side of Soames' ear.

"Holland was a threat to national security," Soames said. He squeezed his eyes shut. He didn't breathe. He felt like he was standing on the precipice and all he needed to do was take one step and he would be free.

"Is that why you killed him?"

Soames twisted his head against the barrel and looked at Hunt out of the corner of his eye, "You killed Holland. The second you saw him in Afghanistan, he was dead. The moment you took that watch from General Patrick. I had no choice."

It was a snarling, vile accusation. Soames was angry. Filled with fury.

"Maybe," Hunt said, "but you crushed his skull. How'd it make you feel?"

Soames'd had enough. The truth was that he was dying to get it out of him. To tell somebody. To put an end to his suffering.

"Good! Bloody fantastic. It made me feel goddamn wonderful. Now I see why you Section Seven killers can't get enough. So, go on! Do it! Do it! Put me out of my own mind."

"What about McKenna's team?"

Soames stopped. He was suddenly very still.

"You heard me," Hunt said. "The intelligence from the informant in Holland ..."

"I don't know anything —"

"No, you know everything," Hunt said. "What was the intel? What had he discovered? The Frenchman had found out that there was a senior member of MI-6 working with a peripheral but influential figure within Russian intelligence. He discovered a mole —"

"Oh, that fat French bastard knew nothing!" Soames scoffed.

"Then why did Mints have Natalia murder a team of field agents?"

"You think Mints' could have orchestrated that?" Soames asked.

"No, I don't," Hunt said. "Which is why that only leaves one person with the motive, means, and opportunity."

"Very clever, Hunt. Not as dumb as you look ..."

"And Crookshank and Allen-Smith in Vilnius?"

"Oh, old school chums. You know how it is ... or maybe you don't. They know what they needed to know. They helped where they thought it would help their careers."

"Why'd you do it?" Hunt asked. Soames heard the desperation in his voice. The first crack in his armour.

"It was a way back in," Soames said. "If I could solve the riddle, and save the nation, I would be back in favour with the people at the top."

"You were willing to destroy the country to do it."

"He was never going to go through with it —"

"Oh, but he was! That crazed eco-terrorist launched a nuclear missile at your own country."

"It wasn't armed," Soames said.

"Yes, it was."

Soames was silent.

"You didn't know?" Hunt asked. "You were a pawn in all of this? You expect me to believe that?"

"Do it, Stirling. Just do it, please, put me out of my misery."

Hunt pushed the barrel into Soames skull so he heard bone grinding against metal. "No," Hunt said and took the pressure of the barrel off Soames' head. "I'm not going to kill you."

Soames turned to look. Hunt reached into his trouser pocket and pulled out a digital voice recorder. He pressed the stop button. Soames groaned when he realised. He'd confessed.

He did feel better though. He'd told someone. He felt relieved.

"They'll never believe it, Hunt, you goddamn provincial. You *nobody*. They'll never believe it!"

Soames rolled over and sat up. While he was bargaining, trying to convince himself, Hunt took Soames' handgun.

"What're you doing?"

Hunt removed the magazine and pressed one nine-millimetre round into it. He reinserted the magazine and loaded the handgun. Hunt placed the gun on the desk beside Soames. The ex-director of intelligence's eyes were wide.

He panted. "What will you do?" Soames asked.

"You can do the honourable thing," Hunt said. "Or, when every official at MI-6 receives this file," he held up the voice recorder, "With your voice on it, admitting that you took pleasure in murdering your friend, one of our colleagues ... well, the shame will make you wish you'd taken option one."

Soames was quiet for a moment. He looked at the carpet contemplatively and said, "What about Reverend?"

The way Hunt looked at Soames, full of pity and shame, made him realise there was no way out. Hunt turned and walked towards the door. Soames glanced down at the pistol and picked it up and aimed it at Hunt's back. The gun shaking in his hand. Hunt stopped for a moment, his head to the side, looking at Soames out of his peripheral vision. Soames could see the back of Hunt's ribs rising and falling.

"What about Kabazanov?" Soames asked.

"What about him?" Hunt said.

"You think it was his idea to hit your family; take out your father, send your mother back across the wall?"

Hunt didn't respond. He just turned his head away. Soames knew, and Hunt did too, even though Gerald D. Soames was capable of extreme conceit, shooting a man in the back just wasn't cricket.

"Stroke of genius, I thought, getting the son to kill the traitor. It wasn't personal—you know—with the scorpion, he just got greedy. Started making threats. I put you to good use, no?"

"Goodbye, Gerry," Hunt said.

Soames watched him leave and pull the door shut and then lowered the weapon and glanced at the pistol in his hand. He had nothing left. It was the end of the game. Nowhere left to run to. No one left to lie to. Fitting, it seemed to him. He was going to have to die too. His greatest creation had become a monster. No one survived Stirling Hunt. They were all like waves crashing against a mighty rock. They destroyed themselves against him. Soames opened his mouth and put the barrel in sideways. He tasted the smooth metallic coldness. His teeth touched the metal.

He didn't want to shoot his brain stem out. What if he survived? He'd live like a zombie. He twisted the gun until the bottom of the handle was pointing towards the ceiling. He tilted it down and felt the tip of the barrel against the top of his mouth. He closed his eyes. The only image in his mind was Tom Holland's dead eyes staring out at him from a bashed-in and bloody face. Soames pulled the trigger.

HUNT HAD PULLED THE LIBRARY DOOR SHUT BEHIND him. His breathing was shallow. He stood outside the stained glass insets of the door panels and listened. Then, a moment later, there was a sudden flash, the report of a gunshot, and a loud thud as the dead weight of Soames' body hit the floor.

Hunt went to the front door and put his fingers on the handle. He cocked his head and heard Reverend whining and yapping upstairs. He sighed and lifted his fingers off the handle and slowly made his way upstairs.

He let the dog out of the room he'd been locked in. Reverend ran out into the corridor and then stood there looking at Hunt with his tongue out and little tail wagging. Hunt went back downstairs and Reverend followed on his heels.

"Okay then, pup," Hunt said. He found a canvas bag in the kitchen and filled it with Reverend's things. He found the dog's lead and clipped it onto his collar. Reverend's tail wagged and Hunt picked him up and held him close to his chest. He went out the back and disappeared into the night.

Printed in Great Britain
by Amazon